POST FACTO

POST FACTO

DARRYL WIMBERLEY

THE PERMANENT PRESS
Sag Harbor, NY 11963

For information, address:
    The Permanent Press
    4170 Noyac Road
    Sag Harbor, NY 11963
    www.thepermanentpress.com

Library of Congress Cataloging-in-Publication Data

Wimberley, Darryl, author.
    Post facto / by Darryl Wimberley.
    First edition.
    Sag Harbor, NY: The Permanent Press, [2018]
    ISBN: 978-1-57962-555-9
        1. Mystery fiction.

PS3573.I47844 P67 2018
813'.54—dc23   2018032624

Printed in the United States of America

PROLOGUE

Believe the reports or don't—fake news or real—makes no difference to me. Whether they were weather balloons or flying saucers or ghosts, I never claimed to see anything, at least not publicly. I'm just the umpire, the reporter actually, though when you're the solo scrivener for a paper with barely a thousand subscribers it's not like you're Rupert Murdoch. The *Clarion* is the smallest newspaper in northern Florida, and barely hanging on. Along with everything else.

It's also the only rag in the region owned by a female.

You might think a small-town gal made good would make some splash coming home to rescue her burg's only free press, but that has not been my experience. Aside from the headline I composed myself, there were no announcements to indicate that Howard Buchanan's daughter had returned home to "take over" the paper. In the two years since, I should not have been surprised to see that the *Clarion* is not valued much differently than the Western Auto right down the street and probably a lot less than the coffee shop behind the high school.

Certainly I enjoy no aura of celebrity. Nobody asks for my autograph. Nobody lingers in thrall for stories of the big city. As for the grist of my work—the exposés of graft, the feud with Speaker Ryan—all go unremarked. More than 80 percent of my home county's vote in the general election tilted for Donald Trump; that constituency is not interested in my elitist opinion—on anything. Nothing like the attention I received in Boston. I was notorious in that Yankee redoubt. Fearless.

"Better to have somebody mad with me than ignoring me," I often challenged my editor, and most times he'd agree.

"But you can never go home again, Clara," my husband reminds me.

"It's not just about me," I reply lamely.

"Don't bullshit yourself, sweetheart—you didn't buy this sheet to rescue anything or anyone but yourself."

Well, there you go. A reality check, courtesy of my husband, Randall. That would be Randall Greene, software wizard and couch potato. One-time lobbyist on K Street.

Randall puts the "T" in Tough Love.

"No one cares about Boston, Clara. Quit expecting them to."

My husband always calls me "Clara," as did my Boston colleagues, anyone in the profession really. In fact, until our exile, I doubt my husband ever heard anyone address me as Clara Sue, but in my hometown, that's my name. Even my maiden name remains fixed and unchanged in the minds of my relatives and neighbors, and why shouldn't it? I kept the family name, after all, even in my big-city byline. For selfish reasons, of course.

Clara Buchanan conveys more gravitas, in my opinion, than Clara Greene.

"You're not the first journalist to lose her column." Randall continued to correct the course of our new journey. "Doesn't make you a goddamned martyr."

It took three days in a U-Haul to relocate from Massachusetts to my homestead eighty miles south of Tallahassee, and the thing that struck me most in the course of that resettlement, aside from a casual indifference to my profession, was a pervading aura of decline. President Trump maintains that he is revitalizing manufacturing and creating jobs nationwide, but that's not what I see in my region. A whole lot of Florida's Big Bend remains an unbroken swath of pine trees and poverty, despite alternative facts cited to the contrary. There are no factories in my little town. There are no theme parks or pizza joints, either, and for a long time the only medical care available in the entire county was a rotating crew of interns from the medical school in Gainesville. Nothing is close to Laureate, Florida. Nothing is convenient.

You can drive a hundred miles and never see a golden arch.

Our biggest employer is a medium security prison just north of town. The ruins of agricultural enterprise are evident in razed barns and rusted tractors all along Highway 27. Flue-cured tobacco was once a major cash crop in Lafayette County. I've spent as many hours stringing tobacco in my lifetime as I have editing copy, and everyone I grew up with worked in those barns and fields, but no longer.

There are very few locals cultivating the Golden Leaf anymore—a good thing in some respects, I suppose—but the decline of that noxious production has paralleled a sharp erosion of healthier enterprises. Take dairies, for instance. There are fewer than half as many dairies working in Lafayette, Taylor, and Dixie Counties as there were ten years ago. There are fewer chicken houses. Fewer truck farms. But there are many, many more acres of pine trees.

Land that used to make hay or pasture Holsteins has been planted in slash pine destined for cardboard and paper.

A topography that used to mix freshwater lakes and sloughs with stands of tidewater cypress and yellow heart pine is largely drained now to feed the need for pulp. Driving to work each morning, I follow a narrow blacktop into a vast maze of pine trees, a featureless grid planted in narrow rows as uniform as a picket fence. Sometimes I'll spot laborers working the needled alleys between. But you won't see ICE agents trolling for the undocumented in Lafayette County. Our illegals are too valuable to be deported, families of Latinos toiling with their children in plain sight and, despite nativist howls to the contrary, indispensable.

I am sometimes disoriented on my daily commute, the sun flashing at intervals between alleys of slash pine like a stroboscope in some giant discotheque. But the families inside are not dancing. They labor—mothers, fathers, even children. Raking straw for twenty-five cents a bale. That's twenty-five *cents* per bale.

Might as well be working for the fucking pharaoh.

At least they're working. A few months back, our local Optimist Club sent an open letter to the *Clarion* chiding local politicos for not getting some of that tourist industry, illustrating yet again the difference between confidence and delusion. There aren't enough vacationers between here and Steinhatchee to field a football team, let alone revive a region devastated by failed farms, foreclosures, and the related flotsam of voodoo economics.

This isn't Panama City. We don't have kitesurfers or bikinis. We don't have golf courses or multiplex theaters. Tourists are not coddled or courted in Lafayette or Taylor or Dixie Counties, at least not inland. It's spotty, even along the coast, though there are signs of incursion. I recently learned that some arriviste from Fort Myers has got a weekend condo replete with Wi-Fi and solar panels rising on stilts off

Pepperfish Keys. And Dead Man's Bay, once off-limits to anyone but fishermen and hunters, is now punctured at more or less regular intervals with beach houses piled over canals that take Jet Skis and powerboats through prairies of turtle grass on their way to the Gulf of Mexico.

Where, as a girl, I used to wade in cutoffs gigging flounder, I now see out-of-towners in sporting apparel on boogie boards, their runabouts kicking up a salty spray beneath the sentinel of pelicans and osprey. Other visitors take to the open water in expensive kayaks, scooping up scallops from the shallows along with bottles of soda pop, Gatorade, and the occasional condom.

Used to be, Roy's was the only restaurant for fifty miles up and down the coast. Then there was Cooey's. There is a little-known resort at Steinhatchee; Jimmy Carter stayed there some decades ago, and I will acknowledge that on that narrow strip of pine and palmetto you can see the impact of disposable income year-round. But as for the rest—?

Failed farms and single-wides. Broken trampolines. Listless children.

Most folks who leave our county, young or old, do not return. Senator Stanton's wife is an exception. Barbara "Babs" Stanton fluttered back to the Keys and her coastal mansion maybe three years after her husband was blown to bits. The house was an abortion when new, a confusion of gingerbread and Venice Beach, but the verandah is spectacular with a view over maybe fifty or sixty yards of lawn to the pier and water beyond. There is a balcony above that verandah and it was from that vantage that Babs Stanton swears she saw her long-dead husband at the dock smoking his cherished cigar.

"It was Rooster, no doubt about it!"

Barbara Stanton drove nearly sixty miles to give me her report face to face.

"He was on the dock in that ratted-out lawn chair I hate so much. Smoking that cigar."

I was the first of many people to whom Babs confided details of her encounter. The stories improved with each telling, which is to be expected. Stanton insisted that I publish the account she gave to me, not needing to mention the certain loss in advertisements and subscriptions if I did not oblige.

"I tore up my feet running out to see him!" Babs elaborated from the counter looking over my army-salvage desk.

"You actually saw the senator?" I tried to drain the question of incredulity. "You saw Senator Stanton smoking a cigar?"

"Big as life," she insisted.

"But by the time I got to the dock, he was gone."

Most everyone who knows Barbara Stanton will tell you she's crazy, and that was before her husband's assassination. "A bubble and a half off plumb," is a common characterization. I tried to steer our conversation to more empirically founded realms, but Babs wasn't having it.

"It was Rooster, Clara Sue. I know it was. Now put it in the paper."

The thing is, Stanton recounted her vision just two days before little Jenny O'Steen's sighting, right before Halloween. Then there was that business at Pickett Lake. And then, just a few weeks later, Hiram Lamb spills his entrails into a slough of stagnant water.

Normally I'd be posting stories about homecoming and ten-point bucks with copy from candidates running for sheriff or tax assessor, the squalls of politicians competing for attention with photos of local sirens on their senior float, or tackles and tailbacks in their red and white pads. The Future Farmers of America posing purple and gold in their corduroy jackets. There might be an occasional column addressed to larger concerns.

Immigrants. Islam. The withering middle class.

The latest tweet.

Not this year. Call it fake news or infotainment I couldn't keep up with the reports. Folks started calling in from all over. But never north of Perry, never south of Cross City, and rarely east of the Suwannee River. I received a report or two from Live Oak, but the vast majority of sightings in whatever variety were alleged to have occurred in Lafayette or Taylor Counties, many of these only a couple of miles from my own modest lanai.

There was no comparable activity anyplace else in the country. California is supposed to be the land of fruits, nuts, and abductees, but those folks were too busy looking for water to worry about UFOs or visits from the beyond. I began to long for the days when rainfall was grist for my own newspaper. What psychosis precipitated these other sightings? These visitations? Maybe it was no more than the fallout of Halloween, unemployment, and coffee shop caffeine.

Maybe.

Whatever the source, the reports multiplied. Sometimes a dozen sightings in a single night, everything from dead relatives to the always-reliable flying saucer. I still don't know exactly what to do with all the material. My little rag doesn't have enough columns to detail every incident, feigned or otherwise. I thought about making a numerical summary and leaving it at that. Or I could go through every message, note, and e-mail, and serialize the whole thing, like Dickens. Except I'd be getting a fuckload less than a penny a page.

Talk about a career change. Here I was an award-winning journalist organizing what amounted to a scrapbook for Area 51. These were not the topics I'd hoped to headline on my

hometown paper. When I worked for the *Globe,* I challenged
the Speaker of the House of Representatives with questions
about tax policy and entitlements and foreign entanglements.
People from K Street to Kansas read my columns. The closest I get to real reporting, now, is the still-unsettled investigation of Hiram Lamb's death. Sheriff Buchanan is awful
closemouthed about Lamb's accident, but then Colt hasn't
been the same since he witnessed that gruesome display at
the lake. He won't admit to it, of course.

"Just a meth-head's hoax." Our sheriff shrugs it off.

And who knows? Maybe Colt's right.

But that's not the point of the story I'm writing, not the
whole point anyway. The angle I'm taking is broader than any
single incident. I'd like to know why people believe anything.
Why do some folks trust a fourth grader's fantastic account,
but not a senator's wife? A known drunkard claiming alien
abduction is taken seriously, but not the testimony of an
entire family bearing witness to a miracle in the pines. Why?

For that matter, why do some folks accept evidence related
to a warming climate while others dismiss that information
out of hand? Why is Darwin still a dirty word in many circles? How often do you hear that cutting taxes creates jobs
and raising taxes kills them? Do these claims reflect facts-
on-the ground or are they only a mirror of what somebody
wants to believe? It seems to me that folks who swear they've
seen alien spacecraft aren't different in principle than supply-
side enthusiasts, because in either case facts don't matter.

Fuck facts. Belief is what matters.

So who are the true believers? Who are the dissemblers?
What makes us trust one person or policy over another?
Because no matter how the apple gets sliced, you either
believe what people tell you—

Or you don't.

Chapter One

Second Grader Spots Little Green Man
The Clarion

The first sighting did not occur, as you might expect, in the black night of some hybrid forest, or in a hayfield scythed to a pattern of alien encryption, but in broad daylight at Butch McCray's candy store. Butch is close to seventy years old and has sold sweets and sodas across the street from our county's only school for as long as anybody can remember.

You'd lose any claim to verisimilitude if you described Butch's place of business as quaint or cute. Truth is, it's a shack, a tiny box of lathed cedar sealed with tar paper. But it's a busy shack. Noontime at Butch's store looks like something a child might crayon onto a piece of scrap paper, the wobbled square of his candy shack splashed yellow and blue, kids emerging by the dozens in stick figures of black or brown, their fingers spread wide like pitchforks to gig bottles of soda or Popsicles rendered in shades of magenta or lime.

I can remember getting an orange Nehi and a PayDay for twenty-five cents, pressing dimes, nickels, or pennies into Butch's gnarled hand, and if you brought him ten wrappers you got a penny off any purchase. Butch has a thing about candy wrappers. There are boxes of wraps stuffed and stacked behind the counter—Mars bars, Hershey chocolate, Snickers—you name it, each foil pressed flat as a daisy in a dictionary. Butch is odd, no doubt about it, a wrinkled gnome with a hump of shoulder and rheumy eyes that remain, even in direct address, fixed on some distant point beyond the long bill of his bib cap. Locals write him off as simple or retarded. The idiot son of parents taken too soon and violently.

It was getting toward Halloween after a summer that seemed never to end when Jenny O'Steen skipped lunch on her way to Butch's store, a second grader in a ruffle-tier skirt bound for a Nehi and Honey Bun. Jenny was diabetic but even so should have been fine. She was allowed a single treat during the day and in any case had received her morning shot of insulin. On the other hand, it was unseasonably warm and by the time Miss Jenny got to Butch's store there was already a line of kids stretching along the sidewalk that girdled the store, all of them sweltering on a shadeless street beneath a lingering dog-day sun.

Laureate Consolidated School sprawls across the asphalt from Butch's place, a complex consisting of a gym, cafeteria, maintenance sheds, and two buildings linked with breeze-ways sufficient to bridge the Hellespont. Secondary grades matriculate in a monolith of cement and jalousie windows built by the WPA in 1931; grade schoolers are located in a more recently completed facility featuring metal roofing, central air, and reliable plumbing, all amenities provided courtesy of those cursed federal funds.

Come lunchtime it's common to see grade schoolers and older students jostling for a place in the queue at Butch's store. By the time I was a high school senior, that line might have run to a dozen kids, but nowadays you can see scores of young people milling around, scrapping for position and singing out orders for Pepsis and Snickers in the quest for a fix of sugar.

The complexion of that daily gaggle has also changed over the years. My father once recalled the first African American he ever saw at Butch's canteen. "Harold Sykes was his name," my father declared. "Boy loved his sodas and moon pies. Played football too. First Negro ever to put on a helmet and pads at Laureate high."

Turns out Harold Sykes was also the first black student to graduate from Laureate high school.

A few months later he was killed in some rice paddy in southeast Asia.

Of course, by now the school is thoroughly integrated, *de facto* if not *in spiritu.* You take a drive past the LCS now and you'll see black kids and Latinos, maybe even an Asian or two, mixing with the scions of white gentry at Butch's candy bank, the Lambs and Buchanans and O'Steens, who have for generations run the county like a fiefdom mixing with poorer blood.

The old tensions that used to play out between blacks and whites is reconstituted now between native crackers and immigrants from Mexico or farther south. Drop by Koon's Coffeehouse & Café most any morning and you'll hear some farmer or businessman loudly condemning those damned illegals even as an undocumented family huddles outside in the bed of some farmer's pickup on their way to crop his tobacco, stack his hay, load his melons, or rake his straw.

This was the labor that I used to do, that damn near every white kid was expected to do, frequently in company with black adults. You don't see that anymore. An influx of cheaply hired and easily exploited labor has freed the sons and daughters of Laureate for milder pursuits, football or

basketball or a Jet Ski along the amber waters of the Suwannee. Maybe a run for booze to Taylor or Dixie Counties.

You can bet that neither Trent nor Danny Lamb ever
cropped a single leaf of tobacco off their daddy's field or
threw a watermelon. The only thing Trent ever threw was a
football, and in fairness he's good at it. Both of the Lamb
boys are ferocious athletes, but Trent is a special joy to watch,
towheaded and tall and liquid as mercury on a football field.
The Laureate Hornets had already won a pair of titles with
Trent taking the snaps, his brother, Danny, running interference like a berserk, as barreled and dark as Trent is lithe and
blond.

Freed from Helots' labor, Trent and Danny toil on friendly
fields of strife to the approbation of a community desperate
for any hero with blue eyes and white skin. A white kid who
can throw or run or tackle can still have just about anything
he wants in Lafayette County, but there's the rub, because
there are only a handful of folks in the county can give you
anything worth having and chief amongst these is the super-
jocks' deacon daddy.

Hiram Lamb inherited over six hundred acres of river-
bottom land from his own father along with a twenty-
thousand-pound allotment of tobacco, and from that base
went on to acquire a construction company, a cement plant,
and a fleet of trucks that ship fertilizer and agricultural
equipment all over the southeast. It was Hiram's company
built the new prison. What he didn't own, Lamb ran or
influenced, stacking the school board and city council and
the commissioner's office with candidates of his choosing,
and running roughshod over anyone brooking opposition.

No challenge was too trivial. A wheel-chaired teacher
once called Hiram from the school to complain that his

dark-haired son had parked a Dodge Ram in her disabled slot.

"He'll be gone by noon," the elder's reply was widely reported. "You can have it back then."

On the morning of Jenny O'Steen's adventure, Trent and Danny were amusing themselves by courting fights with Hispanic students. Edgar Uribe came from Gonzales, Texas, with his family to harvest tobacco and rake straw for the Jackson family. On this noon recess, the undocumented teenager was escorting his much younger sister Isabel to Butch's store. Jenny O'Steen had just let Isabel and her brother take a place in line when the Lamb brothers came swaggering across the street, the quarterback and his brother garbed despite the oppressive heat in the livery of lettermen, fists stuffed inside the pockets of their woolen jackets.

"Out of the way, wetbacks," Trent ordered. "We got a bus waitin'."

Edgar replied by placing a hand on his sister's shoulder.

"Goddammit, move," Danny complained. "We got a game in Cross City and we're runnin' late."

"Then you should haf come earlier," Edgar replied.

Imagine a Hispanic boy of seventeen or so. Baggy jeans. A plaid shirt untucked. Probably one hundred and thirty pounds wet with a limp that testified to a childhood scrape with a front-end loader. This is Edgar Uribe.

Danny freed his fists from the pockets of his jacket.

"Get the fuck out of the way."

"That's not nice!" little Jenny protested.

"Hear that, Trent? Jenny's sticking up for the wetbacks."

"Careful where yer standin', Freckles." Trent spat his words carefully. "You don' wanta pick the wrong company."

At which point Butch leaned over the counter.

"Why, Mr. Trent, whassa trouble?"

"No, trouble, Butch. We got a schedule is all."

Butch's smile vague beneath the bib of his cap.

"Well, I 'spect you better come on up then."

"I feel sick," Jenny complained as the Lambs shouldered by.

"You're always sick," Danny said, snorting.

"*Polla.*" Edgar offered that *maliciondes* at which point reports begin to conflict, some saying it was Danny Lamb started the fracas when he shoved the Latino's sister, others present saying that the "wetback" triggered the donnybrook when he took a swing at Trent.

The only point not contested is that somewhere in the melee that followed Jenny O'Steen disappeared.

She was found on the playground just east of Butch's store beneath an arbor of needled pines. A small girl limp as a rag on a carpet of Saint Augustine. There is some dispute as to whether Jenny actually went into insulin shock, that determination complicated by the second grader's own report.

"I knew I shouldn't have skipped a meal," she would tell Doc Trotter. "And it was hot. And then Trent and Danny were mean, and I started feeling sick and woozy, like sometimes before, and next thing I know I was in the playground with a pine cone stickin' my bottom and there's this little man holding my hand."

A little man? What little man? Did she mean Butch McCray?

"No." Jenny seemed positive in that denial. "It wasn't Mr. Butch. He was old though. And he had a kind of fur all over. Like grass. But not winter grass. Grass like when it's nice outside and I told him he better dress or he'd catch cold and he told me not to worry. 'Just relax,' he said. He had a funny tin-can kind of voice. 'Close your eyes.' And I did and then

I felt better and then I felt real funny. And then I felt cold, like I'd jumped into a spring. Or like somebody poured iced tea all through me and then I opened my eyes . . .

"And he was gone."

Was that when the Mexican girl found you?

"Isabel, yessir. She's in the same grade as me an' she ran to Mr. Butch and he brought me a Pepsi Cola and made me drink some of it and then Miss Hicks come running from the cafeteria, but by then I was awright."

Better than all right as it turned out. A prick to the finger gave the doctor all he needed to determine levels of sugar and insulin and the results were reassuring.

"The numbers for both her insulin and C-peptides were better than I expected," Doc Trotter reported with some surprise. "Thank the Lord for Butch and Pepsi Cola."

Even so, and in an abundance of caution, the doctor went on to recommend that the O'Steens keep Jenny under close observation for the next week or two. Of course, nobody took the account of a nude and benignant dwarf seriously. Jenny had suffered from diabetes for years, as everyone knew. The little green man was the product of a brain starved of glucose, was the accepted explanation. Entirely understandable.

But the child continued to insist that her encounter was real.

"I saw him," she declared with the obdurate certainty of the born again.

"He was nice. And he made me better too."

It would make for a cute story, I decided, and headlined little Jenny's account with Barbara Stanton's, not imagining the chaos to come.

Or the visions to follow.

CHAPTER TWO

Federal Funds Stimulate Local Contractors
The Clarion

Most folks my age remember Monk Folsom's auto shop, a Butler building erected on a concrete slab on the exact axis of Butch McCray's candy store, but on the far side of the school's generous playground. For years, maybe decades, Monk's was the watering hole for the movers and shakers of Laureate's insular community. I should be clear that this population did not include those elusive people of color. If you were black or the very rare Hispanic in those years, you were relegated to a table out back of Shirley's Café on the other side of town.

Monk's patrons were local, white, and exclusively male. Habitués included virtually every elected official in the county. You wanted to run for office, you tested the waters at Monk's. You needed a favor, you were bound to see the mayor, or the sheriff, or, more important, the moneybags of Lafayette County, all convened over a Mr. Coffee on bench seats salvaged from some wreck or another to negotiate in torrid heat or freezing-ass cold beside the altar of Monk's hydraulic lift.

Kissing ass. Sucking up. Wheelin' and dealin'.

Of course, the conversations were not all serious. There was room for recreation, of a sort. Sometimes customers would wander in a gaggle out to the pasture behind Monk's shop, pile paddies of cow dung on top of five-gallon buckets and blow that offal to pieces with shotguns or handguns or, on one occasion, a scattershot of ten-penny nails cherry-bombed from a steel pipe.

Which makes it fair to report that at least a few of Monk's regulars were only there to shoot the shit.

Monk has been dead for years, and good riddance, too, but his legacy is at least partially reprised in Koon's Coffeehouse & Café, a meeting place still devoid of color with air-conditioning ducts snaking over a mélange of tables and stools and chairs crowding the same concrete floor that used to support hydraulic lifts and broken transmissions.

In a metal shed once utilized for the repair of trucks and tractors, espresso steams from beans raised organically in Guatemala, and locals accustomed to ordering grits and eggs call out for doppios of espresso or café au lait in an interior cold as a footlocker with Carl's wife their brown-haired barista, a one-time cheerleader and mother of twins still inviting attention in short shorts and halter.

A scoop of navel over legs tanned all coffee and cream.

"That damn Connie is hotter than a fresh fucked fox in a forest fire," Roscoe Lamb announced.

Making sure her husband could hear.

Roscoe is three years younger than Hiram, which at sixty-nine makes him effectively a century older than Connie Koon, but if Roscoe has not the charms of youth, he brings other inducements. Roscoe backed the loan allowing Carl and Connie to open their business while Hiram shoved a zoning change through the city council to allow a "restaurant" on the site. That double-barreled assistance guaranteed the brothers Lamb free refills on their coffee, and other services.

The elder Hiram and his younger brother cooperated where mutual advantage was served but were otherwise as mismatched as a thoroughbred and a mule. If you didn't already know the two men, you'd never guess they were related, Roscoe idling in soiled jeans and brogans, usually with some T-shirt salvaged from a Garth Brooks concert, Hiram favoring pleated slacks in summer wool, usually Kenneth Cole, and Versini shirts. Roscoe is never guilty of more than random hygiene. Hiram kept his fingernails clean as a surgeon's. Roscoe is bald as a cue ball while Hiram boasted a mane of hair to rival Bono's, though whatever panache might accrue from that blessing was diminished by a birthmark that ran like the sign of Cain from the elder's ear to his jaw.

An independent observer might say that Roscoe looked like a drunk who crawled out of a pig sty and Hiram like a banker bitch-slapped at a brothel, but if you had a mortgage in trouble or needed some credit to fertilize your tobacco or fix your combine or place a thousand dollars' worth of ads every month in your struggling newspaper, you might be inclined to see the Lamb brothers through a more charitable lens.

Beauty, as it turns out, owes to the banker as well as to the beholder.

Hiram and Roscoe Lamb were the alpha males in Laureate's ingrown society—persons less puissant could be ridiculed without penalty. Butch McCray, not surprisingly, was a reliable target.

"If I was ugly as that sumbitch, I'd paint a smile on my ass and walk backward," Roscoe Lamb loved to remark.

Or—

"That boy fell off the ugly tree and hit ever' limb on the way down."

Not the kindest words for an adopted brother. Have I mentioned that Butch McCray was adopted by Hiram and Roscoe's father? Perhaps "adopted" is not technically accurate. In circumstances either unsettling or tragic, Butch's mother, Annette, was widowed when her first husband, Harold McCray, got himself killed. "Hunting Accident Takes Local" read the *Clarion*'s banner. Hiram and Roscoe Lamb had already lost their own mother to influenza; the boys' father, old man Kelly Lamb, took Butch under his roof when he married Harold McCray's widow. Wasn't three months after those vows that Annette Lamb née McCray was found hanging by her neck in a smokehouse.

A bad run of luck, locals clucked.

Just terrible.

Terrible for Butch too. Both Roscoe and Hiram resented having a youngster they regularly derided as a retard in their home and took every opportunity to let him know it. Butch endured that arrangement until he was well into his twenties. Then old man Lamb died leaving the major portion of his estate evenly divided, Hiram and Roscoe each receiving one section of land, roughly 640 acres apiece.

The thing is, every square foot of Hiram's property was taken from the McCray homestead. Butch McCray's father, Harold McCray, worked hard to acquire more than 640 acres of bottom land and pasture west of the Suwannee River. It was a beautiful piece of land, fed with artesian springs and running creeks and bordered with cypress trees and water oak. Was common to see ten-point bucks and red-tailed foxes on that tract. I've seen turkeys roosting in loblolly pines forty feet high and a squirrel could run for an hour in those oaks and never touch the same limb twice.

Some nice fishing holes too.

When Harold was killed, Annette McCray inherited all of his property. Was not a month later that Annette produced a will of her own, and that instrument bequeathed all of Annette's recently inherited homestead to Kelly Lamb. The relevant documents were notarized at the courthouse shortly before she and Kelly married. It's clear from reports in the *Clarion* that Annette's decision to make Lamb her beneficiary was not regarded by locals as unusual. First of all, women in those years and in that region rarely owned estates of any size independent of a male heir or husband. Then there was the matter of Annette's health. Everyone knew that Butch's mother was much too frail to work a section of land on her own. And then there was Butch. The one fact that everyone seemed to take for granted was that Butch McCray could not inherit his father's property. You didn't leave assets that valuable to a simpleton. Locals no doubt viewed the transaction as an amicable quid pro quo, the Lamb brothers' father made heir to Annette's property in return for his pledge to shelter her surviving son.

So it was that decades later Hiram Lamb inherited Butch McCray's birthright.

To compare fortunes, Butch inherited from his foster father a half-acre lot in town where the candy store still remains, and you'd think from the way Hiram and Roscoe reacted that their daddy had robbed them of a gold mine. Hiram, in particular, resented his father's token largesse and used every trick he could think of to ruin Butch's modest business, embracing any pretext in that effort. About a year ago, after recalling the former president's wife using her platform to push for healthier food in school cafeterias, Hiram came to realize that the former first lady had given him an idea which he could bend to his own ongoing campaign.

I was present at the school board meeting when Hiram and his brother loudly proclaimed that it was the board's duty to stamp out all manner of junk food on the school's premises. "Our children deserve to eat healthy." Hiram stood before the board in righteous indignation to deliver that message. "We don't need our children spending their parents' hard-earned money on Cokes and candy."

This from a man whose closest association with vegetables was ketchup.

Butch McCray was not in attendance at the meeting. I'm sure Butch didn't know what Hiram was up to, and even if he did, Butch was not capable of making any contribution. However, Ms. Sheryl Lee Pearson made a point to attend the meeting.

Sheryl Lee teaches chemistry at the high school, one of the few folks educated outside the county who came back to her hometown. About the size of a starling, with a skullcap of hair and thick, plastic-framed glasses, Sheryl Lee lives in a style vaguely bohemian to natives, ignoring the society of churchgoers, county sings, and men for a private vocation devoted to a blind and aging mother and an extended family of teenage students.

"What precisely do we mean by 'premises'?" Sheryl Lee pushed back those enormous spectacles on a long, narrow nose as though exploring the intricacies of valences and bonding, moving on to point out that Butch's store, located on privately owned land, was not on the school's premises at all. Sheryl Lee further established that Butch's shrine to sugar and tooth decay was actually a couple of hundred yards farther from the elementary wing of the school than was Carl Koon's coffee shop.

"So if Hiram is truly motivated by a concern for our students' health, I move we amend his motion to press for a city ordinance that forbids food of any kind being sold within, say, a quarter mile of the campus."

Hiram stalled briefly before retorting that it was Butch's store selling to the children.

"Butch is the problem," Hiram declared with unintended candor. "Not Carl."

"But if you shut down Butch's store, what's to keep our children from going to Carl's place?" Pearson objected. "Junk food is junk food, no matter who sells it. If we close Mr. Butch's business, then Carl's café has to go too."

That riposte got immediate support from the solitary black citizen at the meeting.

"You tell 'em, Sheryl Lee. What's good for the goose be good for the gander."

The Lamb brothers had not anticipated geese nor ganders nor, apparently, Sheryl Lee Pearson. They certainly had never entertained the possibility that a putsch on Butch could backfire, so in a bald *volte face,* and in rare defeat, the Lamb brothers withdrew their petition to close Butch's store. Sheryl Lee's proposed amendment was thus made moot and the board exhaled a collective sigh of relief.

I allocated maybe half a column covering this brouhaha in the *Clarion,* a few lines on an inside fold, but when I contacted Hiram for comment he tore into my ass like Nixon into Woodward, threatening to pull his advertisements along with whatever subscribers he influenced.

I bought our local paper after being laid off from the *Boston Globe.* I had my own column at the *Globe,* "The Daily Take, from Clara Buchanan." Had my picture topping the column, airbrushed to erase ten years from my actual age, a tumble of unkempt hair framing a face windburned from countless hours sculling on the Charles. That was before Hillary's messy defeat and the layoffs at my newspaper. Before my brush with Speaker Ryan and precipitous fall from grace. I came back to Laureate thinking that at least in my own hometown I'd be released from restraints imposed by pusillanimous editors and lawyers. I'd be a free agent. Independent. In no man's pocket! I'd write what I wanted to write without fear or favor, by God. Say whatever the hell was on my mind.

Like Rachel Maddow.

That was before my monthly survival hinged on display ads and the capriciousness of subscribers self-identified as zealots for Jesus, the Tea Party, or the NRA. I stood up to Hiram's extortion for about two and a half seconds.

"How 'bout I just print the minutes?"

"Print one word, you'll lose my ads and anybody else's owes me. I'll make damn sure."

So I pulled the story. Here I am, the big-shot reporter and one-time foreign correspondent, the woman who faced down drug lords and jihadists from Colombia to the Congo, a Peabody winner, not to mention a regular on *Meet the Press*—but with a single threat to my wallet Hiram Lamb put me in a corner. I caved. The brothers Lamb beat me without throwing a punch, but they lost the opening round in their fight to take Butch's half-acre inheritance. For a while, Butch could relax. There was no fresh incentive to take away his land and the Lamb brothers seemed disinclined for a second round with Sheryl Lee Pearson.

But then came an unexpected opportunity.

Was maybe a week after little Jenny's green man bannered my headline that the Honorable Bull Putnal drove over from Madison to meet with Hiram and Roscoe and one or two hangers-on at the majordomo's table in Carl Koon's coffeehouse.

Bull Putnal is the ensconced representative serving our district in the House of a rancorous legislature. I've known Bull from grade school when his name was still "Terrence." I have no idea how Putnal acquired his bovine moniker. The man surely does not look anything like a bull. Our home-owned pol is shorter than average height and soft as putty with a triple chin that shivers like the wattle on a turkey. But he is an edacious son of a bitch. I've seen Bull devour a side of ribs and a pound of brisket in less time than it takes most people to swallow an aspirin. Not a dresser. He uses a Rotary pin to anchor a clip-on tie and I've never seen Terry in a belt. A pair of work suspenders wide enough to tow trucks hitches onto polyester slacks that bag around the man's ankles like socks on a rooster.

But I guarantee you, if Bull Putnal was thrown buck naked into a house full of thieves, he'd come out owning an emporium. I should disclose that I'm not one of Put-nal's confidants. I definitely am not invited to his coffee-table confabs. In fact, during the particular soiree to be reported here, I was snapping pictures in the pasture outside the cof-feehouse. But no conversation stays private for long, and even a rookie reporter could find sources to reconstruct that morning's powwow.

"Mornin', Bull," Hiram greeted the politician as he wad-dled up to join the Lambs and a smattering of other locals.

"Hiram. Roscoe. Gentlemen. Connie, can I get a coffee?"

"Yes, sir."

Connie leaning far over a table to scoop up a tip and display her twin gifts. The family values candidate smiling his appreciation for that favor.

"What you got, Mr. Putnal?" Roscoe Lamb guided the old goat's attention back to the table.

"Good news." Bull settled himself grandly into a chair built for an ass about half the width of his own.

"You found my dog?" Roscoe inquired.

Roscoe had begun the morning's conversation expressing distress over the loss of his favorite hound.

"Best damn deer dog I ever had. Cost me a fortune."

"Cain't do anything 'bout your dog, Roscoe." Bull clucked sympathy. "But I might can help you recoup some of that fortune."

"Roscoe's always up for that," the high school's principal quipped.

Hiram's brother rewarding that familiarity with a cold glance.

"You were sayin', Bull?"

Putnal smiled unctuously. "Ya'll know that federal money the legislature was chewing over last session? For the schools?"

"Ain't the fed's money," Hiram Lamb chimed in to correct his representative. "It's _our_ damn money. Goddamn socialists wanta stimulate the 'conomy, let 'em waste somebody else's earnings."

"You don't take it, somebody else will," Bull replied, smiling.

"The hell you talking about?"

"Four and a half million dollars is all."

"You mean $4.5 million dollars of pork."

The legislator waved his marbled hands over the table like it was a Ouija board. "Call it pork. Call it discretionary or stimulus. Call it whatever yer want to, but it's out there and it's gonna git spent. But you got to submit a bid."

"Bid? What bid?" Hiram was suddenly alert.

Well, it turns out that a grant written by one of those despised bureaucrats qualified Lafayette County for federal funds dedicated to repair and renovate Laureate Consolidated School. Still chafing from losses suffered during the not-so-distant recession, Hiram and Roscoe Lamb were abruptly offered the lion's share of a $4.5-million-dollar pie.

I'm not sure that lions eat pie, but the Lamb brothers—?

Let's just say they were incentivized.

"So we're talkin' a new cafeteria, here?" Hiram snapped open his Mont Blanc.

"And some inside work on the main building. And the basketball court," Bull confirmed.

Hiram scribbling estimates on a napkin.

". . . I can build the cafeteria new and refinish the basketball court for under three million. Two and a quarter. Two and a half, tops. Should leave plenty for the electrical work and air-conditionin' and so on. I don't need those contracts."

"Well, I'm glad to see I've piqued your interest," Putnal replied drily.

"You'll help us out, won't you?"

"I fully intend to lobby for your participation, Hiram." Bull smiled. "Of course, I'm countin' on ya'll to help me too."

"We awready got that cat skinned," Roscoe declared.

"Oh, I know, I know." The state's rep dabbed at a spot on the table with his napkin. "You boys are on board. That's not the problem."

"There's a problem?"

"More like a caveat."

"The fuck is a caveat?" Roscoe turned to Principal Wilburn to answer that question, but the conversation, at least by Laureate standards, kept racing along.

"Got a issue related to landscape," Bull declared, and nodded in the general direction of the school grounds.

CHAPTER THREE

Local Minister Says Evolution 'Voodoo Science'
The Clarion

Carl Koon's Coffeehouse & Café offers two views of our county's consolidated school. One of Carl's wide windows looks west over the playground to the high school, the cafeteria, and Butch's store. The java shop's rear window faces due north across a hayfield to the elementary wing situated on the far side. The field was swarming with activity on the morning of Representative Putnal's visit, a sward littered with crepe paper, bunting and papier-mâché skirting flatbed trailers parked like so many bombers on the deck of an aircraft carrier.

It was football season and the rites of homecoming were on full display. Start with the floats. Every homecoming week at LHCS, students from grades nine through twelve compete for the coveted honor of "Best Float" which means that once a year the hayfield behind the Koons' place of business turns into a project *alfresco* with a fervor to rival Mardi Gras. The week begins with a school assembly and builds over a span of days to an elaborate parade, the homecoming queen and king installed in Confederate colors on some vintage convertible amidst a flotilla of trailers. The school's band leads the procession, marching in full regalia past the courthouse on Main Street and all the way to the water tower on the edge of town.

It's football in the South, a Friday night fever set to peak with Trent Lamb leading the hometown Hornets against the Lake Butler Tigers. "Sting Them Tigers!" Trent and his brother, Danny, were pretending to help a cheerleader staple that banner on a rig of goal posts. Sheryl Lee Pearson was engaged with a pair of Latino students also working on the seniors' float. Edgar Uribe, the man-sized migrant who crossed swords with the Lamb brothers, was completely absorbed in the final touches on an amazingly detailed sculpture of NASA's lunar lander, shavings of Styrofoam lodging on his shirt and in his thick dark hair.

It is the prerogative of graduating seniors to choose a theme for their homecoming parade, those motifs ranging in past years from "Just Say No" to Michael Jackson's "Beat It." This year the theme was positively geek, "Life On Other Worlds," which meant that bales of tissue and logs of Styrofoam would go to the construction of extraterrestrial gags, gimmicks, or similar presentations.

The discipline of students, haphazard even in ordinary seasons, was suspended entirely for homecoming. Freshmen, sophomores, juniors, and seniors were allowed to skip class so long as they were engaged in some approved activity, and if they were working on a float the dress code was greatly relaxed, to the delight of coffeehouse patrons, mostly men edging to retirement, who gathered at Carl's rear window to see teenage nymphs stretched over bunting or hiking up a stepladder to drape a truncated goal post.

Caffeine-primed to catch a flash of leg, belly, or breast.

"Ain't nuthin' wrong with that landscape," Roscoe intoned and Principal Wilburn swallowed an embarrassed laugh.

Bull Putnal waddled around in his chair to face Hiram.

"But it ain't the pasture's in the way. It's this here site. Right chere."

"You mean—the coffeehouse?" Hiram now leaning in close to the pol's ear.

Representative Putnal nodded. "Way the plans work, the school can't expand south, and there's already residences built on three sides. Only way to add construction is out front, toward Main Street, and with easements and all, that means Carl's gonna have to relocate his business to accommodate the new construction."

"Don't tell Carl," Hiram warned. "Or Connie either, for that matter. They'll try to milk the deal."

"Why I'm tellin' you-all now," Bull smiled. "Ya'll oughta be able to convince Carl to move locations. Either that or buy him out. Which just leaves one piss-ant piece of land left to worry over."

"Another caveat? Where?"

Bull pointed a finger fat as a sausage.

"Candy store."

"Butch's store?!" Hiram's birthmark flushed with his face.

"It's in the way."

"A half-acre lot?!" Roscoe practically choked on his coffee. "Hellfire, we can build around him, for Chrissake. We can build over him!"

"Wish you could," Putnal said with a cluck. "But the way the plans work, that street out front—? Is gonna be cut off. The new cafeteria's gonna be built across the street from where it is now. Right on Butch's property."

"Butch ain't gone sell that shack. Not for all the tea in China."

This assessment from Marty Hart, a weasel-thin guard employed at the prison north of town.

"This is a private conversation, Marty."

"Private or not that store is Butch's life," Marty rejoined. "It's all he knows."

Principal Wilburn removed his glasses in a weighty attempt to influence strategy.

"But couldn't Butch's land, or the coffeehouse for that matter, be acquired under eminent domain?"

"Could if the state really wanted it," Bull said, nodding. "Or if this was a federally mandated project. But this is a grant, gentlemen, a dump of federal money contingent on caveats already agreed to by the state legislature. Which means the feds don't pay if we don't play."

Silence fell around the table. Leave it to Marty to voice what everyone else was thinking.

"Gotta be some way to part a half-wit from a half-acre of land."

Representative Putnal pointedly ignored that bait.

"How much time we have?" Hiram asked finally.

"Bids are due first of December." Bull hitched his thumbs inside his out-sized suspenders. "Course, with the holidays and all, you got some more time. But still . . ."

"We can't get the bid till we get the land," Roscoe said, summing up the situation, and Putnal's wattle shimmied with the nod of his head.

"That's about it."

An uneasy silence settled over the table, broken only when Correction Officer Hart in complete non sequitur posed the question on almost nobody's mind.

"What ya'll think about Jenny O'Steen's little green man?"

The table groaned in unison, but then Representative Putnal's reply cracked up everybody at the table.

"Can I get the bastard's vote?"

CHAPTER FOUR

Great Balls of Fire Seen from Porch
The Clarion

About Daddy. I bought the *Clarion* for more than three hundred thousand dollars, two hundred grand of that total borrowed on the back of my father's property. Wasn't a loan, really, I rationalized. Just an advance on my inheritance. Dad sold most of our land after mother died, but he still has a double-wide on one hundred and twenty acres of pine not far from Pickett Lake. That collateral in hand, I went to the bank ignoring any possibility of failure. After all, Laureate's hometown paper has been in business continuously since the thirties. I am only its third owner.

National trends favored me too. It's a curious fact that as big-time newspapers have folded or gone digital, broadsheets and weeklies with local ties in modest markets have hung on. Some have even thrived. Surely the *Clarion*'s ledger would balance roughly the same as it had in earlier decades, I told myself. After all, Laureate's web of kith and kin kept their paper solvent through the Great Depression—why wouldn't they support me now?

In fairness, my father warned me.

"Be sure you know what you're getting into, Clara Sue."

"I'm born and raised in Laureate, Dad," I replied. "Folks will believe me before any outsider."

"Not necessarily."

"What's that supposed to mean?"

"You know damn well what it means. Folks here don't want to hear you ragging on conservatives. Sticking up for queers and trans-whatevers."

"Daddy, I have run maybe three or four columns total on gay rights in my entire career."

"What about that business with Speaker Ryan?"

Okay, *that*.

I may have mentioned that Speaker Ryan and I had ourselves a small contretemps. That kerfuffle unfolded a couple of months before Senator Clinton lost her bid for the presidency when Ryan released yet another proposal to cut taxes and hobble health care. I had spent months looking for sources other than Paul Krugman to debunk the speaker's supply-side fantasies and was surprised to find a broad spectrum of wonks who agreed that the speaker's budget simply did not add up. The underlying assumption that tax cuts pay for themselves was not supported by facts on the ground, but, hey—!

You just have to believe.

"I want to know if Paul Ryan is simply a dogmatist who ignores contrary evidence, or whether he's a shill for big money," I told my editor. "Is he a man of blind faith or a man blinded by faith? Or is he just a liar with a Lon Chaney smile?"

"Don't go there," my editor chided. "No arguments *ad hominem*. Assume unsullied intentions and stick with the numbers. Even Republicans can't change arithmetic."

So the *Globe* sent me to Washington to interview Speaker Ryan. I called in advance to get an appointment and made sure to confirm the date and time. I arrived at the speaker's office ahead of schedule, but a buzz-cut aide informed me that Ryan had been called to the White House and would not be able to meet with me to discuss the details of his latest budget. I asked when I could get our appointment rescheduled and got a vague reply. "We'll let you know," the flunky assured me, but three days and half a dozen e-mails later it became clear that Speaker Ryan had decided to duck the interview.

However, there is one gig the speaker never evades. On any weekday morning you can find Congressman Ryan leading a dozen or more mostly Republican acolytes through a grueling workout. It's one of those pseudo military routines that are popular. P90X is Ryan's go-to. I decided that if I could not get the speaker on record in his office, I'd ambush him at his gym. The problem was that Ryan's gymnasium only admits members from the United States House of Representatives. In fact, until the mid-eighties even women elected to Congress were not allowed inside the House gym and the place remains, in my opinion, a nest of narcissists. You've probably seen Ryan's photo. The wide smile. Barbell and biceps. A baseball cap turned backward and a torso hairless as a newt. Lots of "hormone therapy" going on, it seems to me. Politicians touting family values signing up for testosterone boosters like Boy Scouts for Jamboree.

The lockers are located in a subbasement of the Rayburn Building. You descend into those bowels, show your credentials to a security guard, and proceed down a claustrophobic hallway to find what looks like a wide, sterile cave with a low ceiling of acoustic tile punctured at intervals with fluorescent lighting that makes everything look like stale paste. A vast hardwood floor lined along the periphery with weights, mats, medicine balls. Lots of treadmills. I wangled a day pass from my Massachusetts representative and a little before six thirty in the morning jumped Speaker Ryan just as he emerged from the men's locker room.

"Mr. Speaker."

Took him by surprise, which isn't easy.

"You aren't a member."

"I'm Clara Buchanan, Mr. Speaker. The *Boston Globe*."

"I know who you are, Ms. Buchanan. Mostly from CNN."

"We were on the calendar, sir. You canceled."

"Well, I don't do interviews in the gym," Ryan said, glaring. "This is my time."

"You wasted three days of mine," I countered. "So when can we reschedule?"

"Tell you what," he offered after the slightest pause. "Hang with me for a workout and we'll see."

I spotted a pair of rowing machines not far from the free weights.

"How about the erg? First to six thousand meters."

I was still rowing competitively at the time. Dawn patrol at the Union Boat Club, five mornings a week. That was before the docs found a blockage in my right descending ventricle. Yes, I have a stent in my heart. It's not a huge deal.

At least, not until lately.

In any case, a week after I handily bested Paul Ryan on a Concept2, I was granted an interview in his spacious office. Ryan brought a sheaf of his famous charts to the meeting; I brought a three-ring binder stuffed with articles and a calculator. It's safe to say that the speaker did not appreciate my critique of his arithmetic, but what really chapped him was that somebody with an iPhone had videoed me kicking his butt on the rowing machine.

By the time I sat down to interview Speaker Ryan, that damned video had dominated the news cycle for an entire week. My interview with the speaker—? Was a bust. There would be no coverage of Ryan's plan for cutting taxes. Nothing about budgets or the assumptions underlying supply-side prescriptions. What voters were to believe about the most important questions guiding economic policy was completely ignored.

Instead it was the digital capture of the speaker gasping next to a forty-something woman that went viral. A froth of commentary was spawned, none of it having anything to do with tax cuts, entitlements, or funny numbers. The *Clarion*'s banner boiled down local reaction to the video along with a native misogyny.

Local Girl Embarrasses Speaker

In full disclosure, I should admit that the gray beards at the *Globe* were not impressed with my tactics either. Most regarded my blindside as a badly conceived stunt. The older heads pegged me for a Woodward wannabe. Others saw a diva in the making, or maybe just a bitch. The only person in the ensuing weeks who did not offer an opinion about my run-in with the Speaker of the House was Randall Greene.

I actually met my husband-to-be some years before my infamous interlude with Speaker Ryan. Randall was working for Common Cause at the time and had contacted the *Globe* to offer some inside scoop on coming legislation. I got tagged for the interview.

"Try not to piss him off," my editor admonished.

"It's Common Cause, chief. Nobody cares."

"I care," my boss replied, so I threw on my anorak and headed out.

The day was cold with the promise of sleet. The paper had arranged for me to meet Greene at a local Starbucks. I arrived, as is my habit, a little early, but was distracted by a confection of steam and roasted beans meeting the raw aromas of stale cement and pedestrians outside.

It took me a moment to note the man staring at me from a booth just inside the door. First thing I noticed was the hair. Randall has a great head of hair. I mean, like Robert Redford hair, gold and layered and thick. Then I noticed the eyes—light green with lashes almost feminine. Fair complexion—I am brown as a berry compared to my husband which led me to surmise, correctly, that Randall doesn't spend a lot of time out of doors.

He stood to greet me.

"Randall Greene," he announced formally.

Offering that wry smile.

"Clara Buchanan."

I shucked my anorak and shook the damp from my hair. I expected to see some soft-gutted person in a lobbyists' uniform—the stereotyped fella in a gray flannel suit, as it were—but Randall was lean and compact in pressed jeans and a light wool blazer. I could see he was surprised at my height. Most men are. Some try to hide it.

Not Randall.

"Is that all you, or are there stilts?"

"If that's the best you can do, Mr. Greene, let's just call it a day."

"My bad." He winked an apology. "Please. Take a seat."

I ordered a latte, and with no other preamble the visiting lobbyist began to probe my positions on everything from affirmative action to Citizens United.

At some point I actually raised my hand to stop him.

"Aren't I supposed to be interviewing you?" I asked.

"You are interviewing me," he replied. "Just not for your paper."

I steered the conversation back to his own wheelhouse. It was not earthshaking news, just another cabal in some committee or another trying to defund the Affordable Care Act, which remains Randall's special area of expertise.

After getting his take on that battle, I broadened my inquiry.

"So, Mr. Greene—"

"Randall, please."

"Okay, then. Randall, who will Common Cause back for president in the coming election?"

"We're . . . open-minded," he said, fencing.

"Have you *ever* gone to bed with a Republican?" I pressed.

"Got up with one this morning," he smiled, and with a wink of those Brooke Shield lashes, I knew I'd met my match.

He stayed an extra day, and that day turned into another day, and then another. We had a lot of coffeehouse conversations. I learned that Randall Timpson Greene had worked K Street for nearly twenty years, a scrappy forward pushing position papers and policy manifestos up a hardened court that stretched from the West Wing to the Pentagon. A K Street familiar, but never a Steve Clark or a Susan Hirschmann. Never a real player. In fact, Randall was "let go" a month after I lost my column. He probably could have hired on with some other firm, but here he is with me, laying out photographs of the local 4-H Club and posting minutes from Rotary meetings in a paper that runs eight columns and twenty pages.

I tried to believe that Randall and I were like those professionals who leave high-paying jobs to find fulfillment in a microbrewery or pet store. I strained to imagine readers stimulated by my hometown columns to Jeffersonian debate. A public forum for enlightened citizens. A new estate.

Scratch that.

I found out in a hurry it's not print that readers are look-ing for in their backyard news—it's photography. People scan the copy, sure, the banners, anyway. But it's pictures that keep subscribers happy, not print, and it's easy to see why. After all, who doesn't like to see herself in the paper? Parents love seeing their sons or daughters in the local rag, whether lined up on the football field or that third girl from the right in the back row of the Glee Club. Every youngster who makes Honor Roll gets a picture. Every family reunion generates a half-dozen portraits, and of course hunters will literally kill to get their trophies displayed in black-and-white.

Hunting season always provides an added bonanza, deer season competing with football for the number of pictures published. In fact, from first frost till spring hardly an issue of the *Clarion* hits a kitchen table that doesn't feature a father and son flanking a buck, bear, or boar. "No buck fever here!" That caption accompanies a photo of some boy or girl who's just bagged that first deer, the blood of the slain animal smeared over a smiling young face in joyful commemoration of his or her first and vital kill. Of course, fishermen send in pictures year-round with detailed narratives of the expedition that hooked a redfish or snapper or largemouth bass. These are not the bloody images of a real hunt but are treasured equally with all others.

Trophies of choice have changed over the years, of course. Forty years ago, a hunter was never truly blooded till he bagged a bear or panther. Even gators didn't count. But panthers are now protected and rare as hen's teeth, and bears vary in range and population. Hunters nowadays who are in the running for a trophy of merit take their weapons and dogs in search of wild hogs.

It's hard to beat the challenge posed by a feral hog. These are intelligent and ferocious beasts that range with few natural predators in the acorn-rich loess of the flatwoods, or else gather in sounders in the palmetto wilderness near the coast. A boar can run anywhere from seventy or eighty pounds of tusk and tooth to a three-hundred-pound monster that can charge a hapless hunter at forty miles an hour. Wild hogs feed, forage, and attack in sounders, the sows as mean and dangerous as the boars. These are the new Grendels of the flatwoods, the *Sus scrofa*, a hybrid of Eurasian boars and domestic hogs turned loose from the time of Ponce de Leon. With populations of panther and bear nearly decimated, the wild hog has become the trophy de jour for hunters looking for primal thrills, and the photos these folks send to the paper can be downright kinky.

This morning, for example, I received a digitized photo of a good-looking young lady bursting out of a polka-dot top and denim shorts posing with a two-hundred-pound hog that she killed with her boyfriend's Remington.

"Randall, take a look at this."

There she is, smiling into the camera, a straw hat over strawberry hair. A wink of something metal piercing her navel. I wasn't surprised to see in the file's accompanying text that the young hunter was a coed at Florida State.

I remember when bowhunting was regarded as an exotic pastime; now we have babes in bikinis cruising the woods for the rush of a well-tusked slaughter. College kids used to sow their wild seeds at Daytona or a Grateful Dead concert. Now they hire guides to go after feral hogs.

We can get dozens of these photos in a single week, a Roman triumph of bears, deer, hogs, and fishes freshwater and salty. In the days of emulsion and linotype it would take hours and hours to lay out the visuals for that volume of material, and hours more to arrange the elucidating copy.

Thank God for In-Design and Sheryl Lee Pearson. I don't know how Randall and I would have gotten through our first year at the *Clarion* without Sheryl Lee's help. Pearson has honchoed the high school yearbook ever since joining the faculty and knows more about software and photography than I will ever forget. Virtually everything is digitized. Photos come to the paper attached as a file to an e-mail. Sometimes people walk in and download directly from a smartphone or camera. My newspaper, in case you want to visit, is located on Main Street just down from the courthouse in an overbuilt brick building that used to be a bank. We still keep our cash and valuables in the old Diebold vault, which is a joke, because that stash is always open. Not sure I'd know how to open the damn thing if it shut.

Anyway, there's nothing between the vault and the streetside entry but a half-dozen computers and desks and a maple counter interrupted on one end with a saloon door and a brass-framed mirror. Every now and then I'll find my reflection in that antique speculum, a forty-something female in a pair of stained chinos and a frayed Tamrac vest. A windburned face below a mop of salt-and-pepper hair. Broad shoulders. That and prescriptions for medicine to lower cholesterol describe your intrepid reporter.

A bay of windows older than my antique mirror gives a great view of Main Street. These are huge squares of leaded glass beveled on each side and fitted into oaken frames. The sills are big enough to sit on. The mirror, windows, and pressed-tin ceiling remind me of days gone by, along with some of the paper's archaic equipment. We still have the two-cylinder, water-cooled Johnny whose belted drive used to turn the old press, and job sticks and linotype mount like museum pieces on the walls. Typesetters in those years could read type upside down as easily as right side up, a skill now esoteric and unnecessary.

"You're lingering over that photo, husband."

"A bikini, a gun, and a hog—who wouldn't?"

"You are a priapic old goat."

"If that's what I think it means, I hope so." He smiled. "Oh. And we got another sighting."

"Good Lord."

"Rod Hamlin." Randall retrieved the name from a scrawl of handwritten notes. "Appears Mr. Hamlin was having trouble sleeping last night so he gets up to pee and before he can finish that business he hears something outside."

"Tell me it was a possum. A twelve-point buck."

"Try a ball of light."

"'Ball of light'?"

"What the man said."

"We're talking softball? Baseball?"

"Larger than athletic equipment of any kind, apparently, though Mr. Hamlin was careful to say that it was hard to judge the distance. But he insists this thing was floating over his yard like some kind of jack-o'-lantern, green and round and emitting a steady, high-pitched tone—'Like old TVs used to make.'"

"Drone, maybe?"

"Rod says not."

"I assume the wraith has moved on to *The Twilight Zone*?"

"Or maybe Tampa. Hamlin's saying he observed the thing for a good four or five minutes before he went back inside for a camera. Or was it a rifle? Can't remember."

I unzipped my vest.

"Resurrected relatives. Slaughtered dogs. Balls of light. Has the county gone *Ghostbusters*?"

"More likely the power of suggestion. This *E.T.* theme and homecoming have got people imagining things."

"Balls of light, dead husbands, and gnomes?" I said, snorting. "This in a county with more churches than stop signs?"

"Could be a whole new plane of enlightenment has descended."

"The school board's still pissed off with Darwin, for God's sake."

"So broaden their horizons," Randall rejoined breezily.

"This from a man leering over a half-nude coed and a feral hog."

"And a gun."

"Rifle," I corrected him. "Words matter."

Randall was about to tell me where I could stuff my words when the brass bell anchored above our oaken entry tinkled a warning. I turned toward the complaint of iron hinges and a squeak of neoprene soles to find the sheriff of Lafayette County at the door.

Sheriff Colt Buchanan is my first cousin. Colt inhabits his uniformed tans as lean and hard as a split of rails. A black belt heavy as a lumberjack's cinches onto a waist almost slender to tote a radio, mace, and handgun of formidable caliber. Looking at Colt you're reminded that we live in a place where Creek Indians used to hollow out dugouts from cypress trunks and hunt gators and bears with spears and axes of flint.

Half the people in our county claim to be descended from some Creek or Cherokee or Seminole in a lineage invariably matriarchal. In actual fact, local white residents are more likely to have black slaves in their family tree than Native Americans, but no one rushes to claim that heritage. Much more chic to have a Native American's blood in your veins than a slave's.

But Sheriff Buchanan's ancestry is well documented, Colt's mother being a blood relative and only two generations distant from a Creek woman who married Tink Buchanan sometime in the early 1900s. Martha had a brother and two half-sisters. The sisters married inside the tribe; the brother took a wife in Taylor County before getting himself killed in the Turpentine Wars. There are all sorts of stories about Tink and his gator-skinning wife, but no one doubts her tribe's provenance, that ancestry evident in Colt's mother and in Colt himself.

His face is chiseled in planes, a high forehead with eyes wide set and the color of coffee. He has a nose like the warrior on a can of Calumet baking soda, and perfect teeth. His skin is more dark than red, but the hair is black as the feathers of crows. Blackest black I've ever seen on a human being. Blacker than coal. Preternaturally black.

Colt has been county sheriff for, lessee, three cycles of elections, which is a pretty good run. He presides over four deputies, widespread domestic violence, and a thriving drug trade dominated by the traffic of methamphetamine. The flatwoods offer endless cover for the production of crystal meth, that product easy to brew in RVs or mobile homes or deer camps and invisible in the endless tracts of slash pine that stretch from Perry to Old Town.

Sheriff Buchanan is always busting some lab or another, usually with a local cooker in tow, which always makes for good copy. I suppose I should mention that we used to be close, Colt and I. By that I mean kissing close. Not uncommon in a county where practically everyone is related.

"How's my closest cousin?" Colt greeted me.

"Steady by jerks." I lapsed into local patois and then, "What can I do you for, Sheriff?"

"Dunno. Get me a paper, maybe?"

He took his time strolling to the counter. Worrying a seam of Formica with the nail of his thumb on his way to greeting my husband.

"Mornin', Randall."

"Sheriff Buchanan," Randall acknowledged cheerfully. "I got your birthday request for Miss Briar. Had to squeeze her onto the inside fold, but she's there."

That would be Hattie Briar. Yet another relative.

"How's Aunt Hattie getting on?" I asked.

"She's good," our sheriff replied absently. "Ninety-six years old this Sunday and can't wait for Heritage Week."

I stifled a groan. The town's annual paean to its mostly imagined history always involved a trip to Dowling Park and an interview with the county's oldest native born. Hattie Briar's yearly interview had become a staple for the paper that I could not change, cancel, or discard.

Colt chuckled. "She's not that bad, Clara Sue."

I shook my head. "I've interviewed heads of state and jihadists with no problem at all, but with Hattie—? It's my second time around and I have no idea where to start."

"Set there long enough, she'll start herself. And once she gets goin', forget about stoppin' her."

"Well, that's the damn truth," I acknowledged ruefully, and conversation came to an abrupt halt. Colt just idled there at the counter. Finding another seam of Formica.

"Is there something I can help you with, Sheriff?"

"Prolly not. Cain't make up my mind."

I felt the familiar tingle along the nape of my neck that often presages a breaking story, but I did not press. I did not follow up with a bracket of questions.

A good reporter has to know when to listen.

"Awright, then," the sheriff resumed. "Start with Jenny O'Steen. Little green men, whatever. Ya'll ran a line or two couple weeks back?"

I nodded.

"Well, there's a rumor startin' to mill."

"Kind of rumor?"

"Gettin' around that Butch McCray was the 'little man' Jenny O'Steen saw."

"Butch said himself that he found her with Isabel," I said with a shrug. "Good thing, too, because according to Doc the Pepsi that Butch gave Jenny probably saved her life."

The sheriff nodded.

"But the story takin' a turn on Facebook an' the like is that Butch had something to do with Jennie *before* he gave her the soda."

"Oh, Jesus," Randall protested.

"You don't believe that crap, do you, Colt?" I asked.

"Ain't what I believe that's a problem. It's what other people believe—or more likely want to believe. The Lamb brothers ain't the only ones would love to see Butch lose his store."

"This have anything to do with the construction proposed for the school?" Randall asked. "Because there are boatloads of folks chasing that grant."

"There are," I affirmed. "And Butch's store is right smack dab in the way."

Sheriff Buchanan smiled. "Nuthin' gets by you, does it, Clara Sue?"

Was I blushing? Crying out loud!

"I only know what people tell me, Sheriff."

"Well, if you hear anything that involves Butch, I'd 'preciate your passing it along."

"Anything but my source," I promised.

"Goes without sayin'," he agreed. "Meantime, have ya'll got any more reports similar to Jenny's?"

"Ran that story Barbara Stanton gave me," I answered. "Senator Stanton raised from the dead apparently."

"Saw that one."

"Rod Hamlin called in this morning," Randall spoke up. "Swears he saw a ball of light floating over his place."

"Ball of light, was it? Not a fire?"

"No fire, why? You getting similar reports, Sheriff?"

"Two or three a week," Colt admitted. "Dead relatives. UFOs. One alien abduction. It's like the damn *X-Files*."

"Randall thinks it's just homecoming week," I offered. "*E.T.* and the power of suggestion."

"Beats meth, I reckon."

The sheriff falling silent as he trailed a finger along the brim of his Stetson.

"Colt, what is it?" I prodded. "What?"

He reached a decision apparently.

"Grab your camera, cuz," he told me finally.

"Something I need you to see."

CHAPTER FIVE

Pickett Lake Slaughter
The Clarion

L ast year the county cut three special-education teachers and four classroom assistants from the school's budget, but when time came to update our cop cars there wasn't a whisper of dissent, the old, reliable, and relatively cheap Crown Vic Interceptors replaced on a voice vote with a fleet of Dodge Chargers, each boasting more than 370 horsepower in a hemi engine with variable cam timing that might get twelve miles to the gallon in town with brake pads that have to be replaced as often as socks.

But talk about fun. Every time Sheriff Buchanan brings me along to some crime scene or accident I feel like I'm cruising in the Batmobile, a computer mounted on the cruiser's dash beeping information, calls squawking over radios and chirping from a cell phone mounted amidships with a twelve-gauge pump and radar gun. You look along the door panels you can see where keys and belts and holsters have chewed up the plastic. The smell of leather and sweat. Pine-Sol wafting from behind the welded grille to compete with the effluvium of some felon's vomit.

You can navigate the county by the steeples and bone-yards of our churches. Colt and I passed the First Baptist

Church at the only traffic light in town. Four miles down Highway 27 we shot by the Church of God, and then Airline Redeemer at which intersection we turned off 27 for a series of S-curves to slalom past Midway Pentecostal at eighty miles an hour.

I was pulling Gs like a fighter pilot under ribs of bruised sky. A front of autumn air redolent with ambrosias of pasture and woodlands rushing through the prowler's open windows.

Colt as casual at the wheel as though inching through a car wash.

"WHERE WE HEADED?" I shouted.

"PICKETT LAKE."

Pickett Lake. Our teenage haunt. Our getaway. I'd bicycle to Hatch Bend, stopping along the way to snatch grasshoppers or grunt worms, and then trundle another mile or so to the lake. Colt would meet me with a long pair of cane poles. We'd bait our hooks live on a monofilament line weighted with buckshot, set our corks and our poles.

Then we'd retreat behind the water oaks to neck beneath a bower of moss.

Finding ourselves as minnows nibbled.

We almost always brought home some catch or another. The lake teemed with bass and perch and bream in those years. The water ran clear and cold, routed through countless numbers of sloughs and hammocks and creeks to the lake's sandy-bottomed reservoir. I once landed an eight-pound largemouth bass on a cane pole, and that catch did not rate much above average attention.

Pickett Lake was a magnet for all manner of wildlife. Go early in the morning you could spot gators trolling for breakfast, their snouts leaving wakes that converged in a lazy zigzag on water smooth as glass. Panthers would emerge stiff legged from a canopy of Spanish moss to drink along the shore with white-tailed deer and black bears. You'd see osprey in the one or two tidewater cypress remaining on the lake's northern shore, those singular predators waiting to talon a fish or snake below. And heron stalked pollywogs and craw-fish by the dozens beneath a grove of water oaks that ringed the lake in a breathing architecture as old as Stonehenge. Sometimes we'd fall asleep in that ancient cathedral, Colt and I. Two innocents with fishing poles. That was then.

But now I am married. Colt is widowed.

And Pickett Lake is dry as nun's dust.

We turned off the hard road and lumbered over a cattle gap, the sun breaking through ribs of clouds.

"How long since the lake's held water?" I asked when we arrived.

"Been ten years since it was full," he replied.

In fact, nearly all the lakes that seemed limitlessly fecund in my salad years are now dead, the casualty of a changing climate and the destruction of hardwood forests evolved to shelter a concatenation of natural aqueducts that recharged the lakes and ponds of the region.

My grandfather worked for one of the last gangs to har-vest hardwood in northern Florida, a crew of men who for pennies a day braved snakes and insects and unbearable heat to wrestle giant logs from the swamp with nothing more than peaveys and axes and two-man saws. I have a tintype photo of papa manning an old Clyde skidder to drag in a single tidewater cypress that required an entire boxcar for transport. Trees thirty or even forty feet in girth were common.

Timber was king and a city sprang up overnight, com-plete with stores and bunkhouses and even hospitals, all built in a virtual swamp for the thousands of men who cut, dried, and stacked the dimensioned lumber that gorged the holds of vessels headed to Jacksonville or Havana or farther afield.

But by the end of World War II there was nothing left to cut. Stands of hardwood cypress and pine that took centuries to mature had been harvested to extinction. Local economies died with the trees, lumberjacks and sawyers and yard men losing jobs that would not be replaced until the 1950s when the hardwood forests of northern Florida were replanted with a softer, faster-growing species tailored and tweaked for the production of pulp.

Every paper product you can imagine from transcripts to traffic tickets comes from pulpwood, and it did not take long for slash pine to replace its long-leafed cousin. In less than a decade land once dense with hardwood was carved into a virtual drain pan for vast tracts of *pinus elliottii,* the storied acres interrupted at intervals by fire lanes that stretched in veritable canals to sever the feeding creeks and waterways and divert increasingly fickle falls of rain to the Gulf of Mexico.

Pickett Lake followed Koon Lake and Garner Lake and Sears Lake to become a saucer of blinding white sand ringed with a dark and stubborn sentinel of water oak and scrub that clings to the old shoreline like druids around a pyre.

Bowls of sand dead of thirst.

It had become a graveyard, had Pickett Lake, and its demise was a catastrophe so gradual in the making as to go unnoticed. By the time I finished college, the shore had widened to a boundary of white-hot sand yards distant from any shade. Mallard ducks that used to land in the lake in squadrons for the feast of acorns along the shore altered their timeless migration. Colt told me that in the lake's final days you'd see people dragging baskets to salvage fish dying from lack of oxygen, their gills pleading silent agony.

I had not actually visited Pickett Lake in years. Didn't look like much now. A ragged boundary of distressed water oaks. A shallow crater of loam beyond.

Colt parked the cruiser beneath a beard of hanging moss. "We'll walk her in from here." He snapped off his safety belt and killed the engine. "Unless you wanta chance getting stuck."

"I can walk," I replied testily.

Colt leaned over to break the shotgun from its stanchion. I grabbed my Canon and within seconds both of us were ankle deep in soft, soft sand. I should have worn boots. I could feel grains of sand working warmly through my socks, my shoes. Colt rolling along with no apparent effort. Heading for the center of the lakebed.

"Am I looking for anything special?" I asked.

"Let you be the judge of that."

I staggered to keep up. "I don't see anything."

"There," he pointed straight ahead. "Right along there."

I tried to follow the line of his sight.

"What the hell—?"

It looked at first like somebody had poured oil in a narrow ribbon across the sand. Just a dark stain, maybe six inches wide and stretching to either side. But on approach I saw that this was not a line at all, but a circle poured dark as tar around the center of the lake.

"What is this shit, Colt? Some kind of asphalt?"

"Some damn kind," he replied.

"Kind of circumference we got here?"

"Quarter mile, at least," he replied.

"It is a circle, then?"

"Goddamn perfect, far as I can tell. And see those lines running in to the center?"

The lakebed was so flat I had trouble seeing it.

"Oh, there," I finally confirmed.

"They're like spokes on a wheel," Colt supplied. "'Cept only one goes all the way across."

We broke off to make a short arc around the formation and I saw that Colt was right. The lines ran like spokes in a wheel from the rim to the axle, but were not completely symmetrical.

I laughed.

"It's a peace symbol!"

"Be damn," he said, smiling. "I believe you're right."

"We used to see 'em on those old VW vans, remember?"

"Hippie vans we called 'em," Colt said, reminiscing, and for a moment we were face-to-face.

A long moment. With memories.

I directed my attention back to the lake's bed. Colt cradled his shotgun to pinch a chew of Red Man from a pack tucked inside his belt.

"I don't see any tire tracks, do you?" he asked, directing the conversation to safer topics.

"No footprints either. Other than ours," I said, following his lead.

"It's easy to cover tracks on sand," Colt said, speaking as if from experience.

I unlimbered my camera. "Prob'ly was kids from the school did this. Seniors painted the water tower, didn't they? It is homecoming week, after all."

"Don't jump to conclusions," he warned.

"Not jumping. To anything."

I walked over to the nearest spoke and took a knee. It looked like a perfectly uniform strip of coal-black tar, just a straight line over blazing white sand. I slid my hand along the deposit.

"Asphalt, I'm guessing. Or something like it."

Colt nodded. "I scraped off a sample, but whatever <u>this</u> is—"

Doffing his hat to indicate the larger formation.

"—has got nothing to do with anything peaceful."

"Makes you say that, Colt?"

He extended the barrel of his shotgun toward the center of the formation.

"See for yourself."

We shuffled through the sand to where the separate lines finally converged and at first all I saw was what looked like a large garbage bag and a pair of shovels. That, and a roost of buzzards.

Colt pulled his nine-millimeter from its holster and a couple of rounds later the vultures were dispersed. Slowly, casually.

That's when I saw the gore, the blood.

"Jesus Christ."

A dog was staked out on the hot white sand. Or rather what was left of a dog.

"Jesus, Colt, he's gutted! Disemboweled!"

"Looks like."

The sheriff took off his hat to shoo off a swarm of flies.

"Could have been hogs, I guess." I gagged on the smell as I knelt for a better look.

"Except hogs don't usually paint peace symbols on lake beds," Colt replied drily.

"Coulda been somebody high on drugs. Meth, maybe? Somebody really fucked up."

"Fucked up, for sure."

Colt spit.

"But ain't no druggie went to this trouble. This here is too elaborate. Too damn much work for a hophead."

"Well, then, maybe it actually was a hog got him, or a bear, maybe. Somebody finds a disemboweled dog out in the flatwoods or wherever and brings him here for some kinda weird ritual or burial."

"You got an active imagination for a reporter, Clara Sue."

"Then you tell me where the dog came from."

"From Roscoe Lamb's deer camp."

"This is Roscoe Lamb's dog?! You're sure?"

"Yep. Roscoe paid a thousand dollars for him too."

I can barely tell my own dogs apart, let alone somebody else's.

"I killed me a ten-point buck behind this here hound," Colt went on.

"Have you told Roscoe?"

"Not yet."

My cousin doffed his Stetson briefly. Turned his face to the brooding sky.

"How 'bout forensics? Can you get the FDLE out here?"

I was referring to the Florida Department of Law Enforcement, that intrastate agency famous for assisting sheriffs and police chiefs all over the state.

But Colt was shaking his head.

"Them boys don't come for dogs, Clara Sue." Colt resettled his hat. "Hard enough to get 'em out to homicides."

A breeze stirred. Colt snapped his fingers.

"Doc Trotter," he said.

Dr. D. O. Trotter is a longtime fixture in the county, a semiretired physician and Sunday School teacher.

"I'll take the dog to Doc." Colt spit. "See what he can tell me."

"And what d'you want me to do?" I asked.

"I want a few words and a picture or two in your paper, and I want you to tell anybody that has information to call in. For fucking sure somebody knows what went on here. Maybe we'll get lucky. Can you do that for me, Clara Sue?"

"Certainly. But leave Roscoe out of it?"

"For now, yeah."

"Anything else?"

"Get done with your pictures, you can help me police this mess up."

"You mean—the dog?"

"Well, I cain't just leave him out here."

"Colt, if you'd warned me I'd be shoveling guts in a bag I might've told you to take your own goddamn pictures."

"But I didn't tell you, did I, cuz? And yet we remain such good damn friends."

I had to laugh. "Friends or not, if you'd told me there was a dead hound staked out in a peace symbol in the middle of Pickett Lake, I wouldn't have believed you."

"Kind of thing you have to see to believe."

"I see and I'm still not sure I believe it."

"You're a doubting Thomas, Clara Sue. Always have been."

"I'd have made a bad disciple, no doubt about that."

"Makes you a good reporter though."

"*Made* me," I amended. "Made me a good reporter. Not sure what I am now."

Colt produced a pair of RayBans to filter a breaking sun.

"Why don't you just get the pictures?" he suggested. "I'll manage the rest."

CHAPTER SIX

Field of Dreams
The Clarion

After dropping off his cousin at the *Clarion*, Sheriff Buchanan drove straight to the site of the county's largest employer. The Laureate Correctional Institute and Annex was a state-run prison, but as the sheriff well knew there were Florida legislators eager to see a change of management. These were private-sector zealots who insisted that anything the state managed could be done more cheaply and efficiently by the private sector. Colt never bought into that theory. For one thing, running prisons for profit created a huge incentive to find prisoners. Build a prison and then fill it.

A field of dreams.

Colt left town on Highway 27 heading west and within minutes saw the glint of sunlight off a high fence topped with razor wire. The fence and prison within were situated in the midst of an open field that provided a wide boundary of exposure on all sides. There was nowhere for a would-be escapee to hide on that veldt—no culvert, no trees, no shrubbery. The grass was always cut short and as Sheriff Buchanan slowed his prowler to a crawl, he noted the clear fields of fire for the armed guards mounted on towers set like deer blinds along the perimeter. A series of Jersey barriers forced the sheriff into a maze of turns so tight that it made speeding impossible. Visitors to the prison were routed along the way to a designated lot sprinkled with street lamps and surveillance cameras. A guard waved Colt through to a parking lot that was only slightly more convenient. Visitors were routed to a double-doored lounge inside the fence where they would surrender a driver's license and shoes. The sheriff of Lafayette County was only asked to surrender his sidearm.

"How long do you reckon 'fore I can get in?"

"You awready on the schedule, Sheriff. Shouldn' be but a spit."

Ordinary visitors were required to check in at least an hour ahead of any scheduled contact. A spouse or family member or lawyer would be moved through at least one staging area where a waiting pair of officers would require the purpose of each visit to be recorded and the name of the prisoner to be visited logged in on a manifest as strictly enforced as any harem. No last-minute additions allowed. Visitors could expect to be scanned by one of those full-body rigs common at airports, and wanded, and then a light frisk before bridging the sally port to cross a grassless yard under escort to reach a separately ciphered building within which a windowless room granted entry.

Sheriff Buchanan bypassed wives, husbands, and children huddled with inmates in a cheerless bunker. Cheap, plastic chairs jammed up at odd angles against metal tables bolted to the floor. Ceiling lights buzzed like insects behind wire grids as thick as hockey masks. This was where free citizens and felons communed, a place situated to create a kind of limbo between the gatehouse and units farther inside. You couldn't spend cash in the "Friendly Room," but there was a kiosk to exchange dollar bills for copper tokens with which friends and kin coaxed soft drinks and candy from the several vending machines that were the only source of sanctioned junk food in that bleak house.

But Colt Buchanan did not linger in limbo.

He was headed to the library.

Most prisons maintained a library of some sort, even if it was just a cart stuffed with magazines. Better funded institutions offered classes that were often taught in the library. A surprising number of inmates actually got a GED in prison and everyone had heard stories about jailhouse lawyers. Of all the work details to which prisoners were assigned, library duty was the most coveted, a plum for prisoners desperate for any occupation to pass time. The *bibliotheque* waiting for Sheriff Buchanan, if spartan, was nevertheless a place of books and lamps and tables offering refuge from the brutal sun attending outdoor labor. The library was also a reasonably reliable refuge from sexual predators or other hardened felons. Prisoners generally earned library time with good behavior, the second most popular privilege apart from the yard. You could read at ease in the library. You could even write, though you had to leave your pencil in one of the tin cans scattered like ashtrays on the metal tables arranged below surveillance cameras outside the stacks. There were also computers on hand, not many, a half dozen or so, at which a model prisoner might be allowed heavily filtered access to the Internet.

Tiny Sessions had worked the library detail far longer than any other inmate at Laureate's prison—more than five years of a thirteen-year sentence for manslaughter. Now, if some state auditor or ordinary citizen asked the warden what Tiny had done to earn his long tenure in the stacks, the warden would supply the usual song and dance—good behavior, exemplary attitude, a volunteer for the Christian chaplain who vouched for Tiny at every meeting of his parole board. That was the official explanation. But Colt knew that the primary reason the warden put Tiny Sessions in the prison's library because the library was a safe place for Tiny to snitch.

Only the warden knew that Tiny Sessions was Colt Buchanan's informer and primary source regarding the production, sale, and distribution of crystal meth throughout the Third Judicial District. A pair of guards was required to escort Sheriff Buchanan to his scheduled rendezvous. Most of the guards were local and Colt knew them by name. On rare occasions the warden himself would accompany Colt down featureless halls through cipher-coded doors to reach the lockup's library. But unlike any other visitor, Colt's supervision ended at the library door. Once inside the stacks, Sheriff Buchanan stood alone and unarmed in the company of the largest felon in the prison.

"Tiny, how's life treatin' you?"

Imagine a slender, compact Cherokee in crisply pleated tans speaking to an African American three-hundred-pounds sloppy in prison blues.

Tiny was occupied with a pencil and pad at a book cart. "Got me a Honey Bun?"

"Right here."

Colt tosses the contraband to a table littered with magazines and books and Tiny pulls up a chair.

Maybe a pair of chairs.

"Be nice to have a soda with this thang."

"Don't push it, Tiny."

"Just sayin'."

Colt selects a chair for himself and waits for the inmate to peel his snack from its wrapper, which Tiny accomplishes with the dexterity of King Kong plucking diamonds from a necklace.

He rips off the wrapper.

Takes one long lick down the side.

"Damn, he good."

Tiny wads the Honey Bun into his mouth and swallows it whole. Just one gulp. Like a vitamin pill.

"Shit hot mama!"

"You're gonna choke, you keep that up," the sheriff warns.

"Ain' nuthin' chokin' me," Tiny disagrees and wipes his hands on his striped pants.

"Can I do for you, Sheriff? 'Nother lab? Pusher? I heard 'bout some boys settin' up in Madison. Got one o'them RVs usta belong to the blood bank? Goddamn blood-bank van! Drivin' around in the wide open."

"Sounds reckless."

"Gimme some o'them buns, I get you the puhticulahs."

"I'm not here for those particulars, Tiny. Not this time."

"You juss here to smack, then? Bullshit with ole' Tiny?"

"No. This time, I need you to think outside the box."

"What box? This, here? Ain' no box, boss. This here a lie-berry. This my house, Sheriff. My church."

"And you're doing excellent work, Tiny. Worth a Honey Bun, at least. But I've come across something unusual. Several things, actually. Random shit, all over the county. And now it's turned violent and I'm hoping whoever's involved with this latest incident is connected to somebody inside. Perpetrators love to brag, don't they? Anyway, I need you to sniff around. See if you can get me a name."

"God don't give His name," Tiny declares, jowls hanging like a basset's. "An' neither do I, 'less I get me another Honey Bun."

"Would you like to lose this detail, Tiny?"

"Chu mean?"

"I mean you're my house nigger and if you don't start acting like it, we can put you back in the general population."

"Thass cold."

"That's facts. You ready to take notes?"

For a moment the prisoner smolders, fury and resentment stirred with a rush of glucose.

"Awright then."

He plucks a pencil from a coffee can as gently as a rose from a vase.

Pulls the legal pad off the cart.

"Whatchu got?"

CHAPTER SEVEN

Animal's Death Unexplained
The Clarion

I lingered outside for a moment after Colt dropped me at the *Clarion* and saw that he was heading out of town. I knew my cousin made regular trips to the prison and I'd suspected for some time that he had a snitch inside, but Colt guards his sources as jealously as any journalist. To this day, I've never been trusted with a jailhouse conversation. I can, however, report Dr. David Oliver Trotter's postmortem of Roscoe Lamb's hound practically verbatim because I was there to witness the event. Everybody knows D. O. Trotter, by the way. Besides tending generations of patients, Trotter's Sunday School classes at Laureate's First Baptist Church are famously unorthodox, and popular. For more than twenty years Doc has guided youngsters and adults through the conflicting narratives of the Old and New Testaments. Seeking grace in the ordinary and in the unexpected. Outside of church, he's something of a rapscallion. An interesting combination of parts, is Dr. Trotter.

All kinds of stories revolve around the old man, some more believable than others.

In appearance, D. O. favors his grandpa, or maybe Mark Twain, an aging curmudgeon with a flow of silver hair and an unfashionably exaggerated mustache. Wears cowboy boots with his long, white coat. Doc's supposed to be retired, but you go by his cinderblock office 'most any time from daylight to dusk, you'll see him with a patient or sometimes playing checkers with Judge Simmons. First time I got pains in my chest, I had Trotter check me out. I didn't like his diagnosis. Doc didn't much care.

"You're going to have to do something with this here, Clara Sue. Either that or let it kill you. Which it prob'ly will do anyway, sooner or later."

He's a gruff kind of physician, old school. Trotter respects his patients and his community, but he also expects that deference to be reciprocated. When I reconnected with Sheriff Buchanan at D. O.'s utilitarian digs, Doc was in the midst of a necropsy of Roscoe Lamb's hound.

And he was not happy about it.

"Explain to me how I'm gonna bill this, Sheriff? That be Medicare? Medicaid? Is this an elderly hound?"

"County's good for it, Doc," the sheriff assured him. "Either that or I'll pay you cash myself."

"Cash? Well, that eases the sting. Ya'll do know what 'MD' means, don't you?"

"'Me Deity'?" I supplied and got a glare that would wilt bricks.

I should mention that Trotter is one of only two physicians serving the entire county, and the only native born. Before Doc returned to Laureate, the only medical facility in the county was a part-time clinic run out of a trailer by interns on rotation from the medical school in Gainesville. The only thing you could reliably count on from that bunch was your blood pressure or birth control.

Took years to get any doctor to set roots in town. We still only have one full-time physician. Dr. Cory Aquino jokes that she used to be a Filipino president. She's working off her med-school debt through a federal program that sends medical school graduates to places where there are no theaters, bars, condos, or culture higher than scoring touchdowns or killing hogs. Fortunately, Aquino's upbringing on a rice farm in Baguio leaves her well-prepped for that spectrum of stimulation.

Trotter, by contrast, separated from military service debt free, a flight surgeon transitioning to internal medicine with an HMO in Atlanta. Doc practiced in that high-end market for ten years before returning home to Laureate, taking breaks to join Doctors Without Borders for a dozen deployments worldwide, those interventions proving to be excellent preparation for practicing medicine in rural Florida.

"I regularly diagnose ailments in Laureate that I haven't seen since Southeast Asia," Doc confided to me one morning over grits and coffee.

He was right, of course. Communities in the rural southeast vie with Native American reservations for the most unhealthy populations in the United States.

"Not what I thought I'd see coming home." D. O. stirred another spoon of sugar into his coffee.

"But look at it this way, Doc—" I scratched for a silver lining.

"You're right where you're needed."

Not words of encouragement for a proud man deep in the entrails of Roscoe Lamb's hound.

"I don't even know what I'm looking for."

"How 'bout what opened him up?" Colt suggested. "Could it have been a hog's tusk, Doc? Was it a blade?"

"You need that bunch from *CSI*, Sheriff."

"You're all we got, D. O."

"You've got the damn Pound Lab, don't you?"

The Pound Lab is a hub of forensic diagnosis associated with the Department of Anthropology at the University of Florida. Anyone enforcing the law from Pensacola to Key West is familiar with that laboratory, including Sheriff Buchanan.

"Problem is this here animal's not associated with a crime," Colt explained. "At least, none that we know of. Now, if I could say this animal was materially involved in the murder of a human being, or Medicare fraud, I'd be down to the Pound in a heartbeat."

"Speaking of heartbeats." Doc paused briefly. "We get done here, Clara Sue? I wanta listen at your ticker."

"I'm fine," I said. "Never better."

Doc raised his eyes to Heaven.

"See my problem?"

"Back to the hound, Doc—tusk, you think? Or blade?"

Doc withdrew from the carcass.

"A crude cleaver or hatchet, maybe even a butcher knife could've done this. So could a boar's tusk. I'm just not the expert in that area."

"So you can't really explain what happened."

"Sure, I can. Damn dog's gutted and between exsanguination and shock he died."

"I meant the means."

"I can't specify means, no."

"Or motive," I added.

"Hell, I can't locate my own motives half the time," Doc growled.

"Seems like there's a lot doesn't get explained." I offered what I thought was sympathy and, boy, was that a mistake.

"You know, Clara Sue, you can be one condescending bitch."

Doc dropped a bloody scalpel into a pan shaped like a kidney.

"Come on, Doc."

"Come on yourself. Do you have any idea what happened to this animal? Do you have a story ready to print? Some salacious detail for your readers? Because unlike newshounds, Ms. Buchanan, I work from a method that respects science and method which means that, for a variety of good damn reasons, there are any number of things that I cannot explain."

"Sorry," I said. "Thought I was letting you off the hook."

"If I need rescue from a hook of any variety, I'll let you know."

"Said I was sorry, Doctor."

"Yes. Well."

The three of us let the steam disperse a moment or two. Doc removed his glasses. Colt took that as an opening.

"What's bothering you, D. O.?"

"A slaughtered dog, for starters."

Colt inclined his raven head.

"What else?"

Doc settled down. A long moment passing.

"This has to stay confidential. And I mean confidential. Clara Sue, you put this in the paper without my permission or breathe it to a soul—?"

I threw up my hands. "Not a word."

"Thing is, I saw Jenny O'Steen just a few hours after that episode at the candy store. Principal at the school rushed Jenny to Dr. Aquino right after it happened. Doctor gave her a thorough examination, but the parents didn't want to believe a foreigner, so they brought her on over to me."

"Is Jenny okay?" I asked.

"Better than okay," Trotter answered.

"What d'you mean, Doc?" I stilled the impulse to grab my notepad.

"I mean her beta-cell function and glycemic index were rock solid. And here's the thing, I've followed up with that little girl a half-dozen times over the past few weeks and her blood work hasn't changed a jot."

"Well, that's great news, isn't it? That means she's keeping track of her levels. Taking her injections."

Doc Trotter shook his head.

"No injections."

It took a moment for the import to register.

"No injections. What's that mean?"

"It means no shots—I took her off. Jenny O'Steen isn't getting any insulin other than what's coming from her own pancreas."

Colt rocked back on his heels.

"Doc, are you saying—? Are you saying Jenny's cured?"

"I won't go that far." The old veteran shook his head wearily. "Child could get sick tomorrow for all I know. What I can say is that if you took Jennie O'Steen to the Mayo Clinic today, they'd swear she's never had diabetes in her life."

Trotter let the import of that diagnosis sink in.

". . . I don't believe in miracles, D. O."

"Oh, I know. And I understand the need for proof, Clara Sue. The hunger for certainty. But now and then we need to be humble."

Trotter bowed away from the bloody table as though it were an altar.

"Blessed be they who do not see, and yet believe."

Chapter Eight

Federal Funds Approved for School Construction
The Clarion

When Hiram Lamb dissembled, he stroked the birth-mark along his jaw as though it were a stubble of beard. It was a sure tell. Killed him when he played poker. However, Butch McCray did not see Hiram often enough to be able to read those signs. Hiram's campaign to strip Butch of his store was normally waged through proxies, at arm's length. Both of the Lamb brothers abjured actual contact with their foster brother; Butch almost never saw Hiram or Roscoe face-to-face. That changed when the candy store got in the way of Hiram's bid to refurbish the county's consolidated school.

The elder Lamb ambushed his foster brother late one afternoon as Butch was restocking his plywood shelves for the next day's retail. School was long over, the last bus departed. The last soda and lollipop sold for the day. Butch was easing Cokes and Pepsis into an ice-filled locker in happy oblivion when Hiram pulled up in his Suburban.

Hiram Lamb slammed the door of his vehicle. Paced up to Butch's store.

Ducked his head to enter the tiny shed.

"Butch, we need to talk."

Butch pausing from his labor to see the unfamiliar shirt and tie. Always pressed sharp and clean.

The foster brother oblivious to the rigid posture, the flush in Hiram's face, the birthmark bright below that magnificent hair.

"Why, Hiram. You woan a Coke? Mebbe some peanuts?"

"Not why I'm here, Butch."

"But you woan one?"

"Coke then. Give me a Coke."

"Can or bottle?"

"Does it make a difference?"

Butch paused a long moment to work out the distinction.

"Seventeen cents."

"Pardon?"

"The diff'rence between can or bottle? Be seventeen cents."

Hiram wadded a dollar bill from his wallet onto the long icebox that chills Butch's soft drinks.

"Gimme a bottle."

Butch pulled one from the cooler and produced a church key from his apron to pop the top.

"Here you are, sir. I get you change."

"Keep it, Butch."

"You sure, Hiram?"

"Keep it."

"Why, thass . . . Awful nice. You . . . You awright, Hiram? An' Roscoe?"

"We're good. Couldn't be better."

"Mmm hmmm."

Butch smiling perplexed beneath the long bib of his cap. Hiram half bent over with a bottle of Coca-Cola sweating in his fist.

"Actually, Butch, I came here to make you an offer. A damn good offer."

"Offer?"

"Money, Butch. A pile of money."

"Oh, you don' need to do that. Old Butch, why, he fine. Doin' just fine, yes he is."

"I can help you do better."

"Naw, I'm good."

"Butch I mean to buy your store."

"Buy it?"

"Hard cash. You name a figure."

"But . . ."

Butch runs his hands from his cap to his belt. Over the narrow ledge of the icy footlocker that chills his sodas.

"I cain't sell my store, Hiram. This here's all I got."

"Yeah, but if I paid you—"

"Naw. Huh uh." Butch shakes his head. "Ole Butch need his store."

Hiram crushed the Coke can in his hands.

Soda now fizzing onto the icebox, a brown carbonated stain.

"You fuckin' idiot, I got to have this property, you understand? I <u>have</u> to get this half-acre plot, Butch!"

"But you daddy, he gave me the land, Hiram. You know that."

"I'm not askin' you to give it back, dammit. I'm not askin' you to give it to me at all; I'm willing to pay! All I need's the land. Hell, you can move the store. Move it down the block. I'll even help with that."

Butch shook his head.

"Chirren cain't go down the street. They cain't leave the playground; Principal Wilburn won't let 'em."

"Fuck Wilburn, this is me you're talking to, Butch. Me! I'm the one shared a table with you! Took you in when you didn't have a pot to piss in or a window to throw it out of!"

Butch's hands now shaking on the lid of his cooler.

"I had a house. Mama said ya'll took it."

"You and your Mama! Look. All I'm askin' is that you sell me your lot. I don't wanta take it from you, Butch. I'm offering to buy it. I'll give you more for this half acre than you can make in ten years of sodas and PayDays."

"But then I wouldn't be here."

"'Be here'? Be here for what?"

"Why, for them. When they come back."

Butch turned to pull a candy wrapper from a stack near the cooler.

Smoothing out the wrapper on the icebox lid.

Scanning for some cipher, some sign.

"Is awl here. Right cheer."

"God damn it!" Hiram slammed the lid closed on the ice chest.

"You know, Butch, I didn't wanta do this! I really didn't. But people are talking about you. You and these children? They're talking. And about Jenny too. Jenny O'Steen? You know Jenny?"

For the first time Butch raised his head to meet Hiram eye to eye.

"How's Jenny? How she doin'?"

"What I hear people think maybe you did somethin' to her. What about that, Butch? You found her right by herself."

"No! No, they was another girl there! Little Mexican girl."

"You give her somethin', too, Butch? You like givin' sweets to little girls!"

Butch smiled impassively.

"I brung Jenny a Pepsi Cola. Did'n take no money, neither. An' now she ain't sick no more."

"You're the sick one, Butch, what I hear. And there's no way they're gonna let a man likes little girls stay this close to the school. Just stands to reason. They'll take the store, Butch. Just flat take it away from you and when they do you'll lose everything. Lose it outright! And you won't have a goddamn dime to show for it!

"Better sell it to me. Right away, before they take it. Sell it to me and I'll move you downtown. It'll be all right."

Butch now cradling the candy wrapper as though it were a Torah.

"Jenny saw him, but I awready knew."

The stain on Hiram's face glowed like an ingot in a furnace but Butch is impervious to those signs.

"I been waitin', Lord!" Butch exclaimed. "A long time waitin'. But little Jenny, she saw 'im first. Eyes of a child. Right behind ole' Butch's store."

Butch's own eyes now damp and bright.

"I knew he'd come. Knew it all along."

"What the fuck are you talkin' about?"

"It's all here." Butch displayed the wrapper's bar code. "It's all here, but ole Butch, he can't read it. Not yet."

"You need help, Butch."

"I got to stay. I got to be here when they come."

"You'll be here, all right. And it'll either be the sheriff or the men in white coats comes and takes your ass, but either way you're losing this store, Butch! One way or the other! Take the money, Butch. Take the money, you moron!"

Butch shook his head.

"I doan won't yer money."

Hiram grabbed Butch by the throat.

"YOU FUCKING MORON."

"You . . . ! You hurtin' me, Hiram!"

"Think you're hurtin' now?!"

"Hiram, you—! Lemme go!"

"Remember what happened to your daddy? Your whore mama? It can happen to you too, Butch!"

Hiram dragged Butch away from the flimsy shelves . . .

"SON OF A BITCH!"

. . . and slammed his foster brother into a wall stacked floor to ceiling with candy and snacks. A shower of inventory collapsed to the floor, Butch McCray now gulping for air like a guppy in mounds of Doritos and M&Ms and PayDay candy bars.

Hiram stalking back out to the street.

Snarling over his shoulder.

"Not gonna ask you twice, Butch! Fuckin' retard, you hear me? I AIN'T ASKIN' TWICE!"

ON THE very day that Hiram Lamb took out his fury and frustration on Butch McCray, his younger and unsanitary brother was pushing a cadre of Latinos on a stand of slash pine. The younger Lamb brother had planted this particular grid of slash pine only five or six years earlier on his own section of land. The trees were not mature enough to cut for pulp, but that didn't mean they weren't profitable. You can always sell straw. However, the day's harvest was delayed by weather. An October cold front triggered thunderstorms, which struck unusually early in the day, thunder breaking with enormous bolts of lightning that left the atmosphere with a taste of iron. By midday the storms were depleted, and an unseasonably warm sun broke through to raise a humid and stifling vapor. Roscoe Lamb pulled the sleeve of his shirt

across his forehead as he received a progress report from the
jefe on site.

"Three trailers, full," the foreman apprised the owner
of the day's progress. "Rain slowed us some, but we should
maybe get two more trailers by sundown."

That would be five tractor trailers stacked top to bottom
with bales of straw.

People never cease to be amazed that you can make
money off the adult leaves of pine trees. Through the sixties and seventies, the number-one crop in the county was
tobacco, followed by hay and watermelons. Chicken houses
were big for a while, industrialized sheds hundreds of yards
long pumping feed and antibiotics into tens of thousands
of chicks. No longer. The chicken houses are mostly idle or
razed and land that once yielded nicotine, grass, and melons
has been harrowed to make way for endless tracts of hybrid
pine, the fallen needles of which are harvested for sale to
nurseries, contractors, and road crews.

It takes nine or ten years for a stand of slash pine to
mature enough to be harvested for pulp, but you can rake
straw year in and out and, if you keep labor costs depressed,
you can make a fair profit. There are a surprising variety of
uses to which pine needles can be put, but they are mostly
sold for erosion control and mulch. Straw is light in weight
and attractive, a cheap hedge against assaults of wind or rain.
A bed of needles insulates exposed soil from extremes of
heat or cold, and a mulch of straw reduces the evaporation
of water from unshaded ground.

You see pine straw piled beneath shrubbery bunting private homes and office buildings everywhere, and contractors
purchase baled straw by the ton to prevent erosion along
thousands of miles of roads and highways. That's a lot of
ground to cover, and Roscoe Lamb has a near monopoly on

local supply, his profits measurably enhanced by a cheap and docile source of labor.

It takes people to harvest straw. You can't mechanize the process; the rows between trees are too narrow for any wheeled machine or similar contraption which means you have to recruit human beings to gather the fallen needles. But where to find the workers? You'd never see Roscoe's nephews raking straw into a baler. Trent Lamb never bent his tall, golden frame over a bale of straw, and neither did his dark-haired brother. In fact, you couldn't get any local cracker, young or old, to hunch over a rake and baler for ten hours a day.

Certainly not for twenty-five cents a bale.

Luckily for Roscoe, the county has an undocumented pool to replace the absent hands of native borns. And the *jefe* with whom Roscoe contracts pays his hands by the piece, which relieves Lamb of any responsibility for payroll taxes or social security numbers, not to mention pensions, Porta-Potties, or fresh water.

Raul Herrera and Edgar Uribe were used to these sorts of arrangements. "Big Papi" and his much smaller *amigo* had labored side by side with their parents and extended families to pick grapes in California and beets in Colorado, migrating with the seasons to harvest vegetables and fruit all over the country. Migrants find work where mechanization is either impractical or impossible, where there is no substitute for legs, limbs, and hands. Tobacco, for example, is planted one seedling at a time, suckered one stalk at a time, cropped by hand, and bagged with little to no mechanized assistance. Almost any fruit that grows on a tree requires hand labor. Cherries and peppers are still picked by hand. Machines can sometimes assist, but someone with a strong back still has to heft a forty-pound watermelon onto a conveyor's mechanized belt.

It's always tedious, mind-numbing work.

Raking straw is certainly a backbreaking job, and conditions in the field are deplorable. There are no latrines among the pines. No privacy. There are no cooling stations or refreshment. Often the only water available is what workers lug in themselves, and there are no medics. You sprain an ankle or break a leg, somebody had better be nearby to run for help. Rattlesnakes thrive among the pulpwood trees, and anyone who has raked straw has either seen or suffered heatstroke and dehydration.

Added to these miseries is a unique sensation of isolation more subtle than thirst or ache or outright poison. It starts with a sense of disorientation. Once inside the endless rows of trees, all sense of direction evaporates. There is no horizon. No sky. You can't tell if you're a half mile into the grid or twenty yards from the fence. Workers often report a sense of claustrophobia, dread, or even blind panic. Not easy to calm a man running blind in the pines. Veteran workers familiar with these and other hazards always work in pairs, blazing trails to mark their way, and mothers tie bells onto the waists of *impúbero* prone to wander.

This partly explains why Edgar Uribe's sighting was so easily discounted. You can be forty feet from a neighbor and be invisible, but even if the young Latino had been able to produce a dozen witnesses to vouch for the vision he recounted, it would not have brought a dime's worth of credence to his description. This boy was a Mexican, after all. Undocumented. Illegal. Prob'ly half-stoked on dope.

Roscoe liked to say that if a wetback told him the sun was going to rise in the east, he'd fire him for lying.

People trust messengers before messages, and the tendency to locate belief in persons rather than facts spans all ages and all beliefs, modern-day ditto-heads no less enslaved to their prophets than zealots on the right and left. If you hold that our planet's climate is warming at a rate largely determined by human activity, chances are you're basing that belief on a yen for Robert Redford or a trust in scientists rather than on your familiarity with fluid dynamics, cloud formation, or geology. On the other hand, no scientist is likely to convince a person who admires Rush Limbaugh or Reverend Robertson that God's creation can be unhinged over so flimsy an insult as carbon dioxide.

Edgar Uribe's alleged encounter was not amenable to any sort of rational discussion.

Edgar is the slightest built of the Hispanic teenagers, you may recall, a young man, with an artistic bent, afflicted from childhood with polio. Imagine a slender teenager in a plaid shirt with a knife, twine, and rake limping between tall rows of pine trees. Dragging a baler alongside. A straw baler looks a lot like an outsized dustbin, its forming box maybe a couple of feet wide and a foot and a half deep into which the straw is loaded. A long lever activates the press which compresses the straw into a standardized bale.

Edgar was paired with Raul Herrera that morning, that kid as huge and smooth as a sumo wrestler. The earlier storm left the boys soaked to the bone and freezing, but by midday they struggled to pick up the pace of their labor in a virtual sauna. There was no water. The boys had long before emptied the Gatorade bottle which was their water jug. Hector struck off on a quest to refill that modest canteen, leaving Edgar queasy, thirsty, and alone.

The account to follow is qualified by Edgar's frank admission that at the moment the vision presented, he was dizzy and nauseous.

"We did not eat so good that morning, and I was thirsty," the boy volunteered candidly. "When Hector went for water,

I put down my rake and sat beside a tree. That's when I saw her—the lady. She was beautiful. She float in the air like a hummingbird. Her hair long and shiny like silver. And there was like a light around her head—a halo. So warm! It fill me inside like honey."

Did she speak to you? the boy was asked.

Did she say anything?

Do anything?

"She smile to me," he replied. "An' she say, 'Edgar, I see you care for your sister, which pleases me. But try to be kind as well as brave, *muchacho*. Forgive those who trespass against you.' And then she say, 'I see you are thirsty. Here. Drink this.'"

A drink? She gave you something to drink?

Which connects to the only portion of Edgar's tale that is corroborated because when Raul Herrera returned with his newly filled jug, he found his compadre reclined against the rough bark of a pine tree with a glass of ice-cold water beading in his hand.

Both boys swore they'd brought nothing beside the Gatorade bottle to the worksite, and certainly no ice.

"We din bring nothing." Raul confirmed Edgar in this detail. "*Nada.*"

Edgar had no doubt that his drinking vessel was a gift from the Virgin Mary, but on examination it proved to be an ordinary tumbler, the sort of thing you can get at the Dollar Store for fifty cents.

Too cheap for divine provenance.

"Boy was dehydrated."

Sheriff Buchanan put the most logical gloss on the tale.

"It's hotter than a June bride in a feather bed out here. Boy prob'ly was overheated and low on fluids. I been bear-caught myself, and I tell you what, you get behind the bear you can see some pretty squirrely shit."

So Edgar Uribe got behind on electrolytes and over-heated. Bear-caught, as locals describe the condition. That made more sense than visits from the mother of Jesus. There was, however, one other talisman not so easily dismissed.

Colt Buchanan and I followed Roscoe Lamb to the place where Edgar reported his heavenly encounter. What we found at the tree where the kid located his vision was a circle burned into the straw, a scorch of some unnatural flame that left a jet-black marker like a brand in the earth.

Roscoe was dead certain that his two field hands got bored or pissed off and set a fire.

"Fucking wetbacks. Got nuthin' better to do, they set a fire to my trees!"

"Nope." Sheriff Buchanan's reply was characteristically laconic. "That's not it."

"What was it then?"

Colt took a knee to place his hand on the charred boundary.

"Look here, Clara Sue."

I squatted beside our native sheriff.

"Remind you of anything?"

"Pickett Lake," I grunted to affirm. "This isn't as elaborate, but, yes, it reminds me."

"You been out to the lake? I mean, since you and me was there?"

"No, Sheriff, I haven't."

"I have. Couple times. Damnedest thing, that marker we saw? That circle or whatever it was?"

"Uh huh."

"It's gone."

"Gone?"

"Not a trace. Like the wind blew it away."

"You get a sample to Sheryl Lee?"

"Yep, and you were right. It was tar. Just like ordinary roofing tar."

"I was just guessing."

Roscoe's stamping around clueless to our conversation. Wringing his hands on a Garth Brooks T-shirt like it was a washrag.

"The got-damn hell are ya'll talkin' about?"

Colt rose to his feet, and I followed suit.

"Boy got hisself bear-caught, Roscoe. He didn't do anything untoward. And this here burn around your tree? It's just lightning."

"The fuck you say."

"I do say. And 'less you got a better explanation, Roscoe, it's what we're all gonna say."

I felt some discomfort at that injunction.

"Sheriff, I can't just make shit up."

"Didn't say a thing about what you put in your paper, Clara Sue. You can write anything in that fish wrapper you like, although I would point out that if you tell your readers that a wetback saw the Virgin in the middle of Roscoe's pines, you're gonna make him out to be either crazy or a liar and come Sunday every preacher in the county will be railing about false prophets and Catholics."

"Well, that's for sure," I allowed.

"You can write whatever you want," Colt reiterated. "I'm just suggestin' what you can <u>say</u> to somebody if they ask. What we all oughta say, if asked, is: boy suffered a heatstroke. Made him addled. Made him see things."

I saw a possible solution.

"May I quote you on that, Sheriff? Redacting, of course, the reference to wetbacks."

"You're a pain in the ass, cousin."

"It'd take some heat off the boy if you offered an official explanation," I pointed out. "What about it, Colt? For the record?"

"Shit fire."

He doffed his hat by the crown and a fall of hair spilled nearly to the collar of his shirt. A moment's reflection passed, a beam of sunlight piercing the needled arbor to play along that raven vestment.

"Awright, then dammit, but give 'em somethin' they can understand at least. Tell 'em the boy got caught by the bear. Tell 'em I said so."

He donned his Stetson.

"Folks will believe me before they believe you."

Sheriff Says Boy Caught by Bear
The Clarion

C orrections Officer Martin Hart made sure he had the library to himself before settling down across a stainless-steel table from the prison's enormous librarian.

"Git me the paper, Tiny."

This demand coming from a guard known both to prisoners and guards as The Weasel.

Tiny Sessions handed over the latest copy of the *Clarion* without demur. Strictly speaking, guards were not allowed to use the library's facilities or to have access to anything there, printed or otherwise. But too often the only persons held accountable in a prison are prisoners.

Marty scanned the leading story.

"Hah. Says here some wetback got bear-caught. Overheated from raking straw, it says, an' it ain't even summer!"

Tiny stacking magazines onto a cart without reply. Officer Hart slapped the paper onto the table in disgust, digging into his pressed uniform for a pack of Camels and a Bic lighter.

"Cigarette, Tiny?"

"No smokes inna lie-berry, boss."

"Right you are." Marty smiled and lit up.

Tiny nudged the cart to a roll.

"Don' rush off on me, inmate."

Tiny stopped the cart with a sigh.

"I don't have no juice fo' you, boss."

Marty took a long drag on his cancer stick.

"Whatchu mean, you don't have it?"

"Couple days mebbe I have somethin'."

"Don't need it in a couple of days, dipshit." Marty spit. "I need it now."

Tiny's shoulders rising and falling like a tide.

"My supplier got hisself busted, boss."

"You tellin' me you don' have a stash of your own? Something for emergencies?"

Tiny eased the book cart back to the table.

"I been behind bars for eleven years. Seven of 'em right here. Two months, I keep my shit together, I'm up fo' parole."

"You got this far, haven't you? What's a couple of months?"

"Iss too risky."

Marty fiddled with the radio mike clipped to his epaulette.

"I'd hate to have to turn you in, Tiny."

The giant inmate now freezing in place. Not a movement. Not a twitch.

"Whatchu talkin' 'bout, boss?"

"Oh, I think you know. Word gets to the population that you're snitching for Sheriff Buchanan, you might just be leaving prison earlier than you planned."

"I don' snitch on prisoners. I never!"

"I'm sure the boys'll be entertained with that distinction."

Tiny shivers as if taken with a sudden chill. He drags a chair across the polished concrete floor to take a place alongside Officer Hart. Tiny drags the chair slowly, deliberately. The metal legs squalling like chalk on an oversized board.

The prisoner takes a seat. Lays arms big as pillows on the table.

"I go down I'm takin' you wit me."

"And how you plan to manage that, Tiny?"

"Go to the warden. Tell him you been usin' me to get drugs."

"Oh, I'm sure you'd get an early release for that confession."

"I tell him you made me. Tell him you threaten me if I din."

"But you'd have to prove that, wouldn't you, inmate? I mean that's a hell of an accusation. And, see, there's a big difference in our situations cause anything you accuse me of, you got to prove whereas all I have to do is drop the word behind bars an' in a couple weeks the warden'll be looking for another brother to run his lie-berry."

Tiny leaned back, a slow fury mantled inside that barrel chest.

"Sheriff Buchanan look out for me," Tiny declared. "He know the warden. They friends."

"Does Colt sleep with you, Tiny? Because havin' the man on the outside is not gonna help you in here when you're jackin' off in your rack, or taking a shit, or shootin' hoops or whatever the fuck you do. You'll be a marked man, Tiny, and a rat in prison is a dead man walking."

Tiny lifted his arms off the table.

"I mebbe can get you somethin'. But is my pers'nul stash. No middle man."

"Fine by me. What's the price?"

Tiny shakes his massive head side to side.

"I doan woan no money."

Marty ground his cigarette into the table.

"Up to you. I don't mind a little bite."

"Wait chere."

The Weasel lips his cigarette as Tiny lumbers off into the stacks. A couple of minutes later the prisoner returns with a Ziploc bag.

"This here's awl I got." Tiny tossed it to Officer Hart. "And that's it. They ain' no more. Like I been tellin' you, my middle man's dried up."

Marty opened the bag. Tests the crystal on his tongue with a dampened finger.

"Christ! What is this shit, toilet cleaner? You tellin' me you can't do better than this? Man with your connections?"

"Nobody trust a man's short, boss. You know that. You got to know!"

The Weasel tucked the cached meth inside his uniform.

"Tell you what, hombre, you find me a fresh supplier and we're square. Inside or out, makes no difference to me. But don't fuck with me, Tiny, cause the thing about libraries—? You keep a book too long, you're gonna pay a fine."

～

CONNIE KOON was nervous as a long-tailed cat in a roomful of rocking chairs. She was playing hooky from the coffeehouse in the middle of the afternoon and her appointment was half an hour late. That alone would be enough to unsettle the town's bombshell barista and to heighten her consternation. She was also out of place, installed in her silver Suburban in trespass of city property. Wasn't always off-limits. Laureate's water tower used to be open to the public, its round-faced tank scrawled with generations of graffiti visible from most anywhere in town. The tank sat atop a pentagon of columns rising from a concrete pad poured in the forties. But after Monk Folsom's murder, the tower was declared off-limits to private citizens and the highway entry to the site was block-aded behind a Viking fence always padlocked and chained.

An ancient grove of live oak trees surrounded the rising tower in whose shadow were committed any number of transgressions. Connie always got the heebs as she threaded her way toward the tower, but it wasn't because she was worried about trespassing. The fence had been breached too many times to count, and the town had given up any pretense at regular repair. Every teenager knew the way in. You crossed the tracks to Colored Town, turning at the ruins of the old Negro school to follow a white ribbon of loam through a rent in the chain-link barrier surrounding the tower and the oak trees surrounding.

An arbor as old as Stonehenge brooded inside the fence, those mossy limbs reaching down like the arms of hags set to wrench you from your car or pickup for rituals known only to druids or very old women. At least half a dozen men and as many women were murdered in sight of the tower and God knows how many curses and imprecations had been cast to that mute sentry which made it ideal for teenagers looking for forbidden pleasures. Connie could remember lying in the bed of a battered truck, the stars overhead rolling slowly about the tower's axis as though in some giant planetarium. Listening to the radio. Working on those night moves with Carl and Bob Seger.

It was here that Connie got pregnant with the twins. No question about that. And no question of an abortion either. That was never an option, much less a choice. The only question was whether to stick with Carl or become a single mother, a decision which her father influenced with the threat of a baseball bat. She never told anybody that Carl was her first, her cherry.

No rubber. No pill.

Connie always had a variety of plans that would get her away from Laureate. She would attend the junior college in Madison, maybe. Or maybe go to Daytona. Meet one of those cute boys over spring break. Or catch a plane to Hollywood and get a part in one of those surfer movies. She had the body for the beach, no question. Better after the twins, actually, those still-firm milkers grown to the size of cantaloupes. At least she had the sense to get pregnant late in the school year. She would always be remembered as the homecoming queen, the pinup girl, the hottest cheerleader in three counties.

But there could have been so much more. Connie did not know exactly what else there could have been, but she never doubted that it should have been more than a husband absent every deer season. Something more fulfilling than serving lattes and teasing deacons to unholy passion. Showing off cleavage to a louche politician. Definitely more than a life dictated by the whims of Hiram and Roscoe Lamb.

Connie told Carl to mind the coffee shop, promising as usual to return after completing some routine chore. It was simple to drop a deposit at the bank on the way to her water tower rendezvous, or else gas up the truck, or drop by the Safeway for some sugar or napkins. They were always running out of napkins.

Was easy to alibi a half-hour absence, but not an hour and a half. Carl would be pissed.

"And it's your fault, shit-ass," she complained *sotto voce*, loosening the buttons on her prefaded jean jacket and pulling down the visor's mirror for self-inspection.

Connie recalled being either flattered or reassured on one occasion when overhearing Roscoe Lamb say she was the mama he'd like to fuck. She wouldn't mind hearing that again. But working long hours as a barista did nothing to keep her body in the shape Connie wanted, and each year the tide seemed to recede farther from a shoreline still damp in memory.

Of course, she told herself often, if Carl made any kind of decent living, she wouldn't be stuck under this damn tower. She wouldn't need anything to jazz her metabolism, would she? She'd be able to join the gym in Live Oak and do it all natural.

Maybe the occasional Botox.

Just to keep those lips peach-sweet and full.

Of course, all that maintenance takes time as well as money and between Carl and the business and the twins— Lord, that Donna and Darla would drive anybody insane— Connie had no leisure for gymnasiums or treadmills or Pilates class which was a bitch because Mrs. Koon knew that when women top the hill the only thing waiting on the downside is menopause.

Connie dreaded the day when she'd bend over to pour some man's coffee and have her jugs hanging in her halter like loose socks. Nothing more pitiful than a woman trying to get attention with those assets. Horrible to even think about. No wonder she needed the occasional pick-me-up. Just a hit now and then.

Carl Koon's wife checked her mobile to make sure she hadn't missed a text, then fished out the latest *People* magazine from the center console, checking out the photos that chronicled the latest sightings of George Clooney or Johnny Depp. Somebody said Depp was in Tampa, some film or another. She scanned the wilting pages for confirmation of that claim, lingering along the way to inspect airbrushed images of Angelina Jolie and Jennifer Lopez. Eyeing those photos with what she imagined was a critical eye. Telling herself that with any professional assistance and a good photographer she could look as good as these women.

I mean, these gals were ancient! Connie was still in her prime, or at least close to it. A woman in her thirties could break into the business, couldn't she? There was still time. All you had to do was believe in yourself. And if not movies, what about TV? Or commercials—there was a lot of money in commercials. Gal doing those ads for that insurance company—what was her name Jo? Flo? Had to be thirty years old. Connie could see herself the center of some national campaign. She'd once tried to get into modeling, or at least initiated the first steps to embark on that career, but things fell apart when she couldn't get the required photographs.

She would never forget the snub. It was the day after her thirteenth birthday. She'd seen an advertisement in the newspaper, a modeling agency in Jacksonville casting for "new talent" in the "teenage market." The application required her parents' signatures, which she forged, and a specified set of photographs. Very specific poses and postures. Of course, she had no money and no access to anything like a professional photographer until Clara Sue Buchanan came home for a summer visit.

Connie wondered if the bitch even remembered.

It was at Blue Springs. The spring was a swimming hole always popular with locals, especially in summer. A great place for kids to flirt or neck and a cheap respite from the season's unremitting heat. Connie used to love watching the water actually boil to the surface, an ice-cold torrent fed from an underground aquifer that filled an enormous limestone bowl before spilling over to the shallows that ran fifty or sixty yards to the coffee-brown currents of the Suwannee River.

Miss Buchanan, as Connie knew her then, was at Blue Springs that day, swimming and taking pictures with some kind of Fancy Dan camera. Connie had heard that Clara

Sue was home to help her daddy. Connie envied Howard's daughter. Her body for one thing. She had legs and shoulders like a bodybuilder. Got them rowing, people said knowingly, but Connie doubted it. She'd rowed boats all her life and never got that kind of build. Connie envied Miss Buchanan's height, too, though people said boys didn't really like girls to be too tall.

No danger there anyway.

But mostly the young teenager envied Clara Sue Buchanan's audacity. Alone among the females Connie knew, Clara Sue had escaped Laureate's narrow confines to find freedom and acclaim. Connie didn't know exactly what Clara Sue was doing, but she'd seen her picture in the school library. Some newspaper in Boston. Connie couldn't recall the article Clara had written, but the photo looked great. Connie craved for that kind of recognition, that fame, and Clara Sue Buchanan reminded her of what she did not have. But surely Miss Buchanan would be happy to help her escape Laureate's small-minded community. Surely Clara Sue would understand! But timing is everything, and by the time Connie got up the nerve to ask for Miss Buchanan's help, the journalist had quit her camera to take a turn at the swing rope for a plunge into the boiling cold water.

There are rocks just beneath the water all over Blue Springs which makes diving dangerous, so, of course, folks do. Everybody uses the rope to swing out, a nylon line tied off twenty feet above the spring on a cypress tree that leans over the water. From a narrow, slippery niche at the base of that tree, you sailed out on a slender yellow line for a plummet to the rock-bound pool below. Release too early or late and you could count on breaking a leg or cracking your skull.

Clara Sue was cutting up that day, a grown woman in company with kids half her age swinging over the water to

execute a swan dive or somersault or some hilarious varia-
tion. She'd just completed an Alley Oop to ragged cheers
when Connie took the rope, stretching perilously high on
tiptoes to reach that slick and swaying tether, nothing to
keep her hands from sliding off the end of the rope but a
pair of granny knots.

She made sure Clara Sue had retrieved her camera before
sailing out solid as a gymnast, breasts firm as pears in her
two-piece, to turn a complete one-and-a-half before knifing
without a ripple into the boil.

"Nice one, Connie!"

She still remembered that praise from the older woman.

"Thank you, ma'am," Connie acknowledged as she
climbed out. "What brings you home, Miz Buchanan?"

"Oh, family stuff. Nothing a teenager should worry
about."

"I wonder if you could do me a favor while you're here."

"What you have in mind?"

Connie took a deep breath. "I need me some pictures."

"Pictures? Of you?"

"Yes, ma'am. A head shot and—some other angles."

"Other angles?" Miss Buchanan seemed amused. "And
what do you need with a head shot, Connie? How d'you
even know what a head shot is?"

"I read this ad." Connie still remembered hating herself
for sounding defensive. "In Jacksonville. They're looking for
models for catalogs and stuff. Swimsuits maybe."

Clara Sue just smiled, the bitch.

"Connie, most of those places aren't legitimate. Why
don't you finish school? Plenty of time to model afterward,
if that's what you decide to do."

"No." She turned to hide her embarrassment. "I'll find
somebody else. Shouldn't have expected you to help."

"Hey, now, that's not it."

"You think you're better than the rest of us?!"

People were looking by then. All those redneck farmers and their fat-ass wives looking on. People who would live here and die here and never know anything.

"Settle down, Connie."

"Don't tell me to settle down! I'm not stupid, you know! I'm not gonna be stuck here forever!"

Connie stalked away pretending to ignore the snickers following her away from the pool's cold boil. She didn't need Clara Sue Buchanan or anyone else, was what she told herself. As long as you believed in yourself, that was the thing.

You just had to believe.

Connie was sweating over a pot of black-eyed peas later on that week when her mother walked into the kitchen with a copy of the *Clarion*.

"Looks like you made the news."

Her mother spread the paper flat on the kitchen table for her daughter to see. Connie had to catch her breath. Clara Sue had not ignored her! She'd taken a picture at the spring and sent it to the *Clarion*, and there it was! Front page! A grainy black-and-white framed Connie taut and tanned in her two-piece the instant before her seamless plunge into Blue Springs' deep-fed cauldron. Looking back years later, it seemed to Connie that the single moment frozen in Clara Sue's camera defined the rest of her life. She'd taken the initiative. She made the leap. But in the end she always came up short.

She never made the final plunge.

Connie saved the paper her mother brought her, preserving it between layers of tissue paper for a place in her scrapbook. She still had that fold, somewhere, in some drawer or another. She lowered the window of her Suburban. The legs of the water tower threw shadows like a sundial across the pebbled ground.

What time was it, anyway?! She checked her watch.

"Damn it, Marty," she groused aloud. "You're late!"

Connie set aside her cell phone, rummaging in her purse to find a wallet she'd made all by herself in a leather-working class. A week's worth of tips weighted the handmade pouch. Those tokens along with the tithe she lifted from the cash register were enough to keep her straight till the end of the month. Provided her source made his connection.

"Where *are* you, Marty Hart?!"

Officer Marty Hart was already an hour late for his appointment when he presented his photo ID to the guard manning the prison's sally port.

"H'lo, Ben." He'd known the man since childhood and was waved through with barely a glance, strolling onto the parking lot with a dozen or so other guards dead tired after pulling double shifts.

Someone said something about a bet on the homecoming game.

"You wanta put some money down, Marty? Hornets or Tigers?"

He shook his head.

"I don't gamble."

Martin Hart always reminded himself that the parking lot was under constant surveillance, cameras swiveling from aluminum light poles that gridded the asphalt, their video recorded digitally and fed live to security personnel on duty inside. Marty was careful under that gaze never to do anything that looked interesting, much less suspicious. He never stashed his shit while in sight of a camera. He wouldn't even answer a phone till he was through the gate and on the highway, and Marty never broke that protocol, even if he was running late.

The prison guard heaved into his F-150, turned over the engine, and eased out between barricaded medians to find the exit leading toward Highway 27. The cache of crystal meth made a satisfying weight in his crotch. Once through the gate, Marty reached into his trousers and pulled out the stash that once belonged to Tiny Sessions. A mile south of the prison, Marty pulled off the hard road for a sandy rut that used to lead to the old Calhoun place, stopping beneath a cover of mimosa to stash the meth in a toolbox always handy in the bed of his truck. Moments later he was back on the highway.

The whole detour couldn't have taken three minutes, which would not normally matter except Marty was already behind schedule. He hated being late. You made mistakes when you were behind schedule. Easy to forget your routine when you're running against the clock. It wasn't that he gave a damn about inconveniencing Connie; that was the least of his concerns. But Marty did not want Carl's wife loitering under the water tower for too long at a time. There was always a chance some nosy son of a bitch would start asking questions. It helped, of course, that most locals avoided the place. Even black folk steered clear of the water tower, which was inconvenient as hell for them because the damn thing sat directly between The Quarters and the only black-owned eatery in town.

It was Connie's idea to meet at the tower. Connie Koon! Who'd of guessed that the hot young thing he used to cum over as a teenager was now begging at his knee? She wasn't his biggest hitter, no, but the woman was consistent. Officer Hart could count on Connie to call him at least twice a month. Woman was using regularly which put a wad of cash in Marty's pocket every single month, and after a disastrous run of online poker Marty really needed the money.

He could run tardy on Carl's wife without penalty. Not so with that other crowd. You made an appointment with those boys, you better be on time. Even so, he didn't want the homecoming queen to panic. You could never tell with amateurs. They'd high-tail if the moon wasn't right. Better give the lady a call, but not on his personal phone. Marty wasn't that stupid. He leaned across the truck's bench seat to fish out a prepaid mobile from the glove box. He didn't want Connie getting spooked and anyway it would only take a second to let her know he was on his . . .

FIRST I heard of the accident was off the scanner we keep at the paper. Most small-town papers scan EMS and police frequencies for breaking situations. It helps to keep a page of codes handy. They vary by county. For instance, in our county if I hear a 10-15 I know there's a prisoner in custody. A 10-24 means some lawman needs immediate help. That afternoon I heard the dispatch respond to a 10-47 followed almost immediately by a 10-71 which is a request for an ambulance.

With that information and the officer's confirmation of location, I grabbed my camera and headed out Highway 27 in the direction of the prison. Couple minutes later I saw an EMS van and a fire truck pulled off on the far side of the road, those lights tumbling along with a black-and-tan from the highway patrol. Colt Buchanan's souped-up Dodge rounded out the field.

Where was the wreck?

I crossed lanes to ease my Toyota 4-Runner onto the shoulder south of the scene. The highway runs straight as a string on this stretch of 27. The weather was clear; we hadn't seen a drop of rain in weeks. Across the highway, in fact, a local cattleman was on a front-end loader unloading enormous cylinders of hay from the flatbed of a semitruck to a dust-dry field. A modest billboard overlooked the scene in testament of another sort of drought.

Pray for Our Nation

Returning my attention to the accident side of the highway, I noted a single-wide house trailer half-covered in kudzu that was situated behind a badly kept fence forty yards or so off the road. Housing for migrants probably. I checked the batteries in my camera but until I stumbled past the screen of law enforcement and emergency vehicles, I didn't see the Ford pickup that had clipped off a telephone pole as neatly as a stick of celery before slamming into the iron trunk of a hickory tree.

The whole front end was crushed into the cab like a soda can. The front tires were flat and flared out beyond the fender wells. Steam hissed from a broken radiator, transmission fluid and oil gushing onto the blacktop. A volunteer from the fire department was foaming down the engine block and surrounding grass. Sheriff Buchanan barely glanced up at my approach.

"Sheriff. Looks bad."

"No injuries. One DOA."

I remember thinking at the time that I should have been able to match the truck with its owner, but it's surprisingly hard to place a vehicle pretzeled around the trunk of a tree.

"Driver's killed then?"

"Yep," Colt answered.

"Got an ID?"

"It's Marty Hart."

The Weasel? This was Marty's truck?!

"Jesus, what happened?"

A better question would be what <u>could</u> have happened? It was a clear day. There was no other traffic involved. Could an animal have run out in front of the truck? Many's the driver killed himself trying to dodge a deer or dog or some other critter, but in that case you'd expect to see skid marks from an application of brakes. Either that or a set of antlers on the hood. I drew a line in my mind's eye from the wreck to the road and I didn't see rubber anywhere. Not even on the grass of the shoulder.

"He never touched the brakes," I declared, and the sheriff grunted to agree.

Well, this was getting to be a real puzzle. It wasn't a case of somebody nodding off at the wheel. Marty had just finished his shift at the prison; he couldn't have been on the road more than four or five minutes.

"And besides, we know he was dialing somebody on a cell phone," Colt said.

A highway patrolman nodding sagely from behind his aviator shades.

"Damn mobiles kill more people than alcohol."

I made a note to find data supporting that detail.

"Who has the phone?" I asked and the patrolman nodded to Colt.

"Sheriff's got custody."

Colt didn't seem too happy about that responsibility. I waited until the patrolman was out of earshot to inquire privately—

"What's bugging you, Sheriff?"

"You mean besides having a dead man's family to notify?"

"You know that's not what I mean. It's the phone, isn't it? Something about the phone?"

Colt pressed the brim of his hat.

"Off the record then."

I shrug noncommittally. "Try me."

"It's a throwaway," Colt told me. "Untraceable. Now, I can see why a drug dealer would have a phone like that, or somebody runnin' around on his wife, but you got to ask yourself what'd make a prison guard conceal his calls?"

"Maybe he's just paranoid."

Colt spit carefully. "Maybe."

"Any idea who he's calling?"

"Never finished the dial. We got the local area code and 294, which could be practically anybody in the county."

"Well." I brightened with sudden clarity, "If Marty didn't finish dialing, wouldn't that support the idea that he just got distracted? He took his eyes off the road to punch in a number and just ran himself off the road."

"Could well be." Colt nodded. "Easiest explanation, for sure."

And then without asking me to follow, the sheriff turned away from the scene, crossing the ditch in easy strides to reach a gate in the bounding fence line. He was headed for the single-wide trailer that I noticed on my arrival, but there was no sign of activity that I could see. No kids playing outside, despite a litter of toys, a trampoline, and a soccer ball.

"What are you thinking, Sheriff?" I asked as I hustled to keep up.

"We might have us an eyewitness."

"How you know there's anybody home?"

"Got your recorder?"

"Got my smartphone."

I slung my camera over my shoulder and fumbled through the several pockets of my ragged vest to fish out my Android. I pulled up the Tape-A-Talk app.

"Okay, I'm set."

"Just follow my lead," he directed casually, and placing one hand on the gate's topmost support vaulted that flimsy barrier like a damn deer.

By the time I crawled over the fence, Colt was already knocking on the trailer's front door. He offered a couple of stiff raps and then doffed his hat, waiting for a reply as patiently as a Mormon missionary and I saw a movement at a window. Couple of seconds later a seam opened at the door from lintel to sill. The sheriff murmured some exchange with the shadow inside.

Then he turned to me.

"You coming or not?"

A small, brown woman in a Florida State T-shirt, faded dungarees, and flip-flops ushered us into her home. Large, liquid eyes. No makeup, not even lipstick. She had her hair pulled straight back and secured with some cheap barrette. I was surprised how well she kept the trailer. No fast-food cartons molding on the floor. No mess in the sink. Of course the fact that I expected a migrant's home to be in some state of *sin pudor* is an indicator of my own prejudice, or at least a tendency to stereotype. In fact, the woman's trailer was better kept than my own house, an accomplishment made more impressive as it looked to be accommodating a half-dozen adults, at least, and as many children.

Signs of poverty were evident. A long, ratted-out couch leaned on a leg patched with duct tape. A rabbit-ear television was propped on milk crates and there were clothes and towels folded in piles all over the floor. Even so, the place was warm and inviting. I saw flowers blooming in soup cans, a riot of periwinkles and lazy Susans competing in floral display. A scented candle wafted before the drone of an oscillating fan.

I inhaled that damp vapor.

Pictures and photos festooned the walls in cheap plastic frames, cutouts of Latina celebrities mixed with black-and-whites of family, presumably, those memorabilia looking over a wax statuary of the Virgin and her Son. Crucifixes at odd intervals. These were the iconography I expected to see, or something similar. There was one photo thumbtacked to the wall that grabbed my attention, a black-and-white of a boy who seemed familiar, but before I could fit a name to his face, our hostess ushered us to a kitchen stashed with bags of staples, rice and corn and potatoes piled all over.

I didn't see a refrigerator. I did see a pot of brown rice steaming on a propane stove. A smaller pot boiled water beside that bounty and on the counter I saw a jar of instant coffee. A stick of incense intermingled with the other nectars of the kitchen, a pleasant effluvium. "Please," she said, and Colt and I took chairs at a table mounted on sawhorses. Our hostess spilled some Ritz crackers onto a saucer and fielded a pair of chipped coffee mugs from a shelf busy with paper plates and plastic implements.

"*Gracias, señora.*" Colt accepted a cup of instantly brewed coffee with his cracker.

I was set to pass, but a cluck of Colt's tongue alerted me to the expected etiquette and I smiled as I took a cup of Nescafé from her hand.

"You speak English, *señora?*"

She didn't reply.

Was she Mexican? Cuban? She could be from Peru or Paraguay, for that matter, but her features were more Indian than Spanish.

Not flattering to realize I can't tell these people apart.

"We come from Monterey." The woman read my thoughts with perfect insouciance. "But you do not want to speak with me. You want to hear *mi hija. Venir, hija. Venga aqui, por favor.*"

With that summons a charming little sprite materialized at her mother's side, a pair of ponytails wrapped in rubber bands. She was dressed in a formless smock tie-dyed in a riot of patterns and colors over canvas shoes with white socks and I realized then whose picture it was that nagged me from the wall.

I turned to our hostess.

"Are you Edgar Uribe's mother? I saw your son carving the lander for the senior float. What an eye! And this is your daughter?"

"My Isabel," she affirmed with a pride that embarrassed me.

But Sheriff Buchanan seemed perfectly at ease.

"Isabel. Nice to meet you, *señorita.*"

She nodded politely.

"Can you tell me what you saw?"

The child turned to her mother for permission.

"*Esta bien.*"

Such dignity in a ten-year-old. She nodded to her mama and then returned fearlessly to meet the sheriff's eye.

"I see the truck coming and there is Our Mother."

"Your mother?" I asked.

"Our Mother," the child contradicted.

"Let her tell it her own way," Colt directed me. "Go ahead, *señorita.*"

At first it seemed the child was not willing to elaborate at all. Colt didn't prompt her or respond with the obvious follow-on questions. He just waited patiently and sipped his coffee. I took a sip or two for the sake of appearances. After a long moment, Isabel picked up her narrative.

"She has feeling, Our Mother. I feel her. Edgar, he feel—feels her too."

I turned to her mother. "What does she mean?"

Her mother smiled to me.

"She means to say that she has shown herself to us. To our family."

The last thing I expected to find coming home to Lafayette County was a family of mystics! How could anyone believe such things?

"Our Lady has appeared many times." The mother read my thoughts, which made me wonder if this was actually a warren of sorcerers.

"But the man was not expecting," Isabel continued sadly. "He had a *telèfono* and when he look up he see her and he is surprised. Then he truck, it go off the road and I can no more see because there is the ditch, but the pole breaks and the tree shakes and I go tell *Mama* to call the *policia* because there is a great trouble."

And what of the Lady? Where did she go?

"She stay to help him die," the child answered as if that was self-evident. "And then she come to us. Here. To *mi familia*."

I tried to mask my incredulity but was once again transparent to our hosts.

"She came," the child insisted. "I add her to my picture."

"Can you show us, little one?" Colt encouraged, and her mother answered.

"In her room."

Edgar's younger sister led the way past piles of towels and plaid shirts. Just two doors down a prefab hallway.

"Here."

I stepped into Isabel's modest sanctum and gasped. A vivid illustration as large as a small tapestry occupied an entire wall! The brilliant and varied texture was rendered in a neon tempura alien to me, the Virgin of Virgins smiling over a surreal landscape peopled with children and their families, the hale and the crippled equally represented in startling detail. It seemed impossible that a child could create such a marvel, and yet there it was.

The child's mother regarded me closely.

"You do not drink." She nodded to the still-steaming cup in my hand. "I think you never will."

We thanked Señora Uribe for her hospitality as we left the family's trailer. By that time a gaggle of onlookers was gathered around Marty Hart's still-smoking Ford. Colt hopped the fence and strode over to the wreckage.

"We cleared to get in there, Deputy?"

"It won't be cool to the touch, Sheriff."

"Thanks for the warning."

I followed Colt to Marty's pickup. The door on the driver's side hung on a single hinge. I saw blood and brains on the windshield.

Reminded me of Afghanistan.

"So much for safety belts," I remarked.

"Marty didn't use his," Colt informed me. "Which makes me wonder if there ain't something other than God's mother was distracting him."

The sheriff stepped up onto a buckled running board to inspect the Ford's tin-can cab, squeezing past the passenger seat to check the glove box which I presume sprung open with impact. A couple of road maps were visible. A flashlight. When Colt pulled out, his deputy was waiting.

"Found a toolbox in the ditch, Sheriff. Marty's name's engraved on the box. Must of got thrown from the truck bed when he hit."

"You opened it?" Colt asked.

"No, sir, I's worried about custody."

"Good. I'll sign for it. Get me some forms and bags, you don't mind. Gloves, too, you got a pair you can spare."

Colt waited to formally establish a chain of custody for the evidence before slipping on a pair of latex gloves to attack the toolbox. A thick hasp and padlock secured the small vault, but of course there was no key, so the sheriff sent his deputy for a bolt cutter, which became the firefighters' sole contribution for the day. Within seconds the keep was breached.

I peered over Colt's shoulder to see what was inside.

A tangle of fishing lures and a pair of pliers. A spool of forty-pound tackle and a Barlow folding knife. But then Colt pulled those caddies aside to display the valuables beneath.

"Well, shit," I exclaimed.

The sheriff seemed neither disappointed nor surprised to see a Ziploc bag filled with what looked like clumps of salt.

"Clara Sue, you got a pen?"

I handed over my ballpoint and he teased the bag open. Took a quick sniff. "What I figured."

Colt resealed the bag of methamphetamine with the barrel of my pen.

"You think Marty was using when he wrecked his truck?" I asked.

"Doubt it. But dollars to doughnuts it's why he was using a throwaway phone."

CHAPTER TEN

Crystal Meth Found in Guard's Toolbox
The Clarion

The Tuesday following Marty Hart's wreck, Randall and I were installed before a high-definition monitor to crop and copy photographs of the floats competing for honors in the homecoming parade.

"We need to put this to bed." Randall was complaining about the pace of our work and I agreed, but there was not a damned thing I could do to speed things along.

Running a newspaper is a little like running a dairy. You get up early, there are no days off, and if you quit squeezing teats your enterprise will just plain dry up. I'm not talking about running out of copy. We get more stories than we can handle. We're still in the middle of hunting season and so besides the floats and the parade and all that mess, we've got a dozen camouflaged hunters looking to get their guns and trophies splashed in the paper. Next week we've got Heritage Week, and the week after that the marching band's heading for a performance in New Orleans—can't let that recognition go unheralded.

And then there are the nasty-grams. I've got enough "Letters to Editor" to stuff a landfill, folks pissed off with the federal government, every conspiracy theorist expecting to see his special take on reality featured in the paper. And, of course, there are the Obama haters. That's a well that never runs dry, even though the man is out of office! The FBI actually requires threats against any president to be reported, but if I forwarded every e-mail or letter I get that promises violent retribution against our commanders-in-chief, I'd have feds banging doors day and night.

We are definitely not hurting for things to print. What we're hurting for is subscribers and advertisements. A paper can't survive without readers and ads, and if you don't drum up new business you die. It's a constant process of hanging onto the old as you court the new, and lately we've had very few newcomers to the *Clarion*.

Randall left me fiddling with jpegs and tiffs as he checked the week's classified ads against our expenses.

"We're short," he announced.

"How short?"

"Well, if Hiram renews his ad for the cement plant we'll just about break even."

"He's late."

"He's testing you."

"What do you mean?"

"I mean he's waiting for you to take some position on Butch's place, Clara Sue. He wants readers to believe you're on his side."

"Why do I have to take sides at all?"

"You took sides at the *Globe* all the time. Hell, it was your stock-in-trade."

"It was my stock. But now that I'm the one responsible for paying the bills it's not trading all that well."

"If it's important, there's always blowback," Randall rejoined.

Too true. I remember an occasion at the *Globe* when the staff was debating whether to bump a story about a young marine who left military service after lodging a formal complaint that he had to constantly fake his sexual orientation in order to avoid harassment for being gay. I was still in college when Bill Clinton signed his "Don't Ask, Don't Tell" policy. This latest allegation of mistreatment didn't seem newsworthy to me. The issue had been worked to death. But my editor at the time disagreed.

"This marine is saying that the only way he could be accepted in his chain of command was to lie. What the story is about is whether we as Americans are okay with any military environment that forces any young man or woman to lie in order to serve our country. The lying's the thing. That is the story you ought to care about."

And now, years later, I am faced with another lie and another story.

"Hiram means to get Butch out of the way and he doesn't much care how," Randall said as we butted heads over what to do.

"It's Butch's property," I said, digging in. "Hiram can't make him sell if he doesn't want to."

"Clara, you saw what Hiram tried to pull in that school board meeting over the summer. You think he won't try again now there's money at stake?"

"You have a point," I allowed.

"Readers need to know what's bullshit and what's not. Whatever happened to 'Speak Truth to Power'?"

"The Quakers gave us that one in 1955."

"Still works for me."

"Jesus, okay," I relented. "Tell you what—the school board has to report progress sometime next month. When the discussion goes public, I'll sort out the pros and cons, how's that?"

"Fearless," Randall replied and before I could tell him to go fuck himself, the bell tinkled on our rowan door.

"Mornin' folks!"

In waddles Rep. Bull Putnal, that Rotary pin trapping a clip-on tie to his ample belly, slacks bunched up so loose on his shoes you'd think he'd trip on himself. State Representative Putnal reached the counter smiling like he'd just won the lottery, or at least another election, thumbs tucked inside a brand-new pair of suspenders wide enough to haul an Airstream.

"How you doin', Clara Sue? Randall."

"Mr. Putnal." I offered a smile that I hoped was ingratiating. "How may I help you?"

"Well, you know I got an election comin'."

Jesus, with all the other things competing for attention, I'd damn near forgotten the November races. Putnal gave me a second to recover before pressing his case.

"I know it's a frantic time o' year for you all, but I need to get some of my record noted in your paper."

"Yes, sir. Certainly. How many columns would you like?"

He seemed surprised. "Well, as many as you can give me, I reckon."

It was my turn to be discomfited.

"I thought we were talking about advertisement, here, Bull. Political ads."

He gave me one of those jelly-bowl chuckles. You know the kind. There's no sound. Just that big ole belly shaking along with the triple chin.

"You—! You a pistol, Clara Sue!"

"Oh, I am that."

A final quiver of mirth died.

"I'm sure you want your readers to be informed," he said, smiling grandly.

"I do, absolutely."

"You got a concern, say so, Clara Sue. We can reason together."

This could be tricky. I leaned onto my counter as casually as I could.

"Bull, when President Obama was in office, you were telling your constituents that the prez was a Muslim. I'm just curious—do you actually believe that? Or was that just red meat for your constituents?"

"President has to be a citizen, Clara Sue. That was my point and my only point. And besides, it's water under the bridge."

"I'm just saying that if you *wanted* me to address your campaign in my paper, I couldn't ignore your record, Bull."

"Voters know where I stand, Clara Sue. That's the fire gets me elected."

"Then you don't need the *Clarion* for kindling."

Bull's smile looked awfully tight in that pale of flesh face.

"Awright, fair enough," he broke off abruptly. "Sounds like you aren't willing to volunteer an endorsement. But you will run ads for me, won't you?"

"Of course we will, Mr. Putnal," Randall interjected cheerfully. "Freedom of speech is what we're all about. And we'll give you a good rate too."

Bull grunted like a bullfrog. "I'll let you know."

Putnal turned for the door, but then pulled up short like Colombo, thumb extended from a hand suddenly filled with a cigar.

"Oh, and Clara Sue, one other thing. 'Bout the school? I'm countin' on you to help me get those monies. Be a damn shame to let a candy store get in the way of four million dollars."

"From what I hear, Butch is not inclined to sell," I replied.

Bull's smile was suddenly brittle. "Cain't have a simpleton posing a risk to our children, Clara Sue. Surely our children have to be the guiding priority."

And with a tinkle of our brass alarm he was out the door. Randall leaned back in his chair.

"'Simpleton posing a risk'? 'Guiding priority'? Was that a threat?"

"To Butch, certainly."

"This is a no-win situation," Randall glowered. "If we don't print anything, Butch McCray will be tarred as a pedophile, but in the absence of any evidence we can't refute the rumor. Butch loses either way."

"But a lot of other folks win big, including Hiram and Roscoe Lamb."

"So what can we do, Clara Sue?"

I turned back to a computer screen glowing with pixeled images of floats and football players and hunters in camouflage grinning over guns and antlers and tusks.

"Going to need a shovel," I answered my husband as I exited the screen. "I've got some digging to do."

CHAPTER ELEVEN

Royal Ambassadors Edge Seniors for Best Float
Harvey Sykes Kills Monster Hog
County Commissioners Engage Architect for School
The Clarion

It's frightening to think that with a handful of affidavits, a pliant judge, and a cooperative shrink you can commit almost anyone to a crazy house *cum* "care facility." The Lamb brothers had already decided what sort of care Butch McCray would receive, and though I did not know it at the time, the machinery to establish their foster brother as a pedophile or merely incompetent was well under way. But it turned out that Butch was not the only obstacle threatening the Lambs' already rigged bid, and it was this latter impediment that took Hiram Lamb for a long drive to a fallen woman in a failing mansion on Pepperfish Keys.

I believe I have mentioned that Barbara Stanton returned to her home on Pepperfish Keys a couple of years after her famous husband's spectacular demise. Senator Stanton's homicide, terrible enough, was preceded or perhaps even anticipated by his daughter's brutal murder. The family's fall from grace got international play, a US senator laundering money for a drug lord, his only child faking abuse in a foment of scandal only to be slain herself. It was easy in all that froth to forget that there was a wife involved, and mother.

It was Barbara Stanton who discovered her daughter's mutilated corpse in a bedroom shower. Weeks later, Babs saw her husband hauled off in handcuffs only moments before he was blown to bits. You can still see the crater left by the explosion—right beside the cattle gap at the front gate. The threads leading to those twin disasters are too tangled to unravel here, but for sure it knocked Barbara Stanton off her rocker. Unless you believe she was off her rocker to begin with.

A stark reversal of circumstance, by any estimation. Time was, and within easy memory, when Barbara was the envy of all her Tri Delt sisters, a *nouveau riche* catching the eye of a North Florida cracker who was destined to become a United States senator. Now she's just an eccentric pauper, a has-been in rustication with an unsellable house and a sagging porch in a place isolated from any normal commerce. Of course, I remember when there were no homes of any kind on Pepperfish Keys and no commerce apart from the modest forays of hunters and fishermen.

There wasn't even a road would get you to the Keys in those years. To reach that backwater, you came by boat, and if you were running an inboard you had better watch the intakes. People unfamiliar with Florida's northern littoral come to our shores expecting to find beaches of blinding white sand identical to those encountered at Pensacola or Sanibel with well-defined margins offering an unspoiled view of the gulf beyond.

But there's nothing like a strand at Pepperfish Keys, and even on a good day, you can't be sure you're seeing the gulf. What you do see coming over oyster beds and shallow brine is a vast prairie of turtle grass bounding the last vestiges of Florida's hardwood forest. You see the trees from a distance, modest sentinels of tidewater cypress and loblolly pine.

Sometimes an osprey will roost atop some lightning-shattered bole, scouting for fish along with squadrons of pelicans.

Once off the saltwater and past the boundary of stubborn grass, you reach a terrain that is mostly below sea level, the sammy earth riddled by spring-fed creeks and sloughs that make the place a perfect refuge for turkey and quail and hunting ground for gators and lynx and bear. Last I heard there might even be a panther or two out there. And hogs, of course. Hogs run wild through Pepperfish Keys in sounders that mix feral swine with stock as old as the conquistadors.

Harvey Sykes got his three-hundred pounder on the Keys; I just ran the photo.

I have never hunted the Keys, but I have certainly fished there, just a tomboy with her father and a Zebco reel in a flat-bottomed boat fashioned from plywood and glue and urethane varnish. Imagine sliding off the gulf in that bark, a sinking sun still warm on the back of your khaki shirt, your neck burned red unless you were smart enough to wear a bandana which native Floridians, as a matter of pride, never do.

You're riding the tide in water that might only be waist deep, alert to the threat of oyster beds and to any grass or line that might foul your prop, surprised always at the faint detonation of scallions, those ancient crustaceans breaking the surface for that one inestimably meager sip of oxygen, then to descend trailing bubbles beneath your homemade voyager.

I can still see the rainbow of oil trailing our two-stroke outboard, still smell the gasoline burnt off that overworked Mercury. Other aromas compete for memory, the chum in the bait box mingling with odors of fecundity and decay, a disemboguement of roe contesting the rot of a gutted heron. And of course we fishermen bring our own aromas to the wilderness in pheromones pungent and intimate, a rut of piss and perspiration.

We ended our days thirsty, filthy, and spent, but somewhere past the armor of oyster shells and razor-sharp grass a spring boils ice cold and with my father's gnarled hand at the tiller we navigated channels marked with cypress poles stuck into the silt by generations of fishermen to find our campsite. There to debark, bivouac, and feast.

Sound mixes with smell in my recollection, the sizzle of mullet and bass and bream in cast iron skillets, the explosion of resin from fat lighter kindling. I gorged with my father on the catch of the day. We drank mugs of steaming coffee and I begged for stories. Yarns of thieves and pirates. Of runaway slaves and Billy Bowlegs and Osceola. Fantastic, convoluted narratives!

People see all kinds of things in Pepperfish Keys. Always have. Folks will swear, for example, that they have seen the elusive pepperfish. Caught them, even. In fact, some of the best stories I ever heard as a young girl detailed the wiles and savvy of that fish for whom the Keys are named. Best eating fish you ever had, people said, and they believed it too, believed it all. But as a matter of cold fact there are no pepperfish on Pepperfish Keys because there are no pepperfish anywhere.

The species does not exist.

There is no such thing as a pepperfish, but that obdurate barrier does nothing to shake the testimony of those already convinced. There is something about the Keys that spawns imagination and invention and transmogrification. So Hiram Lamb should not have been too surprised when visiting Senator Stanton's widow to learn that she had received a visit from the dead.

The account that Babs related to Hiram matched the broad narrative I printed in the paper, but with some elaboration. Babs told Hiram that she had fallen into a fitful sleep in the master bedroom below her dead husband's study but woke from a nightmare dizzy with the certainty that some presence filled the room. The Stanton mansion, if you haven't seen it, is ideal to host these sorts of visitations. It rises on sagging piers three stories of confused architecture straddled on three sides by a gingerbread verandah that looks over a failing pier and a channel of silver water cut through a plain of turtle grass. The only smart thing about the house is its respect for prevailing wind; there are french doors at every opportunity, clever passages to encourage cross ventilation, and balconies on three sides of every floor. Of course, the rooms are mostly abandoned, now, the furniture thrown with sheets or plastic.

So much death in that house. So much to cover up. The curtains had long been stripped from the dowels above the balcony doors, so the presence spooking Babs that night did not take shape in a shroud of linen. In fact, according to her, there was initially no visible manifestation of anything at all, no chains dragged across the floor, no whoooooosh or whisper from spirits trapped between ether and earth. The night was neither dark nor stormy. The moon was full through a cloudless sky and from the bedroom's infamous balcony Barbara could see beyond the lawn and pier the silver crescent that was the Gulf of Mexico. But, according to the senator's widow, there was no phantasma or specter at all. Just the sense of a presence in the room.

And then it was gone.

"I felt like some spirit was next to me," Babs insisted. "In bed with me, it felt like. And then it was gone and the air in my lungs was just sucked out. Just sucked out, and there I was gasping like a fish. Scared half to death!"

It should be stipulated that Barbara Stanton has been scared of one thing or another most of her life. Before her fear of scandal matured, a fear of rejection was paramount. Babs knew she wasn't the sort of gal that got boys looking. She's tall and angular with sharp features and a Roman nose. Blotched and freckled skin. Her hair was nice, thick and luxurious, but that wasn't enough to quell the gnawing fear of abandonment by a boy, a club, or a sorority. Babs bought her way into Tri Delt's beehive society, her daddy's checkbook a reliable hedge against rejection from that quarter.

However, no bankroll could assuage the underlying insecurity which was Barbara Ann's default position. The prospect of finding oneself without means warred with a fear of rejection from polite society. It was ironic that Barbara met Baxter Stanton in the summer of love and civil disobedience when slews of young people nurtured or spoiled in middle-class security abjured their parents' bromides for countercultural alternatives. All you need is love, the song went, but Babs was not in tune with that nonsense. Girls could burn bras in California, if they wanted to, or march in Washington or Alabama. Barbara would happily forgo the uncertain benefits of liberation in return for status and security.

She was supervising her sorority's newest bevy of sisters at an afternoon social when Baxter came strolling in with a half-dozen brothers of his fraternity. You don't see these sorts of mixers anymore, unless you matriculate in the deep South, Ole Miss at Oxford, say. Maybe Alabama. But during the sixties Florida State could hang with the best. The white gloves, the diaphanous summer dresses, bared shoulders, and décolletage. The young men in pressed chinos and blazers.

Barbara spotted her husband-to-be the moment he stepped through her house's wide french doors, and she wasn't the only one looking. Stanton had a knack for getting noticed, and it wasn't because he was handsome. He was short. He was skinny. But there was an ineffable charisma about the young man that everyone recognized. He was ambitious and made no bones about it, a cock-of-the-walk who'd tell anyone listening that one day he would represent the Sunshine State in the United States Senate. Babs wasn't much interested in politics, but she did have a father with a bankroll destined to be indispensable to a young man's ambition.

Babs was checking to make sure the punch bowl was not spiked, or at least spiked properly, when Baxter sauntered over. He looked like a bantam rooster, a straw-haired twenty-something strutting up in a light-blue blazer and button-up shirt. Had a loud necktie threaded through the loops of his slacks instead of a belt. She saw the flask in his hand.

"Let me help you out," he said, smiling through a row of crooked teeth and before she could say boo he'd emptied a pint of bourbon into the punch bowl.

"What's your name, dahlin?"

"Barbara. And you must be Baxter Stanton."

"I love it when people know my name," the young man confessed, which should have clued Babs at the outset what to expect from the man she would eventually marry.

Stanton was confident, crafty, and ambitious, but of humble means. He came from Perry, Florida, where his daddy worked twelve hours a day at the pulpwood mill. Barbara's pedigree was no more distinguished, though zealously disguised. She was an O'Steen before marriage, a skinny girl closely related or at least dog-kin to half the penniless families in her county. But Barbara's father amassed a fortune.

O'Steen saved every dime he ever made off tobacco and timber and was one of the first in the region to cash in big-time on federal subsidies of dairies.

The idea was to guarantee farmers a price for milk by paying dairymen to limit production. Barbara's daddy took over a million dollars of taxpayers' money in return for not milking his cows. Of course, the old man loudly denounced federal subsidies of any kind.

So would Baxter Stanton. Naturally.

"Whatever I got, I earned myself!" Baxter always worked that claim into his stump speech, neglecting to mention that an inherited estate seeded by taxpayers' money made his political fortunes possible.

But the charisma came *gratis.* Within an hour of their meeting, Babs found herself following The Rooster upstairs with a Dixie cup of bourbon and a condom. One tumble in the hay got her pregnant. A million fears triggered with that insemination—fear or shame and embarrassment. Fear of hell-fire and damnation and whispers of damaged goods. She had to flee to Georgia for the abortion and was surprised, when returning to campus after the worst Christmas in her life, to find a note from Baxter in her room.

"I'd still like to see you."

She would later have a daughter, her father's spitting image many would say, and for a while it looked as though there was no need to be afraid of anything. Baxter won three terms to the US Senate and was well known as the Sunshine State's favorite son. That was before the crimes and murder which brought his family to death and disgrace as well as ruin.

Barbara insisted that her daughter never left the mansion. She'd swear to anyone that Beth Ann regularly walked the upper stories, late at night, and that Baxter haunted the study, his boudoir, really, the location of countless infidelities. The senator's killer was never found. That's why Baxter could not rest in peace, Babs told Hiram.

He was crying for vengeance.

In the end, she blamed herself. Long before Babs lost her daughter and husband, she knew there was something foul as fish guts about Baxter's associates. Even during the family's halcyon days, she had known there was something dirty about her husband's money. And yet she remained silent. She acquiesced.

In fairness, the cost of running for office encouraged short cuts. Beth Ann was only five years old when Baxter ran for the US Senate, coming from behind to beat a well-known incumbent, but that victory came at the cost of a king's ransom. In fact, that first triumph was the seed of Stanton's never-ending debt, and the machinations which ensued stoked Barbara to premonitions of doom. They were spending more than they were earning, but when she'd raise the issue with her husband, Baxter only replied that the cash was accounted for by the Miami Jew in charge of his never-ending campaigns.

"You're just a worry wart," Baxter said, dismissing her fears. "We're fine. Never better."

And she tried to believe him. She really did. That was her duty, after all, to cherish her husband, to accept his authority. Aside from the social mores enforced at her sorority, the Bible made clear that a woman was completely subservient to her husband. These were eternal truths that Babs had learned by heart. Take Genesis 3:16: ". . . thy desire shall be to thy husband, and he shall rule over thee." Or what about First Corinthians 11:9? "Neither was man created for the sake of woman, but woman for the sake of man."

It was not enough to believe your husband. You had to believe *in* him. That conviction set Barbara apart from many of her white-gloved sisters, most of them, probably. She was obliged to trust her husband.

To protect him.

To honor him.

Even if she hated him.

Babs's father could not understand her anxiety at all. O'Steen loved Baxter Stanton. Couldn't get enough of him. Believed every single thing that came out of Rooster's mouth. Baxter would install her father on the porch swing with a tumbler of bourbon and regale the old coot with privileged gossip or stories of intrigue, largely fabricated, that welcomed the dairyman into a world he'd never dreamed to inhabit. It was not uncommon for Senator Stanton to receive a thousand-dollar check after those soirees, and as the years passed Barbara became invisible to her father.

Baxter Stanton was making his fourth run to the US Senate when Babs discovered their daughter's hogtied corpse. A few weeks later she witnessed her husband's assassination. The press descended on her home, and Babs's fear of shame was realized along with the reality of indigence. There was no money left in the senator's war chest and no asset bequeathed to his widow aside from the now-notorious mansion on Pepperfish Keys.

Babs abandoned the house at the advice of friends and family. Every painting, plate, and spoon got put up for auction. She kept Rooster's shotgun and a few personals, packing those leavings in a travel trunk passed down from some long-dead relative. Then Barbara left the keys with a real estate agent in Orlando and moved to a trailer park, confident that the mansion's sale would stave off back taxes and penury. She lingered in a double-wide for months and months anticipating that relief, but the residence just would not sell. This shouldn't have come as a surprise. The house was in terrible repair, and with a glut of subprime real estate already on the market no one was interested in a firetrap in the middle of nowhere.

So a little more than a year after she left the Keys, Barbara Stanton packed her steamer trunk once again and returned to her gutted home. The local Fox affiliate sent a reporter to cover that pitiful démarche. When asked what brought her back, Babs replied simply that she couldn't stay away, which (who knows?) might be true. And so now here she was alone in this god-awful place when an unnamed presence wakes her from a nightmare.

How many times have you seen the movie where the always-curious coed abandons the safety of comrades and common sense to climb the dreaded stairs beyond which everyone knows Freddy waits with his awful claws?

Well, Babs didn't do that, exactly.

What she did do was leave her bed and the threat of a succubus to unlimber the old double-barrel and creep barefooted to the balcony. This, as she told Hiram Lamb, "To make sure everything was all right."

Not every trip to the balcony was prompted by a sense of dread. How many times had she lingered on this very gallery with Baxter to see the day's troubles cured in a setting sun? Or to watch pelicans flying low over the water like squadrons of aircraft? Sometimes to wave at friends tying off their tony boats at the pier in easy sight below. Her daughter learned to water ski on the silver channel within view of the bedroom balcony. Those were memories pleasant to recall, a balm against nightmares and succubi.

On this occasion a breeze that should have been cool stirred the curtains at the balcony and as Barbara emerged to face a setting sun and amaranth sky she saw a light at the pier, just a moment's flare, like someone lighting a cigarette.

In fact, Senator Stanton often took to the pier in the wee hours to enjoy a cigar. He'd always had trouble sleeping, Baxter had. Babs couldn't count the nights she'd stirred to find him gone. Most times he was just making water, but if she did not hear the familiar flush from the bathroom she might leave her bed for the balcony and, yes, there he'd be. Having himself a smoke on the pier.

Stanton had been dead five years when his wife saw him once again lounging beside the water. When Hiram Lamb drove out to the Keys, Barbara plied him with her latest rendition of the encounter.

"It was Baxter, I'm tellin' you, Hiram. Big as life. Sucking that damn cigar."

Her next memories were not so precise. A sense of running. Of transportation. She left the house, that much is certain. Her feet were cut up—the once-manicured lawn now a treachery of sandspurs and broken glass.

Imagine a hobbled sprint for the pier.

"BAXTER!" She screamed across the grounds like a crazy woman. "BAXTER, DON'T GO!"

But then, as in the movie we've all seen, her husband vanished.

Gone.

Disappeared.

Nothing in sight but a miasma clinging to the slow-churning channel, and nothing to hear but a sough of breeze, a croak of frogs, and a grunt of gators.

"Baxter?" She made one last feeble inquiry, but there was no reply.

Babs probably realized, then, that she was just a silly old woman, an old bag stripped of money and position and driven by boredom or guilt or a collusion of medications to hallucination. She was okay with that verdict actually. Barbara is in some ways a remarkably resilient woman. She is reconciled to her fall from grace and faces with admirable aplomb the notion that she is going insane. But a few weeks after she saw her husband's ghost, Babs returned to the pier where she found a stump of cigar.

Some weeks had passed before Babs revisited the pier. "I was afraid I'd see a ghost, I guess," she told Hiram Lam. "Or maybe I just wanted to get rid of that filthy old lawn chair."

In any case, when Babs returned to the dock she saw something that she missed on her earlier midnight encounter. It was the remains of a cigar. "Was right beside the lawn chair," Babs told Hiram. "Right there on the pier. Here, let me show you." Barbara produced the recovered stogie for Hiram's inspection. It was a Cohiba, Hiram would later report. "Not the Cuban cigar, the other one, the Dominican. Still had the band." Baxter's preferred smoke, left behind like a tease or talisman and burned down to a nub.

Barbara Stanton's repeated accounts did not improve her reputation among local citizens. Various versions of Babs's aborted séance were widely repeated countywide, and even more widely ridiculed. Visits from the Virgin Mary were easier for Laureate's citizens to swallow than reports of Senator Stanton's ghostly resurrection. The skepticism greeting Babs's several accounts did not surprise me. Any self-styled aristocrat in a community as hermetic and defeated as our own is a target for envy and opprobrium, and so it's to be expected that Barbara Stanton, after flying so high and falling so low, would become the butt of coffeehouse banter, our corrupted royalty, our wilted rose, our Emily.

Crazy woman, folks scoffed over their lattes.

Fucking bitch, said others.

"Prob'ly just menopause," Preacher Allen felt free to speculate. "That and all the drugs she's taking."

But Hiram Lamb defended Barbara's evolving account as though it were holy gospel.

"There's definitely stuff goes on at Pepperfish Keys," he'd growl to skeptics. "Has been since God made dirt. You don't believe it, go out there and spend a night yourself."

This sort of chivalry is not what you expected to see from either of the Lamb brothers. Hiram's defense of Barbara Stanton, in particular, was completely out of character. Hiram thrived on schadenfreude. He took glee in the misfortune of those less fortunate.

So why the sudden concern for the discredited widow of a corrupt politician?

I am embarrassed to admit that I neglected to ask that question. It did not occur to me to question Hiram's motive for defending Barbara Stanton. I should have asked myself what prompted him to visit Babs in the first place. Sixty miles is a long way to drive for a ghost story that you can read in the paper. My antenna was rusted from lack of use, is my only excuse, though a cub reporter could have guessed it was not noblesse oblige that motivated Hiram to embrace Barbara Stanton's preposterous story.

In hindsight, it's easy to see that Hiram Lamb wouldn't be offering a single word on Babs's behalf if there was not something in it for himself.

CHAPTER TWELVE

Senator's Ghost Leaves Cigar
The Clarion

When I was at the *Boston Globe* I was responsible for a column a week. Every now and then our chief would assign a story, but by and large I was my own boss. Of course, now that I actually am the boss of my own paper, I have almost no control over what I write. Worse than that, I never have the luxury of covering anything in depth. I have eight columns to fill every week, and any subscriber wanting a print ad or picture gets priority over anything I want to feature in the paper.

Some days I feel like a gerbil in a treadmill, running like hell and getting nowhere. But I have to say that the weeks before and after homecoming provided a ton of low-lying fruit for my modest little rag. Besides homecoming and Halloween, we had the unsolicited sightings of flying objects and virgins and dead husbands all over the county. We even had a crew come down from Atlanta, from CNN, to do a piece on our localized and paranormal frenzy.

Some twenty-something film-school graduate from Emory interviewed me. She had no idea she was talking to a journalist who used to have a nationally syndicated column.

So far as this entitled wo*man* was concerned, I was just a small-town hick with a paper useful for swatting flies. Even so, I have to admit I was caught up in the moment. Been a long time since I'd been on camera for any reason, and I was willing to string the conversation along. In fact, the only reason I broke off the back 'n' forth, was because Hattie's nurse called me away.

Good damn thing too. Because if I'd ignored that nurse's summons, I'd have missed the *real* story altogether.

Hattie Briar was my grandmother's aunt by marriage, the oldest citizen in our county, close to the centenary mark, and a regular contributor to the *Clarion*. She's installed in an assisted-living apartment over at Dowling Park, right there on a high bluff above the Suwannee River. Miss Hattie moved to the Park at her own parents' deaths and is old enough to remember the orphanage that used to be there, old enough, for sure, to remember every aunt, uncle, and cousin in Laureate.

She loves being the center of attention. I can't cover Heritage Week without a paean to Miss Hattie; readers won't let me get away with that. And in fairness it would be hard to find anyone who knows more about the politics and culture of Lafayette and Taylor and Dixie Counties than does Miss Hattie. But you don't exactly interview her. When you go to visit Miss Hattie, you're not a journalist. You're a scribe. You pull up a chair, you sit down, and you try to keep up.

While still ambulatory, Miss Hattie was a recurring guest at high school assemblies and homecoming parades. She remains the doyenne of Heritage Week and loves seeing her mug in the paper. Miss Hattie is very opinionated and dismissive of any authority, which drives her caregivers crazy.

I had an appointment loosely scheduled with Miss Hattie for the following week, so you can bet I was not pleased in the middle of my CNN interview to see Randall trotting up with his mobile phone.

"Sorry. It's for you."

Next thing I know, I'm speaking with some stressed-out nurse at Dowling Park directing me to drop whatever I'm doing and get over to see Hattie Briar. There I was, the big-shot journalist being summoned like a valet.

"Can't this wait?" I grated over Randall's phone.

"I'm afraid not," came the reply.

"Is she dying?"

"I'm afraid not."

I apologized to the newbie from Emory, grabbed a legal pad and a camera, and piled into my foreign SUV. Within minutes I was on a suspension bridge high above the river that Stephen Foster made famous. When Miss Hattie was a girl it was common to see the Suwannee coursing right up to stanchions of the Hal W. Adams Bridge. There were floods in those years, waters originating in the Okefenokee coursing south in combination with other tributaries to inundate homes and farms for miles on either side of the bridge. But now—?

When the Suwannee River is anemic and low. Sandbars that used to be invisible are now small islands sprouting tangles of grass and scrub. You can't even take a Jet Ski through some places on the river, and it looks like that condition is becoming the norm rather than the exception. I used to put my Vespoli single in at the bridge for a scull down to Mearson Springs and back, but no longer. I tell folks that I retired my racing shell because there is too much debris on the river, too great a chance of running up on flint shelves or sandbars, not to mention Jet Skis and powerboats, but the main inhibitor keeping me off the Suwannee is my heart.

I have "some blockage" as Doc Trotter describes it, one of those women with a ticker that sooner or later is going to need tinkering. I rowed competitively through college with never a hint of a problem. I rowed doubles in the Head of the Charles nearly every year I was at the *Globe* and never missed a beat. But when I returned to my hometown I began to notice that I'd be short of breath. Sometimes a bit dizzy. I was rowing toward Branford on the Suwannee when I had my first "episode." It was as though I suddenly could not breathe, like someone put a plastic bag over my head. I was in the middle of the river in a slender shell with rough water and in blind panic. And I was lucky. Lucky to get off the river and lucky to get an accurate diagnosis. Too often, women with cardiovascular disease are misdiagnosed or their symptoms are simply ignored. I got an appointment at Shands Hospital in Gainesville, did the various tests. "You'll need a stent, sooner or later," an intern told me. "Maybe a bypass."

Maybe? That's the best you can do?

I turned left past the bridge and days of glory to find the secondary road leading to Dowling Park. A few minutes later I motored past the stone gate which takes you into a mix of ranch-style houses and institutionalized construction, this last dedicated to the care of folks like Hattie who are in their last laps.

You can't cut a mature tree of any variety on Dowling Park, so anything built, including the homes of retirees, is required to accommodate groves of water oak and hickory. The property is stunning. There are so many dogwoods that in spring you're riding on a carpet of blossoms and the perennials are spectacular, hedges of azaleas broken with groupings of Ligustrum and pyracantha and nandina. Spanish moss hanging like laundry from oak limbs that run, in some places, no more than a child's height off the ground.

I know my way to the "Extended Care" facility and arrived to find Hattie in her handmade rocker at a patio outside. She's ancient and failing. As desiccated as a bag of sticks. I found her draped in a comforter, propped up to face the sun, eyes dark and bright and set as deeply in their sockets as berries pressed into a bowl of dough. A white-uniformed nurse in attendance was retrieving a carafe of iced tea from a lawn table nearby and I saluted to get his attention.

"You have any idea what this is about?"

"No ma'am. 'Cept Miss Hattie said it couldn't wait."

"Any chance I can get some coffee?"

"I'll bring you fresh," he said, nodding, and with that excuse left me alone with Laureate's oldest human being.

"Miss Hattie? Miss Hattie, it's Clara. Clara Sue Buchanan?"

"I see you," she answered dismissively. "Seen you when came thu the gate."

I took another step forward and sure enough, from Hattie's vantage on the patio you really can see up and down the river, all the way to the Park's iron-gapped entry.

"I'm beginning to think you're part Indian, Miss Hattie."

Her arms rustled like vines in her wrap. "Ever'body think he a damn Indian."

"Yes, ma'am." I fidgeted for a pen. "Well, why am I here, Miss Hattie?"

"Cause God put you here," she replied archly.

I took a breath. "I mean why have you particularly brought me here?"

"Got something fo' you. Over there."

She pointed a bony finger and I saw what looked like an antique stagecoach trunk deposited on the far side of the glass-topped table. It was probably a Jenny Lind, a round-topped steamer trunk sheathed in leather and wrapped at intervals with iron bands secured by brass studs. A treasure chest fit for Long John Silver.

"This yours?" I walked over to inspect.

"Usta be," she sighed. "Long time ago I sold that chest to Barbara Stanton fuh fifteen dollars. Hadn't seen it fuh years. Now she done brung it back to me like a bad penny."

I was floored. Miss Hattie is old and revered but she doesn't come from the same social circle as the Stantons. Not by a couple of stratospheres.

"And how do you know Barbara Stanton, Miss Hattie?"

"We're dog kin. Through the McCrays. Barbara was an O'Steen b'fore she married Baxter Stanton. 'Fact, her Granddaddy O'Steen had hisself a house near the gulf not too far from that barn Babs and Rooster built."

Something told me I better find a pen to go with my yellow pad.

"So you are not an intimate of hers, but she drives out here from the Keys to give you back this beat-up old steamer?"

"She did. An' that was after Hiram Lamb offered her a thousand dollars fuh it."

"One _thousand_ dollars? For this trunk?"

"In cash."

"And Mrs. Stanton refused?"

"She tole Hiram she lost track of it. Said it got moved with the other furniture after Senator Stanton was kilt. Then soon's Hiram left, Miz Stanton called me and I told her bring me the damn thing an' I keep it."

"Why would Barbara agree to that?"

"Cause she din' want Hiram to have it, why else?" The old woman clucked in irritation.

I took a second to frame my response.

"Miss Hattie, I understand that Barbara was keeping the trunk from Hiram. But why does Hiram Lamb want this trunk? Is it the box itself he wants, or something inside?"

"They ain't nuthin' inside."

My news meter pegged from intrigued to irritated.

"Miss Hattie, you called me all the way out here to see an empty box?"

She shook her head.

"Ain't what's in the box <u>now</u> that Hiram's lookin' fuh. It's what used to be."

"Okay, and what was that?"

She shakes her head wearily. "All I know is it's got somethin' to do with Annette McCray."

"You mean Butch McCray's mother? The woman hanged herself?"

The old lady wheezed laughter. Sort of like a Chihuahua with asthma.

"Annie McCray never hung nuthin' but laundry."

What? What had I just heard?!

Miss Hattie regarded me slyly. "An' what about Butch's daddy? Whatchu know about Harold McCray?"

"Just that he was killed in a hunting accident," I said, repeating that commonly held knowledge. "It was deer season, somebody missed whatever they were shooting at, and Butch's father caught a round."

"Old Man Kelly found him," Miss Hattie said, picking up the story. "That's Hiram Lamb's daddy, case you don't know, and Roscoe's. Now, those two make a pair, don't they?"

"Pair of something, anyway," I agreed, and the ancient woman laughed.

"Anyway," Miss Hattie went on, "it was December and cold and I was splitting fatwood at the deer camp and Annie was piddlin' over her needlework when Old Man Kelly brought Harold McCray in fum de woods. Had Harold thowed back of his truck like he was hog meat."

"Poor Annette. She must have been devastated."

Miss Hattie spit carefully onto the patio. "Annette McCray was a hussy."

"Hussy?! What d'you mean by that, Miss Hattie?"

"I mean that Annie McCray was getting grits off Kelly Lamb," Miss Hattie declared. "An' that's the God's truth."

I leaned back.

"Well, that puts a different light on things."

"Don't it now?" She smiled wickedly.

"Bolsters the case for suicide too. Annette had to feel guilty as hell for cheating on her husband, and then to see Harold dead in the back of her lover's truck? That'd be enough to throw most anybody."

"I was there," Miss Hattie reminded me. "And I'm tellin' you Annie never missed a stitch."

"I still don't see why Hiram Lamb would give a tinker's damn about a dead woman's luggage, Miss Hattie."

"Ain't a box in the world don't keep secrets," the crone replied, shifting in her rocker like a rustle of leaves. "But not everything a secret. It ain't no secret that Annie inherited the McCray homestead with Harold's death; that's public knowledge. And it ain't no secret that if Annie had died without a will or other arrangement, every foot of that land would of gone straight to Butch, him being her blood and all. But Annie did make out a will, didn't she? Butch's mama made herself a will and named Old Man Kelly her sole heir and beneficiary. Them papers was notarized weeks before Kelly and Annie got hitched."

"You think it was a condition of marriage?" I asked Miss Hattie. "Do you think Kelly Lamb told Annie he wouldn't marry her unless she made him her heir?"

"Could be." Miss Hattie shrugged. "Or maybe Annie used the will to get Kelly to take care of Butch. Or mebbe they was other reasons."

"Other reasons?"

"Three months after that will was recorded Annie was dead."

"Ruled a suicide wasn't it? And there was an inquiry by the county coroner—no foul play suspected. It's all in the *Clarion*."

"Well, if it's in the newspaper it's got to be true," Miss Hattie said, making no attempt to soften her sarcasm. "Just like when Harold McCray got shot. No foul play there neither."

No foul play. But lots of apparent coincidences. And lots of land at stake.

"You have any idea who Annie got to draft her will, Miss Hattie?"

"Could be somebody at the courthouse, but I doubt it. More likely somebody she trusted. Maybe at Shamrock. Annie worked at the mill over there. Putnam Lumber—you familiar?"

"I've heard of it. Over near Cross City?"

"Ah hah. But I bet you a bright penny there ain't nuthin' wrote down about Kelly makin' Butch his ward. Folks thought well of Kelly for takin' in a retard, but I know for a fact the old man tried his best to put Butch out here in Dowling Park, at the orphanage.

"Made Annette mad as a hornet. One time during tobacco season, I was at the barn and I heard Butch's mama and Kelly goin' at it tooth an tongs, and Annie told Mr. Lamb if he wanted to keep her land and her bed, he had to keep Butch too. 'Wills can be changed, cain't they?' That's what she told him, and she meant it too. She always looked out for Butch, yes, ma'am. And then couple months later she's hangin ' in a smokehouse like a side of venison.

"I rode out to the house after the funeral, and there's Butch sittin' on the porch in the middle of his mama's effects, tears runnin' down his cheeks. Mother gone, now, along with daddy. That's when I got Annie's trunk. Her Granpa O'Steen brought it out after the funeral. Said Annie had asked him to keep it for her. Out at his place. Near the gulf."

"Did he say why?"

"Just said she sent it to him from the timber camp. Y'know Annie worked out there for a while, at the Shamrock mill.

"But once Annie was dead and awl, Mr. O'Steen figured he oughta git that old steamer back with the rest of her possessions. Most of her personals that was packed up inside was give away by the time I got there. Dresses and towels. Pots and pans. I got this here trunk along with a milk stool and a washboard."

"But she didn't leave her son anything?" I asked. "Not a thing? Even Kelly left Butch a half acre."

"That was white of him."

I stretched out to tap the brassy trunk with my toe.

"I'd like to take a look, Miss Hattie."

"Go on then."

It was a heavily built luggage, but not overly large, the sort of chest you'd imagine filled with diamonds or rubies or pieces of eight. I slid a bolt from its staple and when I flipped up the hasp was immediately taken with a familiar perfume. The box's unlined interior was constructed of marvelously fitted strips of red cedar and the distinctive aroma of that timber remained undiminished over the years.

I saw a nameplate bolted on the underside of the lid, a strip of brass clearly engraved in an elaborate cursive *Annette*

Elizabeth McCray. But there was nothing else to see. No diamonds or rubies. Not even a speck of lint.

"A thousand dollars is a lot to pay for an empty trunk,"
I remarked.

"Hiram don't know it's empty," Hattie pointed out. "He
must expect to find somethin' in that box, somethin' Annie
put there, an' I know in my bones that whatever it is, has got
somethin' to do with Butch McCray."

I felt hair rising on the back of my neck.

"Pretty gutsy of you, Miss Hattie," I said with a wink.
"Hiding this thing from Hiram Lamb."

"Ain't guts. Money and greed have dragged evil into Laureate. That's why people been seein' things. Hearin' things.
They's signs all over the county, as you know full well. And
now I'm havin' visions of my own. I don't know if they angels
or demons, but I'm too old to risk my redemption. 'Keep
a'holt of Annie's box.' Thass what I hear at night. 'Keep
Annie's hope chest hid away.'"

"But it's an empty trunk, Miss Hattie. What would be
the harm in letting Hiram have it? Why not just give him
the damn thing and be done with it?"

"NO!" She shivered beneath her thin blanket. "Only
thing keepin' Hiram Lamb from puttin' Butch away is the
fear of that box. He find out iss empty, Lord—! They be
nuthin' to hold him back!"

"And if Hiram comes out here looking, what are you
going to do, Miss Hattie? What'll you tell him?"

"Question is, what will *you* tell him?"

She turned to face me squarely, eyes bright and deep and
dark, and I knew then why Miss Hattie had summoned me.

"I don't know, Miss Hattie. I'm not sure I should get in
the middle of this."

She regarded me a moment.

"Somebody tole me you was a big-time reporter."

"Used to be."

"Went after all kind of people, what I heard. Judges and politicians. Mobsters. Movie stars."

"No celebrities," I said. "Pretty much everyone else."

"Well, if you don't break this here story, Butch McCray is gonna be dead in a ditch or locked in a crazy house. You gone let that happen, Clara Sue? Are you?"

What makes you believe one thing and not another? One person, and not another?

All I can tell you is—I believed Hattie Briar.

"I'll do what I can," I promised.

"All anybody can do," Miss Hattie said, ending our pleasant soiree with a dismissal.

It was the last time I saw her alive.

CHAPTER THIRTEEN

Flying Saucer Sighted near Blue Springs
The Clarion

Ileft Dowling Park with a tangle of questions begging for attention, none of which I could tackle until I'd documented the epic contest between the Laureate Hornets and the Lake Butler Tigers. I got back to Laureate ten minutes before kickoff and had just parked my 4-Runner in the sandlot behind the school's stadium when I saw Connie Koon striding over in denim jeans and jacket. I knew what to expect. Donna and Darla Koon had been jointly anointed homecoming queen and their mother had already told me she didn't like the shots I got of her twins during the parade.

"You got 'em mashed all together!" Connie railed anew as I slung my camera over my shoulder. "You cain't tell 'em apart!"

"Well, they are twins, Connie."

Sometimes I get the feeling I'm not reading Connie rightly. I must have wrinkled her peanut somehow or another, though in this case I freely admit that Connie was not the only parent unsatisfied with my photography. I'd never had so many people bitch about my homecoming pics. On the other hand, folks all over the county seemed primed to fight over most anything. Even the normally placid competition for "Best Float" generated a war of vitriol. Hard to imagine that concoctions of Styrofoam and bunting could generate such passion, some parents outraged that the Royal Ambassador's entry beat out the senior float, other parents excoriating a faculty who would allow alien influences in the school's competition, though whether the despised aliens hailed from the Milky Way or Mexico was never specified.

Connie stalked off, finally, and I trailed behind, stumping past pickups and gun racks to reach the freshly mown gridiron, a rising aroma of freshly cut hay and hotdogs redolent in the heavy air. The game started with a temperature in the mid-fifties but the mercury had dropped ten degrees in less than an hour. Despite that chill, Connie had shucked her jacket to bare a drum-tight midriff above the belt line of her Levis. Her husband seemed unusually distracted. It was not uncommon for Carl to ignore his wife, but on this occasion, he was not even ogling the cheerleaders.

I hugged the sideline in my vest and chinos taking shots of players and plays with an occasional nod to the bleachers. It took a while to register that there were no Hispanic students in the stands. Edgar and Raul and their Latino classmates were hedged together directly behind the goalpost in an area where "Negro" students were once mandated to sit. It was odd in the wake of Jim Crow to see the county's newest minority self-segregating.

"Evenin', Clara Sue."

I lowered my camera. Hiram was attired for the big game as he was for the coffee shop or court in pleated slacks and starched shirt, the only concession to the outdoors being a cheap windbreaker and a hat sheltering that mark of Cain on his face.

"Hiram, how are you?"

"Fair to middlin'."

"You enjoying the game?"

"I enjoy it all." Hiram spread his arms like Moses by the sea. "I built this field out of my own pocket, didju know that? I paid for the loam and the turf and the labor. I crowned the gridiron and put in the drainage. Put in the irrigation too. Hell, there are golf courses with less money in them than this here little football field."

"You running for office, Hiram? Cause that'd be a good plug."

He snarled laughter. "No, no. I'm no politician."

I raised my camera to feign interest at a penalty flag.

"Can I do you for, Mr. Lamb?"

"Just wanted to make sure we're on the same page about the school. The renovation and all."

I snapped a shot.

"Shouldn't you be speaking to Bull Putnal?"

"Oh, we got Bull on our side, no problem there. But looks like there might be some kind of hearing required, is all, and I want to make sure you're on board to help us locals nail down these contracts."

"I've got no influence over that."

"You got a voice to the public, Clara Sue."

"What are you fishing for, Hiram?"

"I ain't fishing. I'm huntin'. And whatever little contretemps transpires over the next few weeks, I'm tellin' you straight out I expect you to be fair and balanced."

"Tell you what, Hiram. I can be your *vox populi* or I can be Fox News, but I can't be both."

Hiram looked past me to the contest afield.

"You know the Florida Gators are scoutin' my boys? And Alabama, too, and Auburn and FSU. Now, why is that, Clara Sue? Danny and Trent ain't the biggest boys in the conference, not by a long shot, and not the fastest, neither. So why are all these big schools interested?"

"I have no idea."

"Because Trent and Danny are winners. They don't know what it means to lose, and here's a headline for you, Clara Sue—neither do I."

"Well, before you celebrate, Hiram, the Hornets are down a touchdown and your boy just lost the ball."

The Tigers recovered Trent Lamb's fumble and within two plays nailed a field goal to end the half. The Hornets repaired to their locker room ten points down, and the band took the field with choreography tied to the year's theme, dressing and covering to present a living stick figure of NASA's lunar lander, the module's spindly legs extending on the slides of trombones and the whistle of flutes. I had to take my camera to the topmost tier of the stadium to capture that effect.

Then the twin queens tooled through the goal posts in a vintage GTO to publicly amplified acclaim, Donna and Darla trying without a lot of success to avoid the lockjaw that comes with the sustained effort of a forced smile. Principal Wilburn delivered remarks with a microphone hampered by feedback, extolling the prospects for "our graduates" in the "private market" and noting with approval the excitement of teachers and staff for the coming renovation to "our fine school."

The second half was not kind to the home team. The Hornets fans were stunned to see the visiting Tigers return the opening kickoff all the way to the two-yard line. Lake Butler's offense scored on the very next play. I captured the tailback's plunge into the end zone and was just trotting back up the field feeling pleased with myself when I spotted Butch McCray wandering the stands in his baggy dungarees, a smile vacant below the bib of his cap.

He was selling boiled peanuts. The Booster Club runs the concession stand during home games and enforces an iron monopoly on the sale of candies and Cokes and hot dogs, but Butch is allowed under some ancient dispensation to hawk peanuts at a quarter a bag.

I slung my camera and dug into a pocket of my chinos for a coin.

"Butch, over here."

He scanned the stands to locate that salutation.

"No, Butch, down here. On the sideline."

He turned clumsily, like an overgrown child, edging his way down to the railing.

"Miz Buchanan, yes, ma'am. Be twenty-five cent."

I gave him a quarter.

"You making any money, Butch?"

"A little," he replied, that perpetual smile tugging at the corners of his mouth.

"Butch, have you seen Hiram Lamb lately?"

The smile as fixed as a frieze.

"Hiram, why, sure. He come see me."

I felt something like chilled water in my bowels.

"Butch, you don't have to sell your store. You know that, don't you?"

"I don't want to, but, Hiram, well. I'm 'fraid he'll make me, I don't watch out."

"You've got friends here, Butch."

The smile turned genuine for just a moment.

"Butch got all kinda friends," he enthused. "They tell me 'Thank you, Mr. Butch,' an' 'Mr. Butch, we love you.' And I love them too. Love 'em, ever' single one."

I could just imagine an attorney eliciting that response at some kangaroo proceeding.

"Butch, do you remember your mother?"

"Sure, I do. Talk to her alla time."

"You talk to her? To Annette?"

"Ah hah. And sometime she talk back too."

His smile wavering with that memory.

"But not so much now," he went on. "They's too much inner-ference."

"Interference?"

"Like on the radio. Like when a thunderstorm come and it get all crackly."

"You hear the interference then?"

"Uh huh, but it don't affect the letters none. I keep alla my letters."

"Letters from whom, Butch?"

"I told Hiram, but he wud'n believe me. He just make fun of ole Butch."

I wanted to get back to Annette's letters, but the journalist in me cautioned a slow approach.

"You can show me anything, Butch, I won't make fun."

He brightened. "You promise?"

"Sure."

He glanced about conspiratorially.

"Meet me under the bleachers."

He wandered off then, instantly returned to the persona of the village idiot, a stained paper bag held high overhead.

"Peanuts! Getchu peanuts here!"

I found the gate at midfield which let me off the sideline in a detour around the band and concession stand before I ducked past the public facilities to emerge beneath a lofty display of buttocks. Butch materialized like a leprechaun from the shadows.

He seemed a different person. The posture more erect. The face usually so slack and vacant now mobile and alert.

"Hiram see you coming?" he asked anxiously.

"No, Butch, we're good."

He reached into a stained pocket and fished out a candy wrapper.

"It's awl here."

He pressed a wrapper for a Mars candy bar into my hand.

"What is here, exactly, Butch?"

"Right chere." He turned the wrapper over on my palm like a Tarot card. "Them lines? See 'em?"

"That's a bar code. That's what they scan at the grocery store when they check you out."

"Ain't just that," Butch disagreed. "It's a letter from mama. An' not just her. Others too. They write me all the time. Got one before Jenny O'Steen. Before Marty Hart."

"What do you mean 'before' Marty?"

"'Fore he saw the light," Butch replied matter-of-factly. "Right before they took him away."

"Butch, it's just a bar code."

He shook his head belligerently.

"No, it's a <u>message</u>. You got to believe me, Miz Clara Sue! You got to!"

"Okay, okay." I reached over to settle him down. "But Butch, you can't tell just anybody about this. You hear? Don't show anyone your wrappers. People won't understand."

"They think ole Butch is simple, I know. Or crazy."

He retrieved the wrapper from my hand and was once again, a child.

"But you believe me, dontchu, Clara Sue?"

"Sure, Butch. Course I do."

"You daddy, he always been good to me. I needed somethin' wrote down, he do it for me. And I can tell you daddy anything. Don't matter what, I kin tell him."

"Yes." I tried to keep the frog out of my throat. "He was a good man."

"But it's hard, ain't it, Miz Clara? Keepin' secrets?"

"What kind of secrets, Butch?"

He folded the candy wrapper along the seam, without answering and turned to shuffle away. He was back to being Butch. The slack face. The vacant smile.

I did not know at the time that Butch was not the only person keeping secrets. Carl Koon languished on a bleacher damp with dew beside his feckless wife. Carl looked like he'd been rode hard and put away wet, and Hiram Lamb's approach clearly did nothing to improve that condition.

"Carl, how are you?"

"Watchin' the game," Carl answered perfunctorily.

"Now, Carl, come on," Connie cooed and Carl shrugged off a faux embrace.

"I'm not selling my business, Hiram." Carl cut straight to the chase.

Hiram slipped a thumb inside the waist of his crisply pleated slacks.

"You gonna stand in the way of a four-million-dollar bid?"

"You didn't ask me my opinion before you cut your deal with Bull Putnal, Hiram."

"It's a deal for you, too, Carl. We'd give you a fair price."

"You got me a fair price once b'fore, Hiram, an' I'm still payin' for it."

"I can understand why Butch'd be a problem. He's a cretin. But you, Carl? I always thought you had some kind of common sense."

"I'm not sellin' you my coffee shop, Hiram."

"The hell you think gives you the right to hold out on me?"

"You're offerin' me about half what my property's worth," Carl retorted. "A hundred and fifty thousand will barely cover the loan I already owe."

"Tell it to the bank."

"I'll go to Live Oak. Get my own loan."

"Not going to happen, Carl. And when you go broke and the bank forecloses, every cup and saucer will come back to me at pennies on the dollar."

"I ain't no goddamn Butch McCray," Carl snarled. "You cain't put me in the crazy house or bitch-slap me into somethin' stupid!"

Hiram sighed.

"Don't know why I bothered. A wise man don't need advice and a fool won't take it."

"He'll come around, Hiram, he will, won't you, Carl?" Connie asked, cajoling her husband. "Just give us some time."

"Time's done run out," Hiram replied gruffly as a whistle signaled a penalty on the home team.

I emerged from beneath the bleachers to see Hiram Lamb stalking away from Mr. and Mrs. Koon. Then Connie left her husband behind in a huff, her boobs practically bouncing out of her denim halter. Sheriff Buchanan appeared at my shoulder.

"Now there's a picture for your paper."

"For *Playboy*, maybe."

Colt rested a hand on his holster. "Looks like Hiram and Carl are having themselves a disagreement."

"I don't think Hiram counted on having Carl show any spine. Course, without Hiram's money, Carl'll bust overnight."

"Maybe. Probably."

Colt chewed that over.

"Take a ride with me, Clara Sue."

"Can't. Randall's waiting on these pictures and then we've got copy to write and lay out. Gonna be an all-nighter."

Colt worried a chew of tobacco from his pouch.

"I'll have you back by midnight. You can drop the pictures off on the way."

"Randall will love that."

"Tell him it's a ride-around."

"A ride to what? Some dog gutted on a lakebed? Aliens in corn fields? Car wrecks? What?"

"Call it a breaking story."

I dropped off my camera with Randall at the paper sometime around nine o'clock and came back outside to join the sheriff. First surprise came when I realized Colt was locking the door on his cop car.

"We're taking your vehicle," he informed me, the shotgun already steady in the bend of an arm.

"Well, that's no goddamn fun."

"That's the deal."

"Least you could tell me where we're headed," I complained when settled behind the wheel of my 4-Runner.

"Leb's Place." The sheriff deposited the scattergun carefully in the back seat. "And before you remind me, yes, I know it's not in my jurisdiction."

I pulled out on Main Street and headed north. There are no bars, legal ones anyway, in Lafayette County. We are dry, which means you have to cross county lines to imbibe in anything other than a six-pack from a convenience store. Leb's Place, as it is still called, is located off the main road in Taylor County. Leb himself is long dead, but the business survives, a squalid box of tin with an open porch and barbeque pit propped on the edge of a spring-fed creek where you can get brisket, catfish, and hushpuppies along with your bourbon, Budweiser, and a variety of sexually transmitted diseases.

There are stories galore attached to Leb's, a soap opera flowing from bad hands of poker or the roaming hands of husbands, or their wives. Sometimes a larger conflict plays out. The tin walls are peppered with rounds from revolvers and pellets of buckshot that at nighttime look like constellations displayed in a really cheap planetarium. Step through the single-screen door out front and you enter a juke joint aspiring to be a honky-tonk. There's the obligatory pool table with perennially warped sticks and a juke box hitched up along with a box fan to a power strip. A sawdust floor was improved years back with a slab of cement, but the men still piss in an open latrine out back. Women have a dedicated Porta-Potty.

Some of Taylor County's higher-end prostitutes drift to Leb's on Friday nights to pick up johns frustrated by nubile cheerleaders and notions of past triumph on some field or the other. I've run a source or two to ground at Leb's myself. Not a bad place to rendezvous actually. About as private as a public place can be. Everyone who comes here is ashamed of being here for the one reason, or some other.

Used to, you got to Leb's by following a narrow, twisting rut of sand off the hard road on the way to Perry, but there's a blacktop feeder now that takes you within a quarter mile of the place. There's still no parking lot at Leb's, just a bed of sand for a tangle of trucks, cars, and SUVs jammed at all angles between trunks of water oak and swamp cabbage.

"Why are we in my car?" I inquired.

"Because I need to be discreet," Colt replied mildly.

"So am I going to get reimbursed if some redneck pumps a wad through my windshield?"

"Probably not."

"Jesus. Then at least tell me what we're looking for."

Colt leaned forward, his hair heavy as a towel on his shoulders. "Right there. The Suburban. See it?"

I followed the direction of his pointed finger.

"That's . . . Connie Koon's vehicle."

"Yes, it is."

About that time the Suburban's interior light winked on and, sure enough, there was Connie, checking her lipstick and mascara in her vehicle's rearview mirror. That leather top and jacket. Hotter than a two-bit whore in a ten-cent store.

"So that's it? You drag me out here to see Connie Koon picking up some sausage on the side?"

"Hold your horses. It won't be long."

And in fact I barely had time to unclip my seat belt when a light-colored pickup pulled up on the far side of Connie's Suburban.

"There's our man."

I couldn't make out the truck's make or model at first, let alone who was at the wheel, but then the newcomer got out of his vehicle. I saw the outlines of a man in a baseball cap striding quickly to reach the passenger-side door of Connie Koon's Suburban. Connie's bra sagging with the wealth of her breasts as she leaned over to open the door. The man ducked inside.

"Christ on a crutch," I whispered. "Is that Roscoe Lamb?"

"Yes, it is," Colt confirmed.

"Roscoe's banging Connie Koon?! You're shitting me. Does Carl know?"

Colt shrugged.

"Cause if Carl does know, that could explain some things—like a motive for gutting Roscoe's favorite dog? I can easily imagine Carl taking that payback."

"It's possible," the sheriff allowed. "But that's not why we're here."

"No? Then why are we here?"

"We're going to follow them."

"And who are 'we,' Kemo Sabe?"

"You're Kemo Sabe, Clara Sue; I'm Tonto. We ride together unless you'd like to wait for me inside the hooch house."

About that time Connie's headlights speared the side of Leb's shed and I saw the back-up lights flash on as she threw the Suburban's tranny into reverse.

"Damn you, Colt!"

I could feel my heart hammering. And then that subtle tug in the chest. That mild restriction.

Not now! I told myself. Not now!

"You all right?" he asked.

"I'm fine." I fastened my seat belt with one hand as I reached for the ignition with the other. "But next time, you're driving."

I have tailed a mark before. On several occasions actually. But it's a hell of a lot easier to hide in Boston traffic than on a flat road in the middle of the flatwoods of northern Florida.

"Kill your lights," Colt directed me.

"You fucking crazy?"

"There's a moon. She's got taillights."

So for, I don't know, fifteen or twenty minutes or a year, depending how you measure time, I dragged behind Connie's outsized Suburban like an iron filing pulled by a magnet.

It couldn't have been more than five or six miles up the blacktop that she swerved at some completely invisible inter-section into a stand of pine trees.

"Don't lose her," Colt chided, and I hit bottom following the taillights ahead.

"Where in the wide hell are we?" I asked.

"Flatwoods," Colt answered calmly.

"That covers a lot of ground," I bit back.

"She's slowin' up. Back off."

I fell back as far as I could and still keep Connie's tail-lights in sight. We probably had not covered another half mile when Sheriff Buchanan nodded out his window to an island of palmetto.

"Pull in over there," the sheriff directed. "From here on in we walk."

One thing you lose driving is the smell of your surroundings. I had just come from a football game and could still smell in my clothes the odor of fresh-cut Bermuda grass and mustard and hot dogs. Those lingering aromas were overwhelmed now by the damp belly of a swamp redolent with the fetid rot of leaves and animal life, countless and infinitely small carcasses of bacteria teeming with the bud of growth that was new even in November.

"You all right?" Colt asked.

"I'm fine."

"Can wait in the car, you want to."

"No, I'm fine."

"Come on then."

I had to walk damned near as fast as I could to keep up with Colt's easy lope. The trail we followed snaked for maybe another quarter mile before terminating abruptly in a glade cleared of trees. I spotted Connie's Suburban, parked with a pair of ratted-out pickups beside a goose-neck trailer, at least thirty feet long with push-outs on either side and a satellite dish on top. There were fold-out chairs arranged in a fire pit in front of the travel-trailer, and a pair of recliners. Colt and I worked our way in close, settling finally behind a copse of scrub oak downwind from the fire pit.

"Hell of a love nest," I whispered to Colt.

"I don't think it's that kind of nest."

"What is it, then? Colt—?"

"Shhhh," he warned me, and I saw a blade of light open with the trailer's door. Connie Koon emerged from the interior with Roscoe Lamb right behind. I heard Connie's laugh, high and nervous along with Roscoe's graveled reply.

And then a light went on, an argon light mounted on a pole beside the fire pit, and three other figures stumped out of the single-wide to join Connie and Roscoe. These were young men, Latino, all three dressed like gangbangers in those low-hung shorts with baggy legs. T-shirts untucked and loose as tents. The first two were covered in tattoos; those I didn't recognize, but the third young man was immediately familiar, an enormous teenager, smooth-muscled and sloppy.

I nudged the sheriff. "That's Raul Herrera. He hangs with the Uribe boy."

"Edgar," Colt whispered. "Now listen up."

The three younger men sauntered out to the fire pit with Roscoe and Connie. Connie pulled up a chair beside the pit, chattering some nonsense. One of the tattooed Latinos produced what looked like a corncob pipe and a plastic bag.

"Gimme that shit," Connie ordered.

Tattoo replied in Spanish and his buddy turned over the bag of crystal. Raul Herrera hung back this whole time, hands in pockets, as Connie shook out crystals of methamphetamine into the bulb of the pipe. Roscoe Lamb offered his lighter. Connie took a long pull, then offered a hit to Roscoe Lamb. He shook his head.

"I ain't here for that."

Roscoe tapped the side of his chair with a grimy knuckle.

"*Si, si,*" one of the tattoos acknowledged, and left his posse to reenter the trailer. Connie was laughing when he came back with what looked like a grocery bag.

Roscoe made some demand which I missed. But then he repeated it.

"I said count it for me, amigo."

The Latin kid replied with some curse or insult that brought Roscoe to his feet. Here's a man in his late sixties bowing up to a pair of bangers and Connie doesn't even register what's going on. She is jazzed. Oblivious. Herrera sees what's happening. The kid shifts to take a position nearer the trailer.

"Oh, fuck it, count it for him," the bagman's *compa* directed casually, and immediately things settled down.

The bagman found a seat by the fire and began to sort bills, by currency apparently, into neat piles for Roscoe's inspection.

"I've seen enough," Colt whispered. "Let's go."

I hung at Colt's hip during our long retreat. By the time we reached my 4-Runner, I was shaking like a leaf.

"That was a meth lab, wasn't it? We've got a fucking cartel cooking meth right here in our own backyard!"

"Give me your car keys, Clara Sue. Hand 'em over."

Sheriff Buchanan eased my SUV from its hiding place, the tires digging briefly before finding traction in the soft sand. He checked the rearview mirror to make sure we wouldn't be spotted as we plunged by the light of a fitful moon back to the hard road.

"You okay?"

"There was a time when I'd have been just dandy," I snapped. "Back when I thought I was bulletproof."

"We're safe, Clara Sue. Nobody's following us."

"Have you ever seen that posse before?"

"Only the kid."

"I hate the Herrera boy being involved," I said.

"You don't know that he is involved," Colt cautioned.

"Come on, Sheriff, he was standing right in the middle of it."

"He might have no choice, especially if a relative is involved. Roscoe Lamb, on the other hand—I have an informant who's been telling me for weeks that Roscoe is a player."

"So why were you following Connie Koon?"

"First, you have to agree to keep tonight's episode off the record. *Comprende*, cousin? All of it."

"Certainly," I acknowledged. "This is back story. Deep in the back."

"At least for now." Colt emphasized that point. "But to answer your question about Connie Koon: A few months back I was having coffee at Carl's café and I noticed Connie slipping out the door to take a phone call. Now that behavior in itself doesn't mean a damn thing.

"But then Roscoe made some kind of excuse to leave, and on his way out the door I saw him jabbing in numbers on his cell phone. This happens a couple times, enough to seem like a pattern anyway, so one day I followed Connie's Suburban. She left the café and headed straight for Colored Town. Couple minutes later she eases through that gap in the fence surrounding the water tower. I knew there had to be some sort of rendezvous coming. I expected to see Roscoe Lamb actually. Thought maybe Roscoe was getting himself somethin' from Connie besides a latte and milk.

"But it wasn't Roscoe meeting Connie under the water tower; it was Officer Martin Hart."

"Marty? Marty Hart was banging Connie Koon?"

"No, no." Colt shook his head. "Marty wasn't a lover. He was a shithead and a snake, and if I'm right he was pushing crystal."

"Where'd The Weasel get methamphetamine?"

"I got a couple theories," Colt said, checking his rearview. "I also have a source could be involved, and he's in real danger. I hope you can appreciate that."

"This isn't for print, Colt. You made that clear."

We passed the prison at about that juncture, the spread of dormitories pristine inside that razor-wire perimeter, a glow of Spartan architecture lit in argon. Colt doffed his hat and ran a hand through his hair.

"I have an informant in danger and I have no idea how to protect him. You can bet that Roscoe Lamb's got protection. For all I know, half of my own deputies are on the take, and God only knows who he's got working for him inside the prison."

"Why'd you bring me, Colt? Why'd you want me involved?"

He donned his Stetson before answering me.

"Because if something happens to me, I want you to contact Special Agent Andrew Sandstrom at the regional office for the Florida Department of Law Enforcement in Live Oak. You get hold of Andy, you tell him what you saw tonight along with everything you and I have discussed. You can trust the FDLE, Clara Sue. Those boys are straighter than Eliot Ness, but don't breathe a word to anyone else. Not to Randall, not the Pope—nobody."

"I never gave up a source in my life."

I clenched my hands to still a sudden pain in my chest.

"You all right, Clara Sue?"

"Just get me back to the *Clarion.*"

We didn't exchange another word on the drive back to town. Sheriff Buchanan pulled my SUV into a slot behind his cruiser at the curb in front of my newspaper.

"Twenty minutes till midnight." Colt showed me his watch.

"As promised," I acknowledged weakly.

I could see the cone of my husband's desk lamp through the street-side window. Colt tossed me the keys as I dragged out the passenger-side door. I waited until Colt's cruiser pulled around the corner before entering my place of business.

"It's me," I announced, locking the door behind.

"'Bout time." Randall barely looked up from his monitor.

I hung my keys on a hook screwed into the counter and pushed through the batwing doors on the way to my husband's workstation.

"You and Colt have a nice ride?" he asked.

"Not bad."

I ran my hand through Randall's hair, gold and unkempt.

"I love you, you old coot. I take you for granted too damned often, I know, but—"

He cut me short with a kiss. Just a quick, light buss on the lips.

"Must be one hell of a story you're not telling me about." Randall settled back to work.

I never could fool Randall.

"I can't say anything. Really."

"Long as it's got nothing to do with cousins kissing."

Thank God it didn't.

Randall and I put the paper to bed around three in the morning, barely in time to make the printer's deadline in Gainesville.

"I'm hauling my butt to bed," Randall declared.

"And a fine butt it is too."

"Not gonna get you anywhere, Clara Sue. I am limp as a dishrag."

"See what we can do about that."

CHAPTER FOURTEEN

Laureate Hornets Lose to Lake Butler Tigers
Bid to Renovate School on Hold
Ghosts Seen at Dowling Park
The Clarion

I woke the next morning eager for work. Randall knew I was back in the saddle, maybe a couple of saddles.

"Just be careful," he advised over our morning coffee. "This isn't Iraq. You're not protected by a platoon of riflemen."

My ride with Colt triggered the same junkie's high I used to get when embedded with patrols in Iraq and Afghanistan, but Sheriff Buchanan had made it clear I was off the record for that story. No horse to saddle there. But there remained the campaign to push Butch McCray off his property, and the mystery attached to his mother's hope chest. Those were horses inviting a ride, if I could find a saddle to mount them.

All I had was an empty trunk and a history riddled with loose ends, and my only source was a centenarian in an old folks' home. It's never a good idea to hang your hat on any single source of information, so first thing I had to do was ferret out any documentation that debunked or supported the outlines of Hattie Briar's narrative. I started by paying a visit to Dan Hewitt, Clerk of Court. The *Clarion*, I believe I've mentioned, piles its two stories of brick and wood directly across the street from the courthouse which, along with the fact the court's clerk is a cousin, makes it easy for me to verify things like voter registration, or tax assessments, or, occasionally, wills and deeds.

I spent maybe an hour at the courthouse poring over dusty folios filled with instruments of another age, yellowed parchments penned by hand in flowing cursive. I found Harold McCray's will which left his wife Annie all "earthlie goods and properties." That document was dated in June of 1939 and I was not surprised to see that Hattie Briar's uncle was a signing witness. The coroner's report for Harold McCray was on file as well, a "gunshot wound" cited as the "accidental" cause of death on the 8th of December 1953.

A week before the Christmas of 1953, Annette McCray produced a will making Kelly Lamb her sole heir and executor, effectively ceding old man Lamb the homestead she inherited from Harold. That will was notarized in the county courthouse two weeks before Annie and Kelly were married.

Roughly three months later, Butch's mother was found at the end of a noose.

That chronology, at least, followed Hattie's account. Not that it did me any good. Whatever Hiram Lamb was looking for was clearly not on file with the county clerk. I left the courthouse, crossed the street to the *Clarion* and grabbed my laptop before climbing the rickety stairs leading to my second-story roost. My great uncle used to keep an office on this floor, long before it housed a newspaper, and I had taken the judge's aerie over for my own use. It's not luxurious. A worm-eaten timber panels the walls, and lengths of ancient pine a foot wide plank the floor. It's cold in the winter and too warm in the summer, but I love lounging at my *vargueno* beneath the naked beams of that lofty study, settling my coffee on the sills of lead-paned windows to view the courthouse and street below.

There was still a sampling of Judge Boatwright's notes and formal correspondence filed in a pair of heavy wooden cabinets atop which I lodge my coffee pot and condiments. But what I most treasured was stacked floor-to-ceiling along the walls; these were back issues of the *Clarion* that dated back to the early 1900s. I'd already rummaged those stacks looking for details of Harold McCray's death and his wife's suicide, and I could always return for a closer look. But in light of my interview at Dowling Park and my courthouse research, I doubted any account from the *Clarion* would contradict official records or Hattie's recollection. Those were not the columns of most interest to me.

What I was looking for in the *Clarion*'s fading back issues was some mention of Shamrock and its company-run school. I remembered Hattie Briar mentioning that Annette McCray had been employed for some period of time at the mill in Shamrock. I hoped to discover among the staff or faculty at the school a viable candidate with some link to Butch's mother. Before plunging into those stacks, however, I fired up my modern wireless for a Google of "Shamrock, Florida," and within moments found testament to a vanished city.

Turns out that Shamrock, Florida, was established by Putnam Lumber Company in 1928 within walking distance of Cross City. This was an enormous mill town that confirmed Hattie's description, a community built from stoop to shingle with Yankee money solely for the purpose of harvesting Suwannee River cypress and pine. Growing up in Laureate, I'd heard my relatives or elders make mention of Shamrock, but I'd no clue its operation was so vast or sophisticated.

Or so relentless.

According to the company's history, the Shamrock mill at its peak cut 140 <u>million</u> board feet of timber each year, all hardwood, a mix of red cypress and longleaf yellow pine. I saw grainy black-and-whites of the skidders that hauled in those enormous trees from the deep swamp along with shots of Ross carriers big as buses forking dimensioned lumber in yards that seemed to have no horizon.

Workers toiled round the clock to load lumber and lath thirty railroad cars at a time from immense sheds constructed directly alongside privately owned railroad tracks. A tree that took centuries to grow could be felled distantly, snaked to the railhead, hauled to the mill, sorted, planed, cut to dimension, and stacked to dry within hours.

But by 1959 the trees were gone. An enormous crew of men, not to mention their wives and children, was simply let go and the mill was shut down. However, Annie McCray signed her pernicious will in 1954, which gave me some hope that I might yet discover a reference to the teachers or administrators responsible for running the company-owned school, some detail that would connect Annette McCray to some likely confidant or confederate. By noon I had learned everything I could from web-based sites.

It was time for some old-fashioned legwork.

I decided to bracket the dates of Harold McCray's death and Annette's marriage to Kelly Lamb, which meant I'd need to pull every issue of the *Clarion* from November of 1953 to January '55, but as I made my way through stacks I was captivated by papers that chronicled the years from the Great Depression to World War II. These were papers set up in type cases and printed with honest to god presses and I wondered, reading them, whether I would be capable of such craftsmanship or labor.

It was hard not to linger over the people featured in these aging columns, characters right out of Steinbeck, men and women in khaki or denim posing beside a corn crib or sugar cane mill. The occasional photo from overseas, a cocky local posing beside his Sherman tank or B-17. I was wasting time, of course. The period that I needed to research was nearer to the Korean War. With some regret, I thrashed through another sheaf of newspapers, leaving Roosevelt and World War II behind to reach the 1950s. I was chuckling over a photo of Harry Truman when I spotted an article bannered beneath, "Shamrock School in Crisis."

Turns out that in 1951, Shamrock's headmaster contracted tuberculosis which threatened to shut down the entire school. All the children had to be tested, not to mention their teachers. From the attending copy I learned that the school employed a faculty of twenty teachers, along with janitors, housekeepers, and a nurse. The article continued to an inside fold and that's where I hit pay dirt because accompanying the continuing story was a photograph tagged, "Faculty & Staff Shamrock School."

Staring out from the withered page was a clutch of formally dressed men and women linotyped in a strained pose on some sort of verandah, the gentlemen rigid as statuary in four-in-hand ties and dark coats, the women equally severe in long, gingham dresses with high, white collars. It was hard to make out details; after all, I was looking at a photograph etched and printed nearly seventy years earlier on paper prone to decay. But a caption identified each of the nine persons photographed by name and position.

I mouthed the first two entries silently: Mr. Matthew Lawson—Instructor, Miss Mary Lynn Folsom—Instructor. Any one of these faculty, presumably, could have been Annie's confederate. I returned to the caption and found yet another possibility.

"Reverend Paul Odom—Chaplain."

A chaplain? A confessor perhaps?

I remembered that Hattie Briar alluded to a missionary associated with the Shamrock mill. I did not need a magnifying glass to find Reverend Odom's place on the grainy page before me. It was not hard to spot on the back row a cleric's collar white and bright against a severe, black coat. Reverend Odom was tall and clean shaven in his frock, derby hat, and boots, and he was the only person in the picture sporting darkly shaded glasses. He had some sort of cane in one hand, as well, and on closer inspection I could see that the minister was resting his free hand on the shoulder of a woman standing in front of him. Leaning on her shoulder as though it were an armrest.

The final caption connected the dots—the woman bearing the weight of the cleric's hand? Was "Annette McCray–Cook."

Annie McCray Lamb could not read. She couldn't write. Hattie Briar's uncle notarized the will Annie signed which, at her death, would pass along the McCray homestead to Kelly Lamb, but there was nothing to suggest the judge composed the text of that instrument. For that task, Annie may well have prevailed on some neutral player, someone not related to Kelly Lamb or her dead husband. She needed someone literate, certainly, but also someone bound to keep her confidence.

What better man for that job than a chaplain?

I wondered how far Butch's mother trusted Reverend Odom. Did the minister know Annie was being pressured to deny her son his birthright? Did the reverend know that Kelly Lamb refused to marry Annie unless she named him as her heir? What counsel would a man of God offer a woman who traded her body and her homestead to ensure that a simpleton son would never be orphaned? If Reverend Odom was aware of these circumstances, did he approve? Would he even care? I looked again at the picture in the fading paper. The way the cleric leaned on Annie McCray's shoulder. That familiar contact. Hattie Briar insisted that Butch's mother was a hussy.

Was it possible Reverend Odom was Annie's lover as well as her scribe?

All good reporters spin out hypotheses. We're always looking for ways to connect the dots, but a good reporter never believes anything without corroboration. All I could say with any reasonable certainty was that Butch McCray's mother worked in close proximity over some period of time with a man fully able to compose the document that would disinherit her son, and that, as a minister, he might also be obliged to keep her confidence.

And then it occurred to me—what if Annie changed her will? She had threatened to do just that, according to Hattie Briar. Was it possible there was a revised will secreted away somewhere or another, or some other document that would create a problem for the Lamb brothers? Maybe that was what Hiram Lamb was looking for. Maybe that's why he wanted Annie McCray's steamer trunk.

But this was nearly all speculation. Nearly—but not all. I now believed that Hiram Lamb was afraid of something he believed to be secreted in Annie McCray's travel trunk. It certainly wasn't much of a leap to conclude that Hiram, and probably also Roscoe, knew something about Annette's relationship with their father that was not public knowledge. There was a story lurking just beneath the surface, I could smell it, but how would I ever know for sure? What source did Hiram have that I didn't? What crypt held Annie's last secrets?

How do you search an empty box?

～

IT TOOK me over an hour to make the drive from Laureate to Cross City. You can't actually visit the town of Shamrock anymore—it doesn't exist. The original tidewater cypress and longleaf pine that busied the town's mill have long been cut to extinction along with the community that once thrived alongside. There remains, however, a relic of that era, a kind of visitors' center and museum housed in a lodge that used to be a favored hangout for visiting big shots and dignitaries. What I hoped to find was some local curator or aficionado at the Putnam Lodge who could give or guide me toward more detailed information about the Shamrock School and its faculty.

A tower of bright, shining cumulus was building by the time I turned off Highway 19 and pulled into a parking lot sprinkled with palm trees. Putnam Lodge has been restored a couple of times, two wide wings and two stories of hardwood roofed in green above an exterior painted in a modern and blinding white. I passed through the small verandah leading to the lobby and was greeted immediately by a mid-aged woman lounging behind a long counter.

"Good morning."

She offered a brilliant smile and silver hair.

"Hello." I offered my hand. "Clara Sue Buchanan. I run the newspaper in Laureate."

"I'm Virginia Chauncey." She gave me a firm shake. "Will you be needing a room?"

"No," I said apologetically, "I'm just filling in details for a column I'm writing. I'm especially interested in the old Shamrock School."

"My grandmother attended Shamrock School." Virginia smiled. "She's no longer with us, unfortunately."

I mulled that over. "I read a short piece concerning an outbreak of tuberculosis. You know anything about that?"

"Just the mention from grandma. You might contact Putnam Lumber in Jacksonville; they put out a nice history. I b'lieve we still have a copy or two in the gift shop."

"I'll check. But does that mean the lodge doesn't have an independent archive of records from the school? Letters or contracts? Anything of that nature?"

"Nothing like that, no." She shook her head. "And you aren't the first to ask. It really is a shame to see how much was lost of that early history. We've salvaged what we can but, truthfully? It's only a shadow of what was here."

"Is it all right if I just look around then?"

"Please do."

I strolled through the lobby first, a generous room facing a large fireplace. The walls were famously paneled in pecky cypress, that vermiculated timber now rare and expensive beyond belief. There were tintype photos of the mill's operation scattered about the lobby and halls and several ferrotypes of the managers and staff who ran the mill, but I didn't see a thing related to the company-owned school or its faculty. I had about decided to grab a coffee and custard from the dining room when I spotted the lodge's small gift shop.

The young fellow at the cash register barely looked up. A twentysomething clearly underemployed in a uniform of T-shirt and jeans.

"Morning." I saluted but was not acknowledged.

Most of the items for sale were brummagem and had nothing to do with Shamrock's operation. There were a couple of trays of arrowheads, for instance, advertised as authentic. I didn't know the intrepid crew at Shamrock felled trees with arrowheads. There was some mediocre artwork, etchings and illustrations that were based on linotypes of the mill and surrounding grounds. I saw a few hardwood carvings that were better crafted. I was about to leave for a coffee and custard when I spotted a shelf filled with what appeared to be handcrafted boxes.

"These local?" I asked the unengaged cashier.

"Hmm? Oh, yeah, we got a guy brings 'em in. They're puzzle boxes."

"Say again?"

"Puzzle . . . Boxes," he repeated as though I were deaf.

The boxes were simple cubes or rectangular stained to reveal the natural grain of wood, the lids burned or etched with scenes from the Suwannee or from the Shamrock mill. They ranged in size from a cigarette pack to a cigar box.

I picked up one of the larger pieces and raised the lid. There was nothing like a puzzle obvious to see. Just an ordinary vanity box, except without any lining, not even a skin of felt. I checked the price.

"Pretty steep for an empty box," I noted acerbically.

"Just cause it's empty doesn't mean there's no puzzle." The cashier for the first time seemed to take interest in his customer.

I turned the box over in my hands.

"What? Where?"

"Bring it here," the kid directed and, tamping my temper, I complied.

"Open the box," he suggested casually, and I did.

"What do you see?" he asked.

"A nice-smelling hole," I groused.

"That's all? You're sure?"

"Is there a riddle I'm missing?" I asked, and he smiled with undisguised condescension.

"Watch this."

He took the box without permission, placed his hands inside, and gently pressed the opposed panels. I heard the slip of wood on wood and then I saw—

"A false bottom."

"Yep."

The kid was grinning like a carny as he displayed the well-hidden compartment, the sliding panels concealing a cavity maybe half a foot wide and a couple of inches deep.

"An' every single box on sale opens up in a different way," the kid declared with admiration. "Way cool."

"It's clever," I affirmed even as I declined the purchase. "But it's not very practical. I mean—how much could you actually hide in this thing?"

"You could hide diamonds," he pointed out. "Or jewelry."

"Well, that's true," I granted. "But I don't keep many diamonds around."

"You got a passport?"

"I do."

"Keep your passport safe in here. Or a social security card. Be good for that."

"I don't think so." I slid the box over.

"Or a letter," he went on as if I was not there. "You might have a letter you wanta keep private? Puzzle box'd be great for a letter. Or a diary, maybe."

His sell was getting unexpectedly hard, and I was about to leave when the persistent young man said something I had heard not long before.

"These are boxes built to keep secrets."

I felt a rush of adrenaline.

"Holy shit."

"Ma'am?"

"Nothing. Here."

I fumbled a twenty-dollar bill from my wallet and slapped it down.

"But what about the box?"

"Keep it!"

I hit the lobby at a lope and hauled ass back to Laureate. I burst into the *Clarion* and found Randall cutting the twine that binds stacks of our just-printed paper.

"Could use some help here."

"One second, babe! Give me a second!"

I bounded up the flimsy flights to my upstairs office, threw open the door, and rushed straight to the armoire where I'd stowed Annette McCray's trunk. This wouldn't be like the box at the gift shop, I knew that. I dragged the heavy chest from my wardrobe and sat the lid back on its cowhide restraints.

I saw again the nameplate, Annette's engraved identifier. Was there some keyhole behind that brass herald? I briefly considered prying it off, but instead leaned over to explore the box's cedar interior and when I did my glasses fell from my face to a pleasant report.

"What in the world are you doing?" Randall now standing with crossed arms at the door.

"Help me open this thing."

"It's already open, Clara."

"Not the lid; there's something else. Got to be. A false bottom, hidden compartment. Something. I just have to figure out how to get at it."

"Should be fun," Randall replied laconically, and strolled over.

Minutes later I was straddling Annette's trunk and cursing like a sailor to pound, prod, slap, and otherwise abuse Annie's strongbox, trying to find some pressure point that would reveal a false floor or secret cache. I jammed my hands along the sides and the bottom with no luck. Pulled and yanked the heavy straps and bronze fittings.

Nothing. Nada.

Randall observing at a safe remove and patient as Buddha.

"Here," he offered at last. "Let me try."

I moved aside and my husband dragged a chair over. He took a seat and for a moment just looked the trunk over. Then, without so much as touching the thing, he said, "You haven't tried the lid."

"The lid?" I scoffed. "The hell are you talking about? How could I get inside the box without raising the damn lid?"

"You raised the lid, Clara. You didn't look at it. Hand me your scissors."

"You planning to cut the thing open, you're going to need more than these," I advised.

"Shut up and listen," he said, and tapped the chest's heavy lid with the scissor's handle.

"Hear that?" Randall smiled. "The lid is hollow."

He was right. You could hear the echo of a concealed tympanum inside the lid's rounded architecture. Randall dropped the scissors to the floor and I slumped back humbled as he ran his hands over the ribs that formed the box's top.

"Ah!" He paused. "Help me stand this thing on its end."

I tipped the chest on its end, glad to be of some use, and Randall showed me a notch barely large enough for a pen at the terminus of a cedar strake.

"I'm guessing this'll slide out," he said.

"You're the man."

"Got a pocket knife?"

"Letter opener."

I grabbed the letter opener from my desk and handed it over. Randall slipped the very tip of that slender instrument into the lid's exposed notch and pulled gently—

The rib slid free, and it was immediately apparent that the lid was hollow. The whole top of the trunk, in fact, was a concealed cavity, a false roof.

"I feel something. Some kind of fabric," Randall declared.

He fished out an inch of fabric from the cavity hidden in the trunk's lid.

"Look here!"

Randall pulled out a length of silk about a yard in length. Was *this* what Hiram was looking for? Was a piece of silk worth a thousand dollars?

"Sure there's nothing else in there?"

"Well, let's see."

Randall took the trunk lid apart strake by strake. There was nothing else to find. No will or testament. No document of any kind. There was nothing to be found in Annie's trunk but a length of dimpled fabric.

"Mind if I take a look?"

I took the fabric into my hands. It was silk, for sure, a swath maybe a foot and a half wide and the length of a serape. The material was pipped all over in tiny raised welts that provided an interesting texture. It was the sort of shawl that might have graced the shoulders of some elegant lady at a tony restaurant but could just as easily be a throw for some chair or couch.

"There's some kind of embroidery along the bottom." Randall pointed, and even with that prompt I almost missed the delicate stitch of black thread woven close to the edge along the fabric's width.

"It's not embroidery!" I held the needlework up for Randall's inspection.

This was a signature, a claim to provenance rendered in cursive with a delicate black thread:

Annette Elizabeth McCray.

"Well, I'll be dipped." Randall smiled.

Yes, I'd found Annette McCray's treasured talisman. Her secret possession. A nicely dyed length of silk.

"Is *this* what Hiram Lamb is looking for?" Randall shook his head. "A thousand dollars for a piece of cloth?"

"To hell with Hiram." I dismissed that claim out of hand. "Whatever this thing is, or was supposed to be, it should go to Butch."

CHAPTER FIFTEEN

Prison Guards Searched for Contraband
The Clarion

Tiny Sessions was sorting the latest *Sport Illustrated* into its designated caddy when the prison's librarian approached.

"Inmate, you have a visitor."

Tiny turning his massive bulk in anticipation of Sheriff Buchanan's visit.

"Give us the room, would you, sir?" Colt requested formally, and the guard disappeared behind a closed door and venetian blinds.

"You know why I'm here, Tiny?"

"I reckon maybe."

"Tiny, I'm not here to fuck with you, but goddammit if I even think you're lying to me, I'm going straight to the warden, is that clear enough for you?"

"Yes, boss."

"So first off: Where did Officer Hart get his crystal?"

"From the same people you put in jail. Thass why he was short. Thass why he come to me. I never sold him nuthin' 'fore that. Not a damn thing."

"So that was your stash I found in his toolbox?"

The huge felon spread pie-sized hands on the table.

"Watn't no stash. I don' keep no stash. Just some shit left over from somebody cell is awl."

Colt allowed Sessions to sweat a little before letting that pass.

"You know, Tiny, for a good while now you been giving me the names of mules. Maybe a middleman or two, the friend of a cousin dealing meth out of his backyard or pickup. I've got me a chum's worth of minnows off you, Tiny. Sometimes a bream or perch. But not the kingfish. Not the boss. Is that a fair statement?"

Tiny regarded the scars on his hands.

"Dammit, inmate, answer the question."

"All I get is crumbs."

"Beats getting fucked up the ass."

The prisoner shook his head sadly.

"Fucked no matter what I do."

"How you figure?"

"You think I just up and gave Marty Hart that crystal? I just up and say, 'Here, boss, take some of my shit!'?"

"So how'd it go down?"

"The Weasel tole me I didn' fix him up he'd let the house know I was your bitch. Tole me he'd make damn sure."

Colt shook his head wearily.

"You should've contacted me, Tiny. I could have helped."

"Help me into a coffin maybe. Ain' like Batman, you know. I cain't just shine a fuckin' light. You know how long a day is in here? Or two? Take two minutes for somebody shove a blade in my liver, meantime I tryin' to get you a goddamn message?!"

"All right, settle down."

"You don' know what it's like in here!!"

Colt leaned forward.

"No. I don't. But you don't have to stay here anymore."

"Whatchu mean?"

"I mean I can get you put into protective custody in a facility clear across the state. Even the warden won't know where you are, Tiny. But you got to come clean with me, inmate. Right here. Right now."

A long moment passes between the giant felon and the sheriff of Lafayette County.

"It's Roscoe," Tiny said, finally.

"What was that?"

"Roscoe Lamb," Tiny confirmed huskily. "He get a cut from every cooker in the county. Make his Mexicans his mules. They turn him down, they families lose they jobs."

"I want names and dates. And eventually I'll need your testimony, Tiny. This won't work unless you go under oath."

Tiny nodded. "I do it. Just when you put that mother-fucker away? Make sure he don' wind up in no lie-berry."

～

Now THAT I had pried the lid off Annette McCray's trunk and been rewarded with a silken scarf, I was disposed to turn over the whole kit and caboodle to Butch McCray. Surely Butch had a better claim on his mother's travel trunk and associated property than anyone. But Randall advised me to hold off.

"You turn that crate over to Butch, and Hiram Lamb will have it inside a week."

"So he gets a box and a tallit, so what?"

"If Hattie Briar thought it was safe to let Butch have his mama's trunk, she'd have turned it over to him herself, but she didn't. You have to keep Hiram away from this box; that's what Hattie charged you to do. Maybe after this mess with the school gets settled we can hand it over to Butch, but not now."

"You're right."

I folded the silken wrap and placed it inside the steamer trunk.

"In fact, with this leverage, maybe I should interview Lamb, what do you think? See what shakes out?"

"Tell him you need his picture," Randall offered. "Something for Heritage Week. That'll get you in the door."

"Wish me luck."

I figured the best way to approach Hiram was openly, in public. No better place to spring that ambush than at Koon's coffee shop. I drove over in my 4-Runner and couldn't find a place to park. The joint was hopping. You'd have thought there was a fire sale going on, cars and trucks spilled out to the curb and onto the pasture out back, customers stacked four deep at the tables. But I knew something was wrong the minute I saw Connie slumped at the counter in a modest pair of dungarees and button-up shirt.

"Connie, hey. You seen Hiram?"

"Not today," she answered shortly.

I scanned the shop.

"Where's Carl?" I asked.

"Woods," she replied listlessly, by which she meant out in the woods hunting deer.

Connie turned to face me and I saw the bruise beneath her eye.

"What's going on here, Connie?"

"You're the big-time reporter and you don't know?"

"Why I drove over." I lied.

"Well, for your information, the bank's turning us out."

"Jesus, Connie, I didn't know."

"We were behind, but that ain't the real reason. It's Hiram and that damn business with the school."

She dropped her cup into a bus pan.

"Way it goes, I guess."

"Money troubles," I sighed sympathetically. "I know the feeling."

"You don't know jack," she retorted, all pretense at civility dropped.

"I just meant it can't be easy losing a business, is all," I countered in a simulation of apology. "Specially one you've worked so hard to build."

"There's easier ways to turn a buck, that's for sure," she said, relenting.

"How about Roscoe?" I shifted gears casually. "He in the woods with Hiram?"

Connie turned suddenly cautious. "What's it to you, Clara Sue?"

"I need their pictures for our Heritage Week edition," I said, and then, "I guess your bad news is good for Hiram and Roscoe."

"'Course it's good for 'em!" she snarled. "Who do you think told the bank to foreclose?"

"So now there's only Butch's plot in the way."

"They'll get that spit of dirt, no worries there," Connie predicted tiredly. "I tried to tell Carl, whatever the Lamb brothers want, they get, sooner or later."

Including you, apparently, I thought.

I pushed my coffee away and left a dollar on the table. "You see Hiram, tell him I'd like some pictures."

"Tell him yourself. He just walked in."

I pulled my chair around just in time to see the elder Lamb strolling past in cammies and boots with a vest dragging down from a weight of shotgun shells. First time I'd seen Hiram out of slacks and a dress shirt in years.

"Hiram, how are you?" I offered a smile. "Grab a seat. I'm buying."

"Connie, get me my usual."

"Yes, sir."

Hiram pulled up a chair opposite my own, the shells in his vest tapping the table's ledge. Buckshot, probably. Definitely twelve gauge.

"You must be the last man in the county hunts deer with a shotgun," I said, smiling.

"Who said I's after deer?"

"Just making conversation, Hiram."

"I been hearin' 'bout your conversations."

"Have you now?"

"I was just over to Dowling Park to see Hattie Briar."

"I was over there not too long ago myself." I sipped some java. "For Heritage Week. The obligatory interview."

"She wouldn't talk to me."

"Wouldn't or couldn't?"

"Damn nurse gives me some song and dance, but I saw Hattie out there on that damn patio. She looked fine to me."

"Not sure what 'fine' is like when you're a hundred years old, Hiram."

"Didn't keep you from jawing with her. Heard ya'll had yourselves a nice long talk."

"Old people do ramble, don't they? Just one thing after another. No rhyme or reason."

"Cut the bullshit, Clara Sue. Hattie took something belongs to me and I aim to get it back."

"Belongs to you? That needs clarifying."

I spooned an unneeded sugar into my coffee.

"I don't remember Hattie saying anything about your belongings, Hiram."

You could almost hear a gnash of teeth.

"You better be tellin' me the damn truth, missie."

"That a threat, Hiram?"

"Take a gander around you, Clara Sue. I can ruin you just as easy."

"So much for that crap about the truth setting you free," I quipped. "But, Hiram, if you're missing something that actually does belong to you, why not just tell me what it is and I'll be on the lookout."

"You don't know already, you don't <u>need</u> to know."

I gave him a second or two for his blood pressure to drop. Then I weighed back in.

"Look, I didn't know Carl'd lost this place till I came in here looking for you, and I still don't know how you plan to ease Butch off his half-acre plot. Commit him to a nuthouse? Accuse him of pedophilia? Play that last card right, you might even be able to arrange a lynching."

"You need to mind your own business."

"Anything touching taxpayers' money is a newspaper's business, Hiram. Thing is, you need a certain degree of public support and I have an excellent forum. For example, there's a meeting coming up next week at which, I am guessing, you are going to ask the county to stretch out the deadline mandated by that federal grant.

"You're well on your way to getting control of Carl's property, but that still leaves Butch's lot in the way. I honestly thought you'd have put Butch away by now. Not sure what's holding that up. But in any case, the paper is at the service of parties on all sides. You want a chunk of the taxpayers' money? You have some ideas on how to proceed? I can help you out."

"I've enjoyed about as much of your help as I can stand, Clara Sue."

Hiram shoved his chair back, a gorge of blood staining the mark of birth on his cheek.

He leaned over the table, far over, so that his face was inches from mine.

"Piece of advice, I wouldn't be wanderin' the woods, if I was you. There's lots of guns out there. We don't need any kind of accident."

He pulled back and I affected an air of bemusement, but by the time Hiram was out the door, I was shaking like a dog shitting peach pits.

"Want summore coffee?" Connie inquired listlessly.

"No. Thanks."

I trapped my hands between my legs. "I don't think I could hold another cup."

CHAPTER SIXTEEN

Federal Contract Reviewed
The Clarion

If I went to the coffeehouse uncertain of a course of action that would protect Butch McCray from commitment or incarceration, I left despairing whether anything could be done to keep Hiram Lamb from fucking his foster brother out of his life and livelihood. Not to mention my own. I still had no idea how a cedar chest or a yard of silk posed a threat to Hiram's well-laid plans. I did learn on the QT from my courthouse source that papers of commitment were already in the works which, if approved, would salt Butch McCray away at some ward in Chattahoochee. The apparent delay in the implementation of that writ raised at least three salient questions for me:

First—Why wasn't Butch already in a crazy house or jail? What was holding Hiram back?

Second—How could a piece of fabric stay Hiram's hand?

And, finally—How long did I have to solve this puzzle before the ax fell one way or the other?

I went back to my upstairs office staring at Annie's hope chest and the silken serape in hopes of some inspired insight that would give me leverage against the Lamb brothers.

When that didn't work, I stumped downstairs to find Randall editing copy for advertisements.

"How'd it go with Hiram?"

"Fine," I replied too quickly.

"So he threatened you."

"More or less."

"Was it serious?"

"Doubt he'd warn me if it was. Anything new here?"

"Two flying saucers, an artifact from Atlantis, and a talking pig," Randall replied drolly, but I was too distracted to be amused. "Clara Sue, why don't you get out of here? Go take a drive."

"I don't need a walkabout, dammit. I need something to do!"

Randall paused from work to massage his hand.

"We've got Heritage Week coming. Why don't you get some photos? Tobacco barn, would be nice. Anything remaining of an original dog run or sharecropper's shack. Something like that."

"We could use the pics from last year."

"You know better than that, Clara."

"Hiram Lamb just advised me to avoid the wilderness."

"How long's it take to shoot a broken-down farmhouse? Some outbuildings? An hour? Two?"

"Make it two and I'm on my way to my next Pulitzer."

"Soon as you nab that first one," Randall said, smiling. "Now git."

I should have known the minute I stepped outside the *Clarion* that I'd need some kind of winter wear. Plunging temperatures and high humidity meant that winter had finally arrived. As I left town I could see a blanket of frost settled on pastures and fields on both sides of the blacktop. I briefly considered turning back to grab a coat.

"Screw it, I'll be fine."

I still don't know exactly what possessed me to trespass on the land once owned by Butch McCray's father. It was Hiram Lamb's property, now, private and posted, a section of sandy loam given over to pine trees and pasture. Deep within the property was a hammock behind which the old house and outbuildings were located.

I didn't need to trek onto Hiram's land to get pictures for my paper. There were any number of long-abandoned homes and barns that I could photograph, all within easy view of a road or lane. What used to be the McCray homestead, on the other hand, was far removed from traffic of any kind, a rambling compound of logs and shingles that looked out to a slough peppered with cypress knees maybe five miles north of Pickett Lake.

Invading species play hell with Florida's lakes, ponds, and streams and if you step out onto what used to be Annette McCray's back porch you can see their work. There was once a nice little pond behind the old house that overflowed each spring into the bounding slough. I can recall pulling a pail of bream from that fishing hole in an hour, but no longer. Hydrilla has destroyed the gentle reservoir behind the ruins of Butch's infant home, that noxious grass choking the life and oxygen from countless hammocks and lakes all over the region.

A failing perimeter of cypress and water oak now marks the shoreline of the property's dried-up waterhole, the pond's sandy bed now a Petri dish for islands of arundo and palmetto between which run sounders of wild hogs on the root for grubs and acorns. There are still indigenous deer to hunt, whitetail, mostly, though many locals now drive north to

Georgia or the Carolinas paying thousands of dollars to hunt on leases stocked with more exotic varieties of game.

Hiram Lamb used to keep his dogs out at the old homestead during deer season, but no longer. I followed a winding road which terminated at a sagging fence line bounding the property and then turned off-road to track that winding strand a couple of hundred yards to a gate secured with a rusted chain and padlock. I pulled up to the gate in my 4-Runner and got out, my Red Wings crunching on a frosted carpet of moss and leaves.

God damn it was cold! Winter comes to northern Florida with a vengeance. I saw icicles hanging like spears along the fence, the barbed wire stapled along that line of creosoted posts singing with a biting wind. The clouds overhead looked close enough to touch, cold and bruised and unbroken. The only thing separating me from the elements was a nylon windbreaker and cotton-thin vest. I pounded my hands together wishing I'd brought a pair of gloves, or at least a hat, but I wasn't about to backtrack all the way to town for those petty comforts.

I climbed over the gate and paused to get my bearings. I had to use my imagination to reconstruct the road that once led to the big house some distance away. Sandy ruts that used to snake toward the homestead were vanished, now, covered by the crawl of crabgrass and Bahia and punctuated by islands of the ubiquitous palmetto. The landmarks familiar to me from childhood were long vanished, but I finally decided on a line of travel, and slinging my Canon on my shoulder struck out on what I took to be the shortest path to the McCrays' ancestral home.

Clouds gravid with precipitation threatened a freezing rain, but the air was bright as silver and tinged with a shade of lime. An unnatural light. I shook my camera from its case and snapped a casual shot of the landscape. There was a time that picture takers had to allow for the nearly infinite vagaries of atmosphere. I can remember spending precious time to calibrate f-stops and shutter speeds with a respect for my subject's illumination and the speed of the film in my camera.

Painters over centuries limned their subjects with even more rigorous preparation, mating particular textures of canvas with temperas handmade from egg yolk and dry pigment to catch vagaries of color and light along with the play of shadow and depth of field. Modern technology doesn't pretend to promise the effect of a Vermeer or Rafael, or even Ansel Adams, but it definitely makes picture taking easier. All I had to do was frame a subject in a decent composition, wait for the laser-guided focus to be confirmed, and trigger the shutter.

I am spoiled.

Minutes after breaching Hiram's fence I was a trespasser, blazing a trail beneath pine and cypress through a bog slick with new frost and tangled in an understory of thorn and thistle that disguised or erased checkpoints once familiar. At some point I considered doubling back; I certainly hadn't planned on taking the whole damned afternoon to get a dozen photographs. But I couldn't be far away from the big house, was my reasoning, and once I found that landmark the job would go quickly.

I figured a couple of pictures front and back of the McCrays' farmhouse taken with two or three photos of the crib and the sugarcane mill would be all I'd need. Maybe a smokehouse—there was more than one smoker on the property. That would take care of Heritage Week, I figured. That would be a wrap.

But first I had to find the big house.

Randall likes to say that in matters related to navigation I have a confidence completely unrelated to competence. Even so, a trek to the old McCray homestead should not have presented a serious challenge. I had rambled through those woods and pastures many times as a girl. With Lamb's blessing, I have hunted those flatwoods and fished those sloughs as familiarly as my own back forty. Hiram's property was always familiar territory.

But not that afternoon. The landscape had changed over the years. To take one example, there was now a stand of slash pine planted in what used to be a pasture that offered a line-of-sight approach to the marsh beyond which lay the big house. I might have gotten myself turned around in that thicket, I'm not certain. All I know for sure is that an hour after stepping onto Hiram's six hundred acres I had no idea where I was.

I began to experience that gnawing panic you might recall from childhood, that sense of being lost or out of control. Like being locked in a closet. I reached into a vest pocket for the familiar lump that was my cell phone, embarrassed to consider the possibility that I might need its GPS signal to locate my position for some deputy or volunteer dispatched to my rescue. But when I popped my phone open I saw that "No Signal" was available.

So much for that tether.

I killed another half hour trying to double back through the trees, with no luck. I couldn't even find the sun; the cloud cover blocked that steady reference. Checking my watch, I confirmed that I'd squandered an hour tramping in circles. I had no beacon to deploy. The ground was wet and, in any case, I had no lighter or match to start a fire. I could feel my chest getting tight and my heart began to pound out of time when, abruptly, help came from a completely unexpected quarter.

It was a mule.

I should say, I think it was a mule. Could have been a hinny. And I'm still not sure of the color—a light dun, or even white. He was bridled, but there was no saddle or other tack. No rider either. Probably just got loose from somebody's paddock or trailer and wandered through a breach in Hiram's fence. I was not at all surprised to see horseflesh in the flatwoods. Horses have replaced muscle cars as tokens of status in our community, and in fact there is a cottage industry of trail riders who compete throughout the region. I wasn't sure if mules were allowed on those friendly fields, and, in any case, this looked to be a mount that'd lost its owner.

"Here, son," I called out softly and whistled.

He idled forty yards away in plain sight but seemed oblivious to my presence.

"Here, boy."

The animal ignored me. I considered moving in to make a grab for the reins, but with a snort and a swat of his tail, my sure-footed escort trotted off into a maze of dogwood trees.

"Jesus!" I said and scrambled to follow.

I figured since he'd found a way onto the property the mule might be able to lead me out, but the thick ropes of vine and undergrowth made it impossible to keep up with that riderless guide. I lost sight of my feckless escort, but I could hear him, or at least I could hear something large and deliberate pushing through the tangled understory. At my flank, sometimes, or sometimes directly ahead. At the time I assumed it was the mule making that racket, but I suppose it could just as easily have been cattle or hogs.

I was thoroughly spooked, lost in a terrain alternating between understory and slough, the higher ground a tangle

of cat briar and blackberry vines, the sammy treacherous with
quicksand and cypress knees. I had no horizon to guide my
way. I could not even discern whether I was on a bearing
toward the sun or away from it.

And I was cold. The temperature kept dropping and I
was shivering in a bitter breeze. I was also chapped with
thirst. You need water, even in winter, and I was about to risk
a sip from some puddle or another when I stumbled clumsily
into an open glade. Just a few yards of clearing, a wild lawn
crusted like cake with the frost. It was a bit startling, actually, having pushed through slog and vine to abruptly emerge
onto a plate of unblemished ground. I regained my balance
and glanced about. There was no sign of the mule, but at
the verge where the understory met the meadow I spotted
something I could use—a cedar-shingled smokehouse.

It was near to ruin, a fair-sized box of timber and listing
on a rot of beams. You could still see a jerry-rigged rain cap
rusting atop its stack. I unlimbered my Canon and crossed
a pan of Saint Augustine to reach the abandoned smoker. I
pressed my fingers into the holes where once a pair of hinges
was anchored to the stile, but the door was long gone.

I shook off the cold and took a couple of shots out front
and then a photo out back before stepping into the interior.
It was a very large smokehouse. I could see where hocks of
ham or venison and lengths of sausage had once cured in the
smoke of hickory on racks set along the walls or else hung
from beams a good seven or eight feet off the dirt floor. I
cast about for something to start a fire. A kerosene lamp?
Matches? Flint?

No luck. And even if I'd found working matches, there
was no kindling dry enough to start a fire. The building was
a smokehouse in name only. In fact, by the look of things,
the smoker had been repurposed as a shelter for castoff

equipment. There were antiquated farm implements rusting inside the listing walls, a horse-drawn harrow along with a variety of rakes and hoes. I also saw a pair of saddles draped on a sawhorse, the leather half-stripped from their trees. A saddle blanket alongside was welcome. I threw that wrap around my shoulders like a cape and was congratulating myself for finding some barrier against the cold when I saw an object that seemed oddly out of place.

It was a basket, a large bushel fashioned from palmetto fronds. A faded ribbon wound about the basket's handle and a handful of shotgun shells moldered inside, the shot spilled from casings long disintegrated. Not much left but the brass. Would have been nice to return with a better camera to capture the details woven into that handcrafted bushel—assuming I could find my way out and back again. I shoved that worry aside, checked the flash on my digital Canon, and got to work. I had taken maybe half a dozen shots of the saddles and one or two studies of the basket before I noticed the noose hanging stiff as bone and black as soot from a beam overhead.

"Jesus!"

I recoiled instinctively.

"Jesus Christ!"

It took a moment to gather my composure. I thought at first that the loop above my head was a hangman's noose—that was what leaped to mind, eight tight coils of hemp knotted to a deadly collar. The power of suggestion. However, on calmer inspection, I saw that the rope thrown carelessly over the aging beam above me was only a lariat, the kind of lasso you might use to rope a calf, say, or a horse.

I reached up tentatively to give the hemp a tug. There was no give. I looked down then and saw a stool. Just an ordinary milk stool, three tiny legs in a metal frame, the seat long rotted through. I imagined what it would be like climbing onto that precarious perch. Reaching for the noose overhead. Was it possible I was standing in the smokehouse where Annie McCray was found swinging? Was this the place where, as locals put it, Butch's mama ended her troubles? Did Annie McCray fashion eight tight coils to break her neck or did she strangle to death on the tether of a simple riata? Either way, it seemed a lot to expect from a woman who, according to Hattie Briar, hung nothing but laundry.

What trials did Annie McCray endure that would drive her to suicide? Was it the death of her first husband that drove Annie to despair? But according to Hattie Briar, Annie saw her husband's bloody corpse in the back of her lover's truck and never missed a stitch. So if it wasn't the death of her husband that triggered Annie's fatal decision, and it wasn't guilt over her affair with Kelly, what was the straw that led Butch's mother to end her life?

I had an editor at the *Globe* who used to say that a good reporter is like a scientist who constructs a hypothesis and then ruthlessly gathers data to disprove it. Problem was, the data I had pertaining to Annie McCray and her two husbands was largely based on gossip sixty or more years old, stories and lore which, I realized with some consternation, I had accepted as uncritically as any rookie.

You don't have to be Bob Woodward to know that people mostly believe what makes them comfortable. Certainly it was easier to say that Harold McCray was a good husband who lost his life in a hunting accident than it was to pursue more sinister possibilities. The sole source I had to counter that accepted narrative was Hattie Briar. Miss Hattie had called Butch's mother a hussy in our most recent interview, but in earlier conversations she'd had even nicer things to say about Harold McCray.

"Harold was a sum bitch. Beat up on Annie alla time."

"You sure about that, Miss Hattie?"

"Why she took to wearin' them long-sleeved blouses and skirts. Even in summer."

So that her neighbors would not see the bruises on her arms and legs. The welts on her shoulders from Harold's strap.

I began to feel a tingle at the back of my neck that I hadn't felt in a long time, something atrophied in the coverage of high school sports and hunting trophies. It was an alarm, a warning bell, an awakening. There was a story to be unearthed from this smoky ground, I could feel it, something between Kelly Lamb and Annie McCray long buried that needed the light of day.

I knew that Harold McCray wasn't cold in the ground before his widow made Kelly Lamb the sole heir for every acre she inherited. Six hundred and forty acres makes one hell of a dowry. It made Lamb rich overnight. And then within months Kelly drove to town with the sad news that his newly married wife had taken her own life. Both of Butch McCray's parents died violently within months of each other without a single witness to corroborate or dispute Kelly Lamb's version of events, but it was the exchange of land that suggested an awful hypothesis: Was it conceivable that old man Lamb murdered Harold McCray to get his land? And if that was true, **if** it was true—

Could Annie have been Kelly's accomplice?

I walked out of the bitter-cold smokehouse and onto the white-laced meadow. I could imagine Annie McCray setting out on some sure-footed mule not unlike the animal I'd already encountered to rendezvous with her abusive husband, perhaps on a field like this one, white with frost. I recalled Annie's tintype photograph to imagine a good-looking woman saddled and shivering on her pale mount, a skirt of gingham or calico riding high to display legs long and white and louche.

Harold McCray leaves the cover of a heavy thicket to meet his wife in that open glade. He is a dark man, in my imagination, swarthy and unbathed. He has a carbine careless in the crook of an arm. By the way, Harold did own a rifle, an octagonally barreled .30-30; I've seen the very weapon on the gun rack of Hiram Lamb's truck. I can imagine that old repeater in McCray's arm along with a jug of cider or something stronger slung by a cord over his shoulder.

There's Annie, pulling the beribboned basket off the pommel of her saddle, him offering her the jug in return. She takes a long drink, a silver spill of water or cider bright on a neck as fragile as a flute.

But what then? What direction might the story take?

Maybe he wants the jug back. Yes, that's it. Harold gestures for the jug impatiently; she tosses that demijohn down and, with a kick of her heels, drives her mount into a kind of capriole. The mule breaks clear, leaving Annie's husband exposed in the center of the glade.

That's when Kelly Lamb takes his opportunity. I imagine Hiram's father, and Roscoe's, stepping from the tangled understory at the meadow's boundary, a clean-shaven man more slender than Harold McCray, fair-haired and lethal. He levels his carbine without warning. I see an amber flash and a jet of white smoke, and then an explosion echoes with the slug that catches Annie's husband squarely in his back. Harold McCray pitches forward like a sack of grits onto the grass, blood gushing from his chest and mouth as a bounty of hoecakes and sausage spills from its wickered keep. I can picture Harold bleeding red into the white frost of that killing field.

As for Annie? Well, what would a hussy do? Not to mention a murderess. She slides from her saddle, ignoring her slaughtered husband to police the litter of sausage and hoecakes scattered about. With that evidence returned to her homemade basket, Annie swings back into her saddle, those legs flashing promiscuously, long and white and firm as a colt's, Kelly reaching up to pull her down for a rough kiss. A slap to the flank of her mule ends the scene. Annie's off at a trot, back to the deer camp where Hattie Briar will see her stitching unperturbed until Kelly Lamb arrives much later in the day, a husband's corpse stiff in the bed of his Model T.

Not a bad plan, actually. Annie could marry her lover and provide for her idiot son safe from Harold's fists and any suspicion of foul play. Neighbors and friends were all too willing to believe that Harold McCray died in a hunting accident. Everyone except Hattie Briar. I was indulging in speculation, of course. A line of conjecture fueled by looming hypothermia and an imagined gallows. A tableau posited by a woman cold, tired, and lost.

But what if it was true?

That question would have to wait. The weather was turning colder by the hour and I had to find my way back to my vehicle. I had just gathered my camera and blanket and stumped out of the smokehouse when I felt the first warning cramp in my chest, my athlete's heart.

"Come on, Clara!" I groaned.

I clutched my arms to my breasts, stamping my feet on the ground to encourage circulation. A shift in the clouds seemed to reward that effort. The sun broke through, briefly, just above the trees. So that was west. I knew if I headed east long enough I'd hit a fence line or road and so, turning my back to the sun and pulling my pilfered blanket tight, I left the smokehouse and plunged once more into the darkening flatwoods.

I must have walked in circles for hours. I remember mud sucking up through my shoes, the sudden swallow of unexpected streams and creeks, my pudenda shrinking to the size of a prune in ice-cold water. Scrambling from those streams I stumbled back into the understory, my face and hands and shins shredded in a gauntlet of catbriar and stinging nettles. In and out of water as the temperature continued to plummet. My teeth chattered like dice in my mouth, and then my bowels let go. With equal parts of shame and astonishment, I realized I'd soiled myself.

And then I felt it. Not an ache, but a lance. A pain deep in my chest.

"Shit."

I fished out my cell phone and stabbed in a 911—but the bars on top told me I still had no signal. And then, abruptly, I could not breathe. I sank to my butt on the soft ground beside a pine tree, the defecation beneath me warm and sour. I opened my mouth to find air. Then again. And then I felt another spear in my chest and I knew—

I was having a heart attack.

There was no question of hiking anywhere now. Even if I knew the route back to my vehicle, I couldn't walk. It took every scrap of energy I had just to recover my breath.

You're going to die here, I told myself. Of all the fucking places. To survive hell-holes in Iraq and Afghanistan and the Congo, only to expire on land you once romped in pigtails. I tried to imagine how they'd find me, frozen beneath a blanket on a bed of my own shit. That's *if* I was found. I had about resigned myself to that ignominy when I saw a ripple of palmetto nearby and a mule emerged from the slough.

It was the same mount I'd seen earlier, I'm sure of that. More white than gray, I decided. Still no saddle, but this time the mule had a rider.

A woman riding bareback. She looked like someone who spent a lot of time outdoors, with a broad face beaten by wind and sun. The temperature by then must have registered in the twenties, not counting the chill of a steady wind, but she seemed perfectly comfortable in some kind of denim jacket over an old-fashioned granny smock. A pair of brogans, but no socks. Her hair was pulled straight back in a golden braid so long that it tapped her mount's flank in time with the mule's casual progress. Then I saw the basket slung onto the pommel of her saddle, the splints still green, a garland of bright-colored ribbons spiraled about a handle fashioned from palmetto fronds.

"Help?" I addressed the vision tentatively.

She smiled.

"I got you," she said.

I remember riding double without a saddle, my arms wrapped in an intimate embrace around my savior. She had wide hips and a narrow waist. A woman smelling of smoke and magnolia. I leaned onto her back, hoarding the heat rising from her body. Like a fireplace, she was, a furnace. We pushed beneath a stand of mulberry trees and frost fell like snow on her shoulders.

"Aren't you cold?" I asked, and she turned her head to smile.

That's all I can recall until the moment I looked up to see Colt Buchanan leaning over me just outside Hiram Lamb's rusted gate.

"Easy on, Clara Sue. I got an ambulance coming."

"You are one good-looking man, you know that?"

"You've looked better."

Hard to sustain a romance when you're shivering in a salad of defecation. Luckily, when things get truly miserable, shame goes out the window.

"I got lost," I apologized.

"Yes, you did."

"How'd you know?"

"Randall called me. Said you'd been gone way too long and you weren't answering your cell."

"How'd you find me?"

"Your cell phone," he replied. "GPS."

"I couldn't get a signal," I said and then saw the mobile in his hand.

"Working fine now."

I must have tried my phone once more when I reached the fence. I must have, but I can't remember. Maybe my rider dialed for me.

"Where is she?" I asked.

"Where's who, cuz?"

"Woman who rode me out," I replied, and tried to find my feet.

"There weren't nobody here but you, Clara Sue," Colt corrected me, and I might have let it go, except—

I pointed to the frosted field just inside the gate.

"What's that then?"

You could see them clearly, a set of tracks impressed on the hoary pasture beyond the rusted gate. A passage preserved in the freezing chill—one set of tracks coming to the gate, a separate set of tracks heading back to the understory beyond.

"You see the tracks, Colt?"

"I do."

"That was her!" I declared. "A woman on a mule!"

"Take it easy, sweet pea."

"I couldn't walk out on my own, Colt. My heart!"

"I hear you, Clara Sue," he said, soothing me gently. "It's all right."

I heard a siren wailing up the sandy road and the next thing I remember after that was waking up in a hospital bed in Gainesville.

Randall holding my hand in both of his. "Hey, babe."

"Hey."

"So you had a walkabout, what I hear."

"Something like," I nodded.

"And a rider found you? Woman on horseback?"

"I . . . think so. Must have."

He pressed my hand to his lips. "Too bad you didn't get her picture."

That's the story behind the stent in my heart.

CHAPTER SEVENTEEN

Trail Riders Host Competition near Lamb Property
The Clarion

A few days after my heart attack and subsequent "procedure," I stopped by Doc Trotter's office for a routine inspection of my groin. My surgeon snaked the stent to my heart through the femoral artery—standard procedure. You just want to make sure there's no infection or clot afterward. It would take me an hour at least to drive to Shands Hospital in Gainesville for that post-op examination, not to mention the wait once I got there. Lucky for me, Trotter was closer by and equally competent.

"When do I get off the blood thinners, Doc?"

"Week or two at a guess—but that's your surgeon's call."

"How am I looking otherwise?"

"Like a woman in denial. You had a heart attack, Clara Sue, not a hang nail."

"I know, I know."

"The hell were you doing out in those woods anyway?"

"Taking pictures," I replied evasively.

"Hope they were worth it," Doc grunted.

"Couple of them maybe," I said, hedging. "There was a smokehouse way distant from the residence. I shot a pair of saddles inside should turn out nice. Didn't expect to find tack in a smoker."

"Prob'ly converted to a stable," Doc replied absently. "The McCray family loved to ride. All except Annie's husband."

"Harold didn't ride?"

"Scared to death of horseflesh, according to my grandpa. Not Annie, though. She loved to take the reins. In fact, Papa once sold her a mount. This was before Harold got killed."

I sat up straight.

"Your grandfather sold Annette McCray a horse?"

"Not a horse. A mule."

"A mule? You're sure?"

"Papa sold all kind of animals but this one stuck out."

"Why?"

"It was an albino."

I felt a stir in my bowels. "An albino mule?!"

"Pale as death. Papa sold Annie a saddle, too, but that was a waste of tack."

"A waste? How's that?"

"Because Annie McCray rode bareback."

CHAPTER EIGHTEEN

Riderless Mule Sighted near Convict Springs
The Clarion

I trusted Doc Trotter and Sheriff Buchanan to hear what I'd experienced on Hiram Lamb's property, but I was not about to broaden that audience. I brushed aside casual inquiries—"Had a heart attack. Don't recall much else"— and froze out everyone else, including my husband. Randall didn't push for more, which surprised me a little.

"You're back. You're alive," he declared through a mop of hair. "That's all I care about."

Suited me fine. I would have been happy to write off my equestrienne encounter as a product of hypothermia and cardiac stress. Not enough oxygen in the brain, I told myself. Just because a hallucination feels real doesn't mean it's not a hallucination.

But the thing that still nags is—it did feel real.

There's also an undisputed fact that has to be taken into account which is that I damn sure did not walk out of those woods on my own.

So what part of my experience was real and what wasn't? It got to the point that I could not say, and that insecurity began to affect my confidence in all sorts of ways. I began to second-guess the simplest of decisions at work, and delayed action on others. Randall tried to help me by filling the days with distraction. I passed the time on light duty cropping photographs for the Henderson family reunion or the Rotary Club meeting or the honor roll. It was a sensible tactic, but in the end, it didn't work. Rightly or wrongly, I had seen something I couldn't let go, even if it was a product of my own imagination.

But I couldn't talk about it openly and I sure as hell couldn't write about it in the *Clarion*. Barbara Stanton could report that she'd seen her murdered husband smoking a stogie without penalty, but if I wrote a column in the *Clarion* claiming I'd ridden bareback with Annie McCray's ghost, my credibility as a journalist would be destroyed.

No matter what anybody tells you, nobody trusts a reporter in congress with dead people.

And, in any case, how could I use my backwoods epiphany to help Butch McCray? So what if Harold McCray was murdered by Hiram Lamb's father? So what if Butch's mother colluded? Even if I had incontrovertible proof of those crimes, I didn't see how Butch could benefit. There'd be a dent in the Lambs' halo, of course. In Lafayette County, the sins of the father still visit his sons to some extent, but Hiram Lamb wasn't trying to acquire Annie's steam trunk because he was worried about his father's reputation.

If a crime was concealed, it had become a secret without significance. Hiram and Roscoe might be discomfited to see their father's stature diminished, but how could a decades-old homicide figure into Hiram Lamb's bid for Butch McCray's half-acre plot? And what relation did any of this have to do with a silk shawl in a cedar chest?

There was something I was missing—had to be.

But I could not imagine what it was.

"You're not going to let this go, are you, Clara?"

It was midweek. I'd been staring at a picture of some-body's baby for half an hour.

"Let what go?"

"You saw something, Clara. So let's talk about it."

"Why? It's not real. No different than seeing dead rela-tives or UFOs."

"And yet you can't let it go."

Well, he was right about that. I took a deep breath. "Okay."

I spread my hands as though warming by a fire. "You know about the smokehouse."

"Where you found the noose."

"A lariat, actually, but it got me thinking. Speculating, really. Come upstairs with me."

Randall followed me up to my lofty retreat. I wanted another look at the issue of the *Clarion* that featured the faculty of Shamrock's mill town. I especially wanted another gander at Annette McCray's tintype. I spread out the fading paper. There she was, just as I remembered, though of course the long fall of gingham in the paper's printing gave no glimpse of her legs. Those gams would remain a construct of my imagination.

I took more time to pore over Reverend Odom's stark visage. He was handsome behind those dark glasses, stoic in the long wool coat and formal tie, tall and lean and white as ivory. The other faculty and staff stared stiffly anemic and straight into the camera, but not Odom. His head was turned just slightly, as though distracted, the long fingers of his hand resting on Annette McCray's modestly covered shoulder.

"Is that the shawl?" I asked my husband. "Is that the fabric we found in Annie's trunk?"

"Lemme see." He leaned in close. "Could be, I guess. Hard to tell from this."

"I don't suppose Reverend Odom could have been Father Odom," I mused.

"No indication. Is that important?"

"I just wonder if Shamrock's chaplain took confessions," I answered.

"Whose confession?" Randall asked.

"Annie's," I answered, but did not elaborate.

Was Annie McCray a hussy or a saint? Did she even have a sin worth confessing? Was the long-fingered hand on her shoulder a gesture of intimacy or absolution? Or did the reverend's casual contact mean anything at all?

I returned the newspaper to a pile on my desk and pushed my roll-around over to Annette McCray's hope chest. I'd only had the trunk and shawl a couple of days, but I knew I couldn't keep them much longer. Annette's luggage and autographed scarf were clearly Butch McCray's property, and I had no right to keep those artifacts without Butch's permission. On the other hand, I did not want Hiram Lamb anywhere near those relics. I had already left a message with Thurman Shaw Esq., Thurman being one of only three lawyers in Laureate, indicating in general terms that I'd come into possession of property belonging to Butch. Thurman was probably the only lawyer in the county who wasn't in Hiram Lamb's pocket. I was sure that once he'd digested my message, Thurman would expect me to immediately hand the chest and shawl over and with that surrender I'd lose any chance to ferret out their significance—assuming there was any. The shawl might only be a length of silk, and the trunk no more than an empty box.

But something kept pushing me to take one more look.

I opened Annie's trunk and lifted out her autographed scarf, and for the umpteenth time inspected the fabric end to end hoping against hope to see something of significance, something other than Annette's black-threaded signature.

"See anything different?" Randall asked, and I shook my head.

"Nothing."

I was about to put the fabric back into its keep when Randall stopped me. "Wait a sec."

"What?"

"Close your eyes, Clara."

"What?"

"Close your eyes. Run your fingertips across the fabric."

So I closed my eyes and brushed my hand absently over the welted silk, the raised pimples teasing the tips of my fingers—

And then I knew.

"Well, I'll be damned!"

The tiny pimples which textured Annie's shawl were not, as I had supposed, decorative; I knew now, as surely as shit stinks, what the purpose of that needlework had to be. And I knew as well why Reverend Odom required Annette's steady shoulder to locate his photographer.

"Randall, you're a genius!"

"So what're you gonna do now?"

"I think it's about time for Butch McCray to see what his mother left him."

Randall helped me load Annie's trunk into my 4-Runner. By the time I reached Butch McCray's candy store, the last of his customers were gone. It was cold outside, but clear. The school's parking lot was empty leaving the grounds vacant and unnaturally silent, but Butch remained, as usual, to stock his modest shelves and count the slender pile of bills and change derived from a day's enterprise.

"Miz Clara Sue! Brings you to ole Butch?"

The old fellow looking up from a calculation of pennies and nickels to welcome me with genuine delight. "Woana Pepsi Cola? Popsicle? I still got some Popsicles."

"Pepsi sounds good, Butch."

"Can or bottle?"

"Bottle, I think."

"Cold ain't it?" he burbled, plunging a raw hand into a footlocker of melting ice.

"Cold as hell," I agreed.

"Be fifty cent."

I placed a pair of quarters on the counter along with Annette McCray's shawl.

Butch jerked away, startled.

"It's okay, Butch. It's all right."

"Where you get this? Where?!"

"It's your mother's then? You recognize it?"

"Sho, I do! Mama used to make 'em at the school over in Shamrock. She be in the kitchen knittin'. And Preacher Odom too. He'd take 'em and doll 'em up."

"Doll them up?"

Butch looked to his left and right as if wary of goblins and then waves me over.

"They's little pickles; you feel 'em?"

"I do feel them, yes. And you say the preacher put these on?"

"Yes, he did," Butch smiled happily. "Tole me they was a message from my mama. Tole me wherever I went, no matter what happen, mama would send me messages. Thass how come I save my candy wrappers; they the same thing, cain't you see? No different than these here."

"I can see where you'd think that, Butch, I can," I agreed.

"Can I keep this?" he asked innocently.

"It belongs to you," I tell him. "But, Butch, this isn't just a shawl. It's a letter or document of some kind."

"From MAMA!?"

"I believe so." I had to chuckle. "Your mother stitched it onto the fabric. Can you feel these little bumps? It's a language called Braille, Butch. It's made for blind people."

"Preacher Odom was blind," Butch offered eagerly. "Blind as a bat."

Of course. That was why the school's chaplain wore glasses as opaque as tortoise shells. Why he needed Annette McCray's guiding shoulder. I couldn't tell if it was a rush or relief, but it felt like a barrel of wet cow shit was suddenly jerked off my chest.

"Butch, I know someone can read this shawl like a book."

Butch brightened. "Read it to me? When?"

"Tomorrow afternoon."

I reached for the coded scroll, but Butch clutched it to his narrow chest.

"I wanna keep it! It was mama's. It belong to me!"

"It is yours, Butch," I assured him. "But you need to keep this shawl out of sight until we can get it read. Okay? No one can see this, especially not Hiram or Roscoe. You understand, Mr. Butch?"

His head bobbed like an apple on a string.

"You know Thurman Shaw, don't you, Butch?"

"Mr. Thurman, sho. He hep me with my sosh security check. My Medicare."

"I believe it'd be smart for you to let Mr. Thurman keep this for you, Butch. It won't be long. Just a day or two."

"But it's mine, ain't it?" Butch's voice quavered. "Mama meant it for me!"

"Of course she did, Butch. Absolutely. But there's a message from your mother on this shawl and it could be very important. Something your mama very much wanted you to hear. You don't want to chance losing that, do you?"

"No, no!" He recoiled at the prospect. "I wanna know what mama said."

"Good man. But you can't tell anyone about this business, Butch, and I mean no one. Nobody. Especially not Hiram or Roscoe Lamb."

"No, ma'am. Not Hiram."

"All right then."

With that capitulation, I opened the chest and Butch tenderly laid his mother's shawl inside.

"I'll drop these off at Thurman's office. And then tomorrow? We'll see what Annette had to say."

CHAPTER NINETEEN

Roscoe Lamb Arraigned
Federal Contracts Stall
The Clarion

The next day Butch McCray followed Sheryl Lee Pearson and me into the warren of Thurman Shaw, attorney at law. It was about ten in the morning, the first of December on a gorgeous North Florida day, the sky clear and blue and windless. Thurman keeps his office in a frame house right off Main Street on a lot right behind what used to be West's Drug Store. On one wall you'll see plaques of appreciation from the Rotary Club and Booster Club and PTA; the other walls are speckled with diplomas and certifications and photos of Thurman in his glory days on a basketball court, these last always striking me as hilarious since Thurman stands about eye level with a rooster.

I was never convinced Thurman wanted to be a lawyer, though he seemed to enjoy his years as a prosecutor. For sure, Thurman hates being tied to an office. Until the Koons lost their business, you'd find him at the coffee shop, the only customer there aside from Bull Putnal in a suit and tie. Most often, though, Thurman takes his breaks from tedium at the counter of Dr. West's drugstore, kicking back with a Cherry Coke and a newspaper, the *Tampa Tribune*, mostly, or sometimes a *Wall Street Journal*. It's Thurman's attempt to broaden a horizon typically defined by divorce court and foreclosures.

"Mr. Butch, good to see you."

Thurman left the space heater beside his desk to usher Butch and me into his office. Sheryl Lee Pearson was already waiting. I knew that Sheryl Lee had been reading Braille for many years, that skill acquired in the course of tending her blind and aging mother.

Laureate High's long-time teacher took off her outsized spectacles to smile a greeting.

"Butch, how are you?"

"Fine, Miz Pearson."

Butch doffed his molding cap with automatic courtesy, but I knew what he was looking for.

"It's on Mr. Shaw's desk." I nudged Butch in that direction and he crabbed over in that duck-walk he has. We all watched as Butch bent over the shawl to trace with aging fingers his mother's finely sewn moniker.

"Signature's legal, by the way," Thurman announced. "That is, if it was voluntary and properly witnessed or notarized."

"But we can't assume it's a legal document," I cautioned. "Might be nothing but a letter."

"We'll know soon enough." Thurman extricated the shawl from Butch's inspection. "I'm just giving this to Miss Pearson, all right, Mr. Butch? So she can read it to you."

"You want to hear what she had to say, don't you, Butch?" Sheryl Lee inquired sweetly and with that the old man parted with the shawl, though with reluctance, like a priest handing over a relic.

"Everybody ready, then?" Thurman asked, but we were all too anxious to reply.

"All right then. Let's see what this is all about."

"Give me just a minute or two."

Sheryl Lee making that request as she smoothed the fabric over Thurman's desk, her fingertips scanning back and forth, back and forth.

Butch waiting anxiously.

"It's fine," she reassured him absently. "In fact, it's beautiful. A bit archaic. Like reading a Bible in the King James, if you know what I mean."

I saw her pause over the ciphered text.

"It's definitely from your mother." Sheryl Lee took a moment to offer Butch that encouragement.

"Does it say she loves me?" Butch asked Sheryl Lee, and I thought I'd lose it right on the spot.

"Why don't I just read for you, Mr. Butch? And you can hear for yourself."

Sheryl Lee settled back in a hard-backed chair and from her translation a voice emerged as if from another world, a presence speaking to us that was as real and vital as a separate and living person in our midst:

I, Annette Elizabeth McCray, being of sound mind do here in this document amend and change my previous will and testament.

"Good Lord!" Thurman breathed.

I watched as Sheryl Lee's fingers coaxed speech from cloth.

I first want to confess that I have sinned in my life. I have sinned against my first husband, Harold, who though abusive to me and mean did not deserve to be murdered. I did what I did thinking that the good would outweigh the bad, that Kelly would take me and my precious son and liberate us from the hard life and the hard man I had grown to hate.

Forgive me, Jesus, I am a fool as well as a sinner. I helped my second husband, Kelly Lawrence Lamb, kill my first husband, Harold McCray, on our own land in a little meadow just north

*of the fishing hole. I did not start out meaning to hurt anyone,
much less Harold. I used to see Kelly at prayer meetings and
after his first wife died we'd meet after church. Before long I was
giving him more than my husband. He seemed tender to me, even
to Butch who amazes me daily with acts of kindness rendered
with no ken of getting nothing in return.*

*Kelly Lamb was always looking to improve his circumstances,
and one time after we had slept together he talked to me about
what a shame it was me being married to a man of property with
no interest in his wife or idiot son. What a waste it was. That
planted the seed and it weren't long before we decided what to do.*

*We waited till deer season. I lured Harold down from his
stand with a mess of biscuits and then Kelly shot him. Kelly
told me to go back to the camp and wait for him, which I did,
and then Kelly tarried a long while before bringing Harold in.
Nobody challenged me and nobody would raise a hand to Kelly
even if they did suspect foul play, so I thought I was finally free
to enjoy my 640 acres of land and my precious boy, not to mention a warm bed.*

*We were supposed to wait a decent interval and get mar-
ried, that is what Kelly and me agreed to. But after Harold was
buried, Kelly gets me off by Pickett Lake and tells me he won't
marry me at all unless I turn over all my land, every last acre
that I inherited at Harold's demise.*

*"You need to make a will," Kelly told me. "In case something
happens."*

*I didn't mind about the land, really. I was in love; what
did it matter? But Hattie Briar made some remark about Butch
being left out of the deal. "A retard can't inherit," she said, or
something like that and so I told Kelly I would will my house
and land to him, but only on condition that he foster my son,
and make arrangements for Butch so that he'd not be penniless
in his majority.*

Kelly did not agree right away. In fact, he said if I got picky he'd tell the sheriff I killed my husband all on my own. What could I do then? Lots of people knew about Harold and me and besides nobody will take the word of a woman over a man, especially a woman sleeping around. If Hattie Briar called me a hussy, I knew others shared that opinion, if silently.

But I stood my ground for my boy. "You take care of Butch or I'm going to the sheriff myself," I told Kelly, and finally he gave in. Some lawyer from Dixie County drew me up a will that made Kelly my sole heir. Kelly wouldn't marry until we got the papers witnessed and notarized at the courthouse.

It didn't take long for me to realize I had misjudged my new husband. Kelly liked me in bed, but that was all. And his boys, those two young hellions, made life miserable for Butch. They'd take him hunting just to have him feed the dogs and clean the guns and then leave him alone in the woods without supper.

I came from behind the crib one summer day to see Butch screaming on a bed of fire ants, Hiram and Roscoe there with tobacco sticks to beat off any retreat. That was the straw that broke. I blistered those boys' hides and that night Kelly come to me and slapped me across the face and I told him he touched me like that again I'd put us both in jail. "I'll tell the sheriff how Harold got killed, I will," I told him. "I'll go to jail, I don't care," and then Kelly, he beat me and there I was, no better off than with my first husband.

That's when I started taking Butch to work. It wasn't much pay, being a cook at a lumber camp, but the teachers at Shamrock were nice to me and my little boy. I thank Preacher Odom from the bottom of my heart for all the kindness he has extended to Butch and me and also for guiding my hand in the language of the blind. I wish the mill was not shut down. We could have had a good life in Shamrock.

But Kelly is getting meaner all the time. I came home one day and there's a buck strung up in the smokehouse and Kelly says it would be as easy to gut me or Butch as any deer and that's when I knew I had to confess my sins and change my will. I may not deserve happiness but my little boy does. He deserves his birthright, even if he is simple.

So now, in sound mind, I do declare that the will executed under my signature in the days before my marriage to Kelly Lamb was made under threat and duress and is null and void, that all properties inherited from my first husband, Harold McCray, and all my personal possessions now and in future are at my death bequeathed solely to my only beloved son, Michael Joseph McCray, nickname of Butch. I swear that I render this will and testament freely, without reservation and under no threat of duress or reprisal.

I have asked that this document be kept secret until my death. Part of the reason for that is that I am a coward. Hattie Briar has always suspected me and Kelly of killing my first husband and I live in fear that one day I'll be found out on that score. And even if I escaped earthly justice for killing Harold, I could not bear the shame of living among neighbors who knew my crime. I could not bear it.

The other reason this document cannot be revealed is that if Kelly knows or even suspects that I am changing my arrangements, I am convinced he will kill me and my only child. For these reasons, I am hiding this will and have prevailed on Preacher Odom to keep its location in confidence until my death.

I further name Preacher Paul Odom my proxy and representative and charge him, at my death, to deliver this final will and testament to the elected judge of Lafayette County, doing all that is legal and proper to ensure that my son, Butch, who is ignorant in these matters, receives his rightful inheritance.

Until then, however, this shawl must stay hid. I trust my confessor to know its whereabouts. No one else.

A word to my precious little boy. I am so sorry I have not been a better mother to you, Butch. You deserve more than what I have given you, but at least now I know you will not grow up a pauper.

I love you now and until the day we meet Our Father in Heaven.

Witnessed this fourteenth day of February 1954,
   Paul Odom, Th.D
   Chaplain: Shamrock School, Putnam Lumber Co.
   Shamrock, Florida
Signed this same day and hour,
   ANNETTE ELIZABETH McCRAY

Sheryl Lee finished the reading and for a moment no one said anything.

Butch's eyes were cups of tears. He looked old and tired. How long had he endured the penury and ridicule his mother had anticipated and contrived to prevent? How was it that we his neighbors or putative friends had not noticed?

"Would you like to hold your mama's will, Butch?" Sheryl Lee left her chair to press the silk into the old man's hands and he cradled it reverently.

"Mama's will," Butch repeated, but then I noticed Thurman Shaw tapping his desktop with his pen.

"Thurman—? What is it?"

"It's the will."

"You think it can be contested?"

"Never get that far. Annie has confessed to abetting the murder of her husband. You can't inherit your spouse's land by killing him. Annie never had legal title to the McCray homestead to begin with. None at all."

"Oh, Lord!" Sheryl Lee sighed.

But Thurman wasn't finished.

"Hold on, now. I said the will's no good. But if a court rules this confession valid, that means Annie never had a legal right to bequeath the McCray homestead to her second husband. Old Man Lamb never had legal title to the property. The deed he got from Annie McCray isn't worth a spoon of salt."

"Which means—?" Sheryl Lee prompted the attorney.

"Which means that the only person with a clear and legal claim to his father's property is Butch McCray."

Sheryl Lee breathed a sigh of relief. Butch looked up briefly with no apparent indication he'd followed our conversation.

Thurman loosened the tie at his neck. "But why didn't this Preacher Odom do what Annie asked him to?" Shaw wondered aloud. "'Cause I guarantee you if that preacher had got this document before Judge Boatwright, Kelly Lamb wouldn't have got a foot of Harold's land. That homestead would have gone to Butch, hook, line, and sinker."

"I have an idea," I spoke up. "One of the things I found when poking around Shamrock was Putnam's published company history. The company still exists in Jacksonville, or a remnant of it, and the archivist over there told me he had a ledger which recorded salaries for everybody at the mill, cooks and faculty and clerics along with everybody else.

"Those records indicated that Annette McCray and Reverend Odom were employed at the Shamrock mill in the early fifties. I thanked the man for that corroboration and was about to hang up when the archivist mentioned that another item saved from the old mill was a ledger from the dispensary."

"By that you mean their hospital?" Sheryl Lee asked.

"Close to it," I answered. "And in between snakebites and amputations I saw an entry for Reverend Paul Odom. Turns out Odom died of influenza three weeks before Annette McCray was found hanging in her smokehouse. He carried Annie's secret to his grave."

"So when Odom died, her confession and will stayed hidden in the travel trunk," Thurman said, picking up the thread.

"Good Lord," Sheryl Lee sighed. "All these years gone by, and nobody knew?"

"Maybe not 'nobody'," I cautioned.

"What do you mean?"

"Hattie Briar," I replied. "Hattie didn't know exactly what was in that chest, but she knew something was there and that it was important. And she knew Hiram Lamb was after it, too. That's why she pushed it on me."

"Maybe Kelly Lamb suspected something all along," Thurman speculated. "Maybe he told Hiram."

"Or maybe Hattie shot off her mouth," I said, shrugging. "We'll never know."

This whole time Butch is holding his mother's comfort in his hands, oblivious to new revelations.

"I wonder," Sheryl Lee mused, turning privately to Thurman. "Would a jury in those years and in that community take Annie's word over Kelly Lamb's? Would Annie's confession have been enough to convict the old man of Harold McCray's murder?"

"Hard to say," the attorney shrugged, and then I interjected—

"But it might have prevented Annie's."

Thurman and Sheryl Lee swiveled to face me like a pair of owls.

"Are you suggesting Kelly Lamb murdered Annette McCray?!" Thurman mouthed quietly.

"I think it's possible," I replied. "I'm not sure I ever fully bought the story that Annie hanged herself. A woman who, in her own words, was afraid of a noose?"

"Good Lord," Sheryl Lee whispered.

"Well, the old man would have had a strong motive," Thurman mused. "He had means."

"He certainly did," I agreed. "And he had killed once before—in cold blood."

"Lord, Lord!" Sheryl Lee said.

I turned to Thurman. "So tell me, counselor. How's this confession going to affect Hiram Lamb in the here and now?"

"It'll put Hiram in court, for sure," Thurman predicted. "The title for the property will be in dispute, certainly, and my guess is Hiram's either gonna have to pay Butch for the land or lose a big chunk of it or come up with some combination of the two."

I nodded. "We have to get this confession to somebody in authority."

"Not a prosecutor," Thurman said, reaching for a legal pad and pen. "Before I go to a state attorney, I want Judge Walker's opinion and he's out on a deer lease for the next week, at least. But b'fore anybody sees anything, we all need to remember that this shawl belongs to Butch McCray. Neither you nor I nor anyone here can give that silk to anybody without Butch's permission, we clear on that. We can advise Mr. Butch what we think is best, but it's his property. I'll get to work on a brief for Judge Walker. Meantime, I vote we keep this business to ourselves."

"Absolutely," Sheryl Lee agreed, and I raised a hand to second the motion.

Butch had not followed a word of our conversation, of course. He had the shawl pressed to his face as if searching for his mother's smell.

"Butch?" I walked over to get his attention. "Butch, we need to put it back in the trunk."

"No. I'm owna keep it myself."

"You can keep it here. See, it's a very important kind of letter, Butch. It's a letter we have to be careful doesn't get lost or damaged in any way."

Butch looked to Thurman for help.

"We really do have to take special care of it, Mr. Butch. It's yours, no question, and you can see it any time you want, but for now it needs to be kept here."

"You understand, Mr. Butch?" I asked, but the concern seemed past the old man's comprehension.

"Let me." Sheryl Lee squatted beside the old man. "Butch, you love your mother, don't you?"

"Yessum."

"And you love her words. But you need me to read them, don't you?"

"Yes, ma'am."

"Well, these are very special words, Butch. And your mother's letter is special too. I can't read it anywhere but here. But, like Mr. Thurman says, you can see your mother's confession anytime you like, and I can read it whenever you want me to, but it has to be in Mr. Shaw's office."

She disengaged the shawl from his hand gently. Butch gave it up, finally.

"Thank you, Mr. Butch." Thurman accepted the closely woven text and with that delicate negotiation completed, I ushered Butch McCray out of his lawyer's office. It was a Saturday. Even so, we all had work to do. Sheryl Lee with final exams to grade. Me with a paper to print. But first I had to get Butch settled.

"Let's get you home, mister."

"Be fine," he assented without enthusiasm.

Sheryl Lee trailed us out the door. We reached the curb and she peeled off, and when I turned to offer a parting thank you I caught the glare of the morning's bright sun on a windshield. I shaded my eyes and there was Hiram Lamb's pickup, directly across the street from Thurman Shaw's office.

It was Hiram in the cab, for sure. Even if you didn't know his truck you could not mistake that rock-star hair, or the blotch that marred his face from birth.

"Come on, Butch." I eased Annie's precious son toward my foreign ride. "Let's get you home."

CHAPTER TWENTY

Fatal Accident Shocks County
The Clarion

The week following the meeting in Thurman Shaw's office was hectic for the *Clarion*'s doughty staff, which means Randall and I were swamped. Seemed like everything was hitting us at once. A grand jury indicted Roscoe Lamb for trafficking crystal meth, which was a huge story for our local paper and one I ached to cover in detail, but then there was Heritage Week to cover as well. Heritage Week comes smack between homecoming and Christmas at the height of deer season, and already folks were calling me from City Park where vendors and other enthusiasts were erecting booths to sell everything from mayhaw jelly to handcrafted banjos and bowie knives.

Other people had booths set up to demonstrate early crafts and carpentry, every farrier, wheelwright, and knife maker clamoring for a photo or article, and then the county commissioners, who never do anything, picked that very week to announce a proposal which would move Heritage Week from its early December slot to early summer, which generated howls and counter howls, all sides demanding the *Clarion*'s endorsement.

I was busy as a bee in a tar bucket and to be honest didn't think too much about Butch McCray, or the fallout sure to follow from the discovery of his mother's confession. In my own defense, I had done all I could do. Thurman Shaw was actively pursuing the matter and was more than competent to represent Butch's interests. Sooner or later the dispute would reach a court, and when that happened I'd be ready to cover the story. Until then I was at Laureate's city park shooting reconstructions of sawmills and sharecropper shacks, and sampling venison sausage as kids and grown-ups fletched homemade arrows to attack silhouettes of bears painted on bed sheets.

"Come on, Clara Sue, give her a try," Sheryl Lee Pearson said, teasing me, and I had about made up my mind to take a shot when I felt the tickle of my phone's familiar vibration in my pocket.

"One second."

I pulled out my mobile and recognized Thurman Shaw's number.

"Mr. Shaw. What can I do you for?"

"You need to get over here." His voice was tight. "Hiram Lamb came in ten minutes ago with a court order and Butch McCray. I had to give 'em the confession, Annie's confession."

"How the hell did that happen?!"

"Hiram talked Butch into it. Wasn't hard, I don't expect."

"Hiram's going to destroy that shawl, Thurman. That's got to be his aim."

"I considered the possibility. I even called Judge Walker to voice that concern. But it's Butch's property, ultimately. Not a damn thing we can do about it."

"Jesus fucking Christ!"

I stalled over my phone a moment. "But wait a minute. Even if Hiram destroys Annie's rag, <u>we</u> could be deposed, couldn't we? You and Sheryl Lee and me? We can swear under oath to the contents of Annie's confession."

"We could, but Judge Walker is not about to take a section of land away from Hiram Lamb and give it over to Butch on the basis of what we say was in a missing confession. No way. Won't happen."

"We've got to get the judge to read Annie's confession, Thurman. We've got to convince Butch to turn it over."

"Good luck with that."

"You say Hiram brought him to your office?"

"He did."

"Any idea where he is now?"

"You mean Butch? He's still with Hiram."

"You sure?"

"I am, but you're not likely to find 'em."

"Why?"

"They're off hunting."

"You're shitting me."

"Butch said Hiram invited him."

"And you believed him?!"

"He's been off with Hiram before. Plenty of times."

What was it that Annie wrote—? Something about feeding dogs and cleaning guns?

"I don't like the sound of this, Thurman."

"Clara Sue, please—"

"You see Butch, or hear from him, let me know right away."

I ran our town's single red light on the way to the coffee shop. I hoped to find somebody, anybody who could tell me where Hiram intended to hunt for the day. It would be impossible to find him otherwise. When I was a girl, hunters rarely left the roads that gridded the huge stands of pine planted by Buckeye. Come deer season, half the county deployed in teams along those sandy meridians, their trucks or jeeps converted to deer blinds as they waited for a meet of hounds to push a buck into their field of fire. This was back when we hunted deer with shotguns and dogs and the timberlands were free for man and animal to roam.

Hunters nowadays pay thousands of dollars to lease sections of land for similar recreation. There is very little free land left to hunt, so my first thought was to find out if Hiram was hunting with a club or on privately leased land.

"He's got a lease in Georgia," Carl Koon told me over a purchase of darkly roasted coffee.

Carl wasn't looking too well, his eyes bagging and bruised. An employee, now, of a business he once owned. I noticed the twins busing the tables.

"Hiram goes to Georgia to hunt deer?"

"Georgia, Alabama, the Carolinas. Goes to Wyoming for elk. Montana too. He's got leases all over."

"How about local? Is there any place local he'd hunt?"

Carl shook his head. "Not 'less it's on his own land."

I was about to leave when another thought came to mind. "Where are Hiram's dogs?"

"Fuck his dogs."

I had wondered who butchered Hiram Lamb's favored hound. I was pretty sure now that I had a candidate.

"But would Hiram go hunting without his dogs, Carl?"

"No. He's not patient enough to sit a blind."

I left the coffee shop at a jog and rang Thurman Shaw at his office.

"Dogs?" Thurman seemed puzzled at my question.

"In Hiram's truck. There's a cage in the bed, am I right?"

"Dog cage, sure."

"Yes, but were there any dogs?"

"Damn if I believe I noticed."

"This is important, Thurman. Walk it back. See if you can remember."

"Lessee. I did follow Hiram and Butch out of the office. Fact I walked 'em to the curb. I was trying to convince Butch to leave me the confession, but he wasn't having any of it. 'I'm goin' huntin' with Hiram,' Butch told me, and then they got in the truck and Hiram peels off some rubber, and . . ."

"Thurman?"

"No."

The lawyer's voice was suddenly confident.

"No, Hiram didn't have any dogs with him. Not a one. As he pulled away I could see Butch looking back at me through the cage."

"Thank you." I signed off and hit the road.

If Hiram Lamb had actually taken Butch to go deer hunting I never would have found him. Even if he decided to poach on Buckeye's land, or take a day lease in Taylor or Dixie County, Lamb would be tramping amidst tens of thousands of acres. I wouldn't even know where to start looking for him.

But I didn't believe for a moment that Hiram had gone hunting, not for deer anyway. He already had what he'd been hunting for. Only question for Hiram would be how to separate Butch from his mother's confession long enough to destroy it. That was a task best done privately. You didn't want some neighbor or out-of-towner stumbling along in the middle of that sort of transaction. What you wanted was seclusion and privacy, and where could a man better hide in private than on his own posted land? I had a good idea where Hiram Lamb had taken Butch McCray and if I was wrong there'd be no point looking anyplace else.

I returned to what used to be the McCray homestead under a slow, cold rain. I was glad to be in a winter coat and boots. It was not much over forty degrees that December day and cold as a well-digger's ass. I felt the tires of my 4-Runner slipping on rain-slick clay as I slid along the fence line leading to the property's padlocked gate.

But it wasn't locked that morning.

The padlock that secured Hiram's gate hung open on a length of chain draped casually around a crossbar. I could see where the Bahia grass beyond was pressed down by the passage of what almost certainly was Lamb's truck. In any case, the trail was easy to follow, and for that I breathed a prayer of thanks. I opened the gate and drove my 4-Runner through, following the freshly pressed tracks across the pasture and past a skirt of mixed timber. Breaking out on the far side of that woods, I found the fishing hole I remembered from childhood. The big house had to be nearby and, sure enough, a minute or two later I found the broken fence marking the limits of the yard at what had been the McCrays' cedar-shingled home.

I pulled my 4-Runner over and killed the engine. Hiram's pickup was parked just outside the front-yard fence, a dog cage empty in the truck's ample bed. I got out of my SUV bareheaded and barehanded to brave the winter rain, realizing it was the second time I'd forgotten to bring a pair of gloves. As I got closer, I could hear the radiator of Hiram's truck ticking away, a vapor rising from the hood to tease the boughs of a mulberry stretching overhead. I glanced into the cab to make sure there was no one inside. Then I scanned the porch beyond—no one to be seen there either. I breached a yard gate hanging useless in a vine of fox grape and was halfway across a rude lawn before I noticed smoke curling from a listing chimney.

"HIRAM? BUTCH—? IT'S CLARA SUE. CLARA SUE BUCHANAN."

No answer. I sure as hell didn't want to startle anyone equipped to kill, so I tried again.

"HIRAM—? BUTCH?"

There was still no reply, but when you see smoke curling from a chimney, you know sure as hell there has to be a fire.

"Jesus."

I stomped up the front porch steps as loudly as I could, crossed the verandah, and pounded my bone-cold fist on the unlatched door.

"Anybody home?" I called out, but less aggressively than before.

Then I heard something, some sort of movement just inside. The McCrays' old home is raised off the ground on stumps of pine, its bedrooms and kitchen branching off the dog run of a long breezeway. I pressed my ear to the door-frame and once more heard a complaint of flooring on the other side.

I pulled back. Swallowed the knot in my throat.

"I'M COMING IN."

I opened the front door cautiously and hearing no challenge stepped into a hallway reeking of wood rot and smoke. A door to my right was wide open. I edged through and found Butch bending from a stool over a small pile of pine knots likely collected for kindling.

"Butch, you all right?" I asked, but he did not answer.

His mother's shawl was folded neatly on the floor.

"Where's Hiram?" I asked.

Butch shifted on his improvised stool and I saw a box of Number-One buckshot on the wide-planked floor. A box of ammunition newly opened and dry. Then I noticed his coveralls tucked sloppily into a pair of galoshes still wet and muddy.

"Butch, where's the shotgun?"

"With Hiram." His reply was unsettling.

"But where is Hiram? What's happened here?"

"They was an accident." He smiled puckishly, and I felt a flush of ice in my gut.

"Kind of accident, Butch? Butch—?"

He turned away from the fire and toward the rear of the house.

"Out by the fishin' hole."

I hit the dog run at a lope and dropped off the porch in a jog for the long-dead pond out back.

"HIRAM—?"

I reached the soggy hole calling out Hiram's name, and craning for some reply, but all I could hear was the clatter of rain on fronds of palmetto.

"HIRAM LAMB?!"

I found him lying on his back on the far side of the bog. I ran over and took a knee.

"Hiram?" I tried again knowing it was a waste of time.

A burgundy stain pooled with the unfiltered water collecting beneath his body. He'd been shot in the chest. It was a shotgun did the job, no doubt, and from close range. His ribs were burst from their cage like staves from a broken barrel, the lungs inside exposed like a wilt of lettuce.

I'll never forget the eyes. They stared straight up as though surprised, unblinking under the spatter of rain. The scarlet scar which had distinguished Hiram's face was now insignificant in competition with his other wounds. How long was he dead? I leaned over to take Hiram's hand. It was clammy and cold. I stood up fighting a wave of nausea.

A Remington over-and-under was half-buried in the muck at Hiram's feet, a twelve-gauge shotgun with a ventilated rib. There was also a 30-30 nearby; that'd be the hex-barreled carbine passed down to Hiram from his father. I had an impulse to retrieve both firearms, but then realized better. I'd have to call the sheriff, there was no doubt about that. I rummaged the pocket of my trousers with bone-cold hands to find my cell phone and was grateful to ring right through.

"Sheriff's office."

"This is Clara Buchanan. I'm at the old McCray homestead, at the house."

"Yes, ma'am."

"Tell the sheriff there's been an accident."

CHAPTER TWENTY-ONE

Hiram Lamb Killed Hunting
County Loses Federal Grant
The Clarion

Sheriff Buchanan picked up Doc Trotter on his way out to the Lambs' property. An EMS unit wasn't far behind. The sheriff directed the techs to stay with Butch in the farmhouse. Doc made it clear he wouldn't mind a fireside job himself.

"I'm a coroner, not a damned medical examiner," Doc groused as I led our group through the rain to Hiram's body.

"I need more help, I know where to find it," Colt replied.

County sheriffs routinely contact the Florida Department of Law Enforcement for forensic support, especially where gunplay is involved. The FDLE has mobile units and crime scene investigators on call for just such circumstances. Of course, sheriffs are in no way obliged to invite outside investigators into their counties; even so I was a little surprised to see Colt dismiss that assistance out of hand.

Colt insisted on managing the crime scene himself, taking multiple photos of the body and scene as Doc Trotter examined Hiram's corpse, making sure the chain of custody for the rifle and shotgun was well documented.

"Were both barrels fired on the Remington?" Doc asked at one point.

"Only one, the bottom barrel," Colt called back. "And neither shell's been shucked."

"We're talking about a single shot then?"

"Way it appears. Less you see different."

Doc shook his head wearily.

"Can't say as I do."

A steady, cold rain and mud don't make the best palate for a crime scene, but Colt slogged it out, working in a spiral out from Hiram's body and only when that work was finished, did Sheriff Buchanan trek back to the big house to confront Butch McCray.

The EMTs were dismissed to the hallway and I was not allowed to attend the interrogation that ensued. Couldn't have been much more than fifteen or twenty minutes that had passed when Colt rejoined Doc and me on the front porch.

He appeared genuinely perplexed.

"What about it, Sheriff?" I stood to ask. "We have an accident, here, or a homicide?"

"Be damned if I know." Colt pressed his hat onto his skull. "Butch shot Hiram; he admits it freely. But he says it was accidental. He says Hiram stopped at the house and told him to get a fire goin' so they'd be able to warm after hunting. Then Hiram makes Butch clean the shotgun, but when they get ready to leave Hiram grabs the rifle and tells Butch to bring along the Remington and shells."

I perked up. "So Hiram had Butch bring along shells for the shotgun?"

"Well, he would have, wouldn't he?" Colt grunted. "An over 'n' under only gives you two shots."

"Sounds like Hiram too," Doc Trotter interjected. "Making Butch his butler."

Colt raised a shoulder. "Maybe. Way Butch tells it, Hiram's got him toting the over 'n' under and a box of Number Ones as Hiram leads the way around the old water hole for the woods beyond."

"Are there actually any deer back there to hunt?" I asked.

"Sure there's deer. There's turkey too. Fact, Butch says Hiram spotted a gobbler roosting way up in one of those pines by the old fishing hole and he gets all excited and drops the rifle and reaches back to yank the shotgun away from Butch. He grabbed the damn thing by the barrels, is the way Butch tells it.

"And when Hiram jerked the gun away, Butch's hand got tangled in the trigger guard and the weapon discharged straight into Hiram's chest."

"Tangled in the trigger guard?" Doc Trotter frowned. "That's what Butch told you?"

Colt spit a wad of Red Man carefully.

"Awright, look. This all could go either way. They's lots of unknowns, no doubt about it. But I can tell you this: We're not gonna learn shit more about what happened out here than we know already, not on this ground with this weather, not even if we had every lawman in three states looking, and for damn sure I don't want a lynch mob milling outside my jailhouse, so here's what we're goin' to do.

"Clara Sue, you're gonna make sure anybody reading the *Clarion* sees a preliminary finding of accidental death with no foul play suspected. That fly with you, Doc?"

"I expect it will," Trotter replied tersely.

Not a ringing endorsement, but good enough. The sheriff turned his attention back to me.

"You can say an investigation will be made as a matter of course, but I don't want to see any other details in the paper."

I chewed that one over.

"May I say the death occurred in the course of hunting?"

"That's about as far as I'd go."

Colt made that reply scuffing the floor of the porch with his heavy-soled shoe.

"I get my own report wrote up, I'll shoot you a copy," he went on. "You can print anything you want to off that."

"Fair enough," I agreed too quickly.

There I had a story unfolding right in front of me, blood, guts, and intrigue, but I wasn't nearly as interested in Hiram Lamb's death as I was in Annette McCray's confession.

"Sheriff, did you see a shawl on the floor beside the milk crate?"

"Looked to me like a sheet."

"No." I shook my head. "And it's much more than a shawl. It's a confession, Sheriff, Annette McCray's confession, and Hiram wanted it badly."

"Stop right there." Colt raised a hand. "Just hold up. I don't know anything about a confession, you hear me? *Nada.* You can come by later on and make any kind of statement you think is relevant. You can certainly contact me directly with any information that might bear on Hiram Lamb's death. But not today. Not now. Are we agreed?"

Doc looked at me. I looked at him.

"We hear you, Sheriff."

"Good." Colt spit another plug off the side of the porch. "I'll have our EMS take Hiram to the morgue in Perry; that'll buy us some time. I need to get Butch's prints. Prob'ly have him sign a statement, or at least make his mark. Somebody should call Thurman Shaw."

"I can tell Thurman to meet you in town," I offered.

The sheriff nodded.

"Awright, then, let's get after it."

The sheriff strode back into the house. Couple of minutes later he came out with Butch, who's hanging onto his mother's wrap as though it were life itself.

"Mr. Butch," I began as gently as I could and was amazed when the old man reached out to press the riddled silk into my hands.

"Keep it fo' me, will you, Clara Sue? Keep it safe."

"I will," I promised.

It was still raining when Sheriff Buchanan put Butch into the back seat of his cruiser. Looked like dimes bouncing off the roof.

"Think I'll hitch a ride with you, Clara Sue." Doc Trotter hung back.

"Sure thing."

"Maybe on the way you could tell me what the hell is goin' on here."

"Be happy to give you a lift, Doc. But as for the rest?"

I tucked Annie's confession dry and snug inside my vest.

"You're gonna have to buy yourself a paper."

EPILOGUE

Sheryl Lee Pearson Retires
The Clarion

Hiram Lamb was buried with near-papal ceremony in the cemetery behind the church at Midway that my own grandfather helped build. Naturally, the circumstances surrounding Hiram's violent death provoked comment and speculation all over the county, but nobody outside us principals knew or suspected that Hiram Lamb lured Butch to his property for the purpose of destroying Annette McCray's well-stitched confession. That claim was never leaked to the public by me or anyone else. In fact, it would be many weeks before Annie McCray's confession even came into the public record. Consequently there was no conjecture in the days following Hiram's death that Butch McCray had a motive to kill his foster brother.

Listening to the coffee-shop gossip that ensued, I heard very few folks disputing Butch McCray's account of the incident. The man was a retard, I heard that characterization over and over from regulars gossiping over coffee. Everyone knew the signs, the crabbed gait, the cretin's speech. We'd seen those gelid eyes under that ridiculous cap. The perpetual thousand-yard stare. When Doc Trotter ruled that Hiram

Lamb's death was caused by a shotgun wound inflicted accidentally, he only confirmed what most folks already wanted to believe and with that backing Sheriff Buchanan closed his official investigation of the case.

Butch McCray was never arrested, much less indicted. He never faced a grand jury.

Hardly anybody believes Butch McCray is capable of murder.

There were a few voices in dissent, naturally. Hiram's surviving sons were not inclined to credit any account that left their father responsible for his own death. "Daddy would never grab a gun by the barrel," Trent Lamb claimed to anyone who'd listen, but even those most sympathetic to his family blamed Trent's father for trusting a shotgun to the village idiot.

"I don't know what Hiram was thinking," Principal Wilburn lamented.

You could have sold tickets to the funeral. There must have been a half mile of cars and trucks up and down the road, those rides spilled over from vehicles parked bumper to bumper on the church grounds. No surprise there. The fall of aristocracy is always more interesting than the trials of the unwashed.

But the real story followed Hiram's interment and took months to wrap up. Hiram had a will of his own, naturally, but relatives eager to inherit a chunk of land were flummoxed to learn that the title to that 640 acres was being contested on the strength of a confession stitched onto a length of silk. Judge Walker admitted Annie's unusual parchment as evidence relevant to a possible homicide and testimony from an unexpected corner bolstered the state's claim that Annie and her second husband murdered Butch McCray's father. Roscoe Lamb, seeking to reduce a prison sentence following his conviction for trafficking methamphetamine, testified that just a few days before Annie's death he and his brother, Hiram, heard their father tell Annie that he'd "shut her up for good" if she breathed a word about "their business" with Harold McCray. "Me and Hiram always knew Annie had somethin' over daddy," Roscoe admitted. "They was always rumors inside the family that daddy killed Harold McCray."

Annie's unusual parchment became the centerpiece in a paroxysm of civil litigation. An action taken on Butch McCray's behalf went all to the way to Florida's Supreme Court. Hiram Lamb's would-be heirs engaged a firm from Miami in a last-ditch effort to deny Butch his birthright. Thurman Shaw represented Butch's interests. It took a state-appointed arbiter to settle the mess and when it was all dusted, Butch wound up with something like four hundred thousand dollars in a cash settlement, along with four hundred acres of his original birthright, all carved out of Hiram Lamb's ill-gotten estate. Roscoe Lamb learned of that verdict as he languished behind bars in Raiford. He'd be leaving prison in seven years with nothing but a Social Security check for support.

The *Clarion* had the scoop on the whole shebang, of course, and at first I planned to serialize the whole story in soap-opera detail, beginning with Annette McCray's affair with Kelly Lamb. I mean, this was the kind of story that could go viral. The story that would put me back on the map! But then I started finding ways to put it off. There was always something. In a single week, the Glee Club got an invitation to the Sugar Bowl, Edward Henderson's grandson reeled in a twelve-pound bass out of some pond in Madison County, and the Morgans enjoyed their seventeenth family reunion.

Not every story brought fodder folksy or comforting. Barbara Stanton lost her home, by no means the only foreclosure in our region, but easily the most notorious. The property was auctioned off soupspoon to water heater this past February. Closer to home, Connie Koon went in for drug rehab and Carl probably should have. Edgar Uribe's mammoth compadre Raul Herrera managed to avoid jail time for muling methamphetamines, which was heartening, but the experience tore apart his family. No one knows where the Herreras got off to, and they're not the only migrants to pull up stakes. In fact, there has been an exodus of the undocumented from our county. Sheryl Lee Pearson told me that Edgar Uribe dropped out of school not two weeks before graduation. I drove out to the young sculptor's trailer home and found it abandoned. Nothing remaining but a candle and the scent of prophecy.

That and the miraculous mural on a bedroom wall.

Hopes for local glory took a big hit when Trent Lamb ripped an ACL his second day in pads at Florida State. Hiram's elder son limped home with shattered dreams to a decimated seigneury and never recovered. Trent's at the pulpwood mill in Buckeye, now, working a caterpillar alongside his thickset brother.

In other developments, the Koon twins are pregnant. With twins.

As for Butch McCray? You can see Butch most days in a porch swing at his single-wide watching the traffic of children across the street as he feeds a scurry of squirrels in a well-shaded yard. But though Butch is retired, his store is not. A well-documented couple from Laredo took over McCray's tar-papered shack and within weeks the new business was thriving, to the point that *Jarritos* and tacos have now displaced the domestic sodas and candy familiar to generations of Laureate's youth. People who never gave a damn about Butch or globalized trade are raising hell over this fresh and foreign incursion, but at least we know it didn't come from outer space or the nether regions of Hell. No, sir.

It came from Mexico.

Hiram Lamb would turn in his silk-lined coffin if he knew that Butch gave away his half-acre plot to Senor Sanchez free of charge, though I understand Butch did exact a price for inventory still on the shelves. "Man never went broke showin' a profit," Butch said, explaining the wisdom of that transaction.

Some of us were worried that Butch would be incapable of handling his newly gained wealth. Thurman's right there to help, of course, though truthfully Butch doesn't much lean on Shaw's counsel. In fact, Thurman told me just the other day that his sometime client is a lot smarter about dollars and cents that any of us would have credited. Of course, seeing Butch day to day in those overalls and cap, you'd never guess that capacity, but then you'd never know who paid for the town's new baseball field, either, nor the identity of the *patron* behind the Thurman Shaw Scholarship for graduating seniors. I get a kick thinking about some kid who'll go off to college never knowing her benefactor was a man who once sought enlightenment in the wrappers of candy bars.

I dropped in on Butch just the other day. A nice spring day. Baby blue sky. A hint of cumulus building like cotton candy in the sky. I saw McCray rocking back and forth on his porch swing and on pure impulse pulled over beneath the shade of a pecan tree that shelters the old man's modest porch. A hedge of honeysuckle climbing.

"Mr. Butch, how you doin'?" I called from my 4-Runner.

"Miz Clara Sue," came the reply from beneath that long bib cap. "Come sit with me a spell."

So I did. The smell of honeysuckle redolent. The gentle oscillation of his swing as comforting as a sea breeze. The pleasant *squeak squeak* of chain on iron.

I took a rocker opposite Butch's swaying perch and accepted a glass of sweet tea.

"I halfway expected you to offer me a Pepsi, Mr. Butch."

He plucked a chew of tobacco from a moldy pouch and laughed.

Was not an idiot's laugh. Was not the laugh of someone who'd missed the irony of my remark. And when I looked up I saw that Butch was looking me straight in the eye.

"You drop in for, Miz Clara Sue?'

"Me? Why, no particular reason."

"Ah hah."

Suddenly I felt a little uncomfortable. I could not ever remember Butch challenging me, or anyone, for any reason. Probably just a consequence of independence. No need to kiss butt when you're comfortably retired, after all.

"I just saw you on the porch and thought I'd drop in," I explained.

He didn't say anything. But those idiot eyes were not wandering now. There was no deference, no turned head or Uncle Tom shuffle.

Butch McCray was looking at me as though I were a target.

"Always nice to have company," he said.

"Looks like your old store's doing well." I steered my remarks toward what I thought was neutral ground and was shocked at the elder man's reply.

"Goddamn store." Butch broke off his gaze. "Fucking near killed me."

I have rarely been caught off guard in any interview, but Butch's comment left me completely flummoxed.

". . . I guess we all have a tendency to take other people's work for granted," I rejoined lamely.

"Never took yers for granted," he contradicted, those eyes now returned with purpose to meet my own. "We on record, here, Miz Clara Sue?"

I sat there stunned.

"Clara Sue? We visitin? Or is there somethin' else?"

"I . . . I don't know what you mean, Butch. Honestly!"

"You hadn't been by in all this time," he pointed out. "Not a 'Hello.' Not a 'How you doin.' Fact, I don't think you spoke to me since that day in the woods."

"Butch, really—I'm not here for anything."

"We're just folks, then? Just shootin' the breeze?"

"We are, of course, but—" I began to feel some heat of my own. "Butch, you do remember that I played some role in helping your situation? I'm not asking for a medal, but I went to bat for you, Mr. Butch—I hope you recall."

"I recall plenty."

He dragged a boot along the porch's floor and spit.

"An' I do 'preciate ever-thing you done, Miz Clara Sue. You and Colt both. An' Mr. Thurman. I don't take none of it for granted."

I pulled back, speechless. Then he leaned over with a long sigh. The swing resumed its gentle rhythm; a breeze brought the sweet nectar of honeysuckle and in a minute or two I was lulled to some desultory topic or another. The weather. Spring gardens, sweet corn and okra. By the time our colloquy was finished, Butch was back to being the old coot with whom I was familiar.

"Nice seeing you, Mr. Butch," I offered as I made my way down the wide, pine steps of his porch.

"Anytime," he replied vacantly, those eyes returned to some distant horizon.

I didn't know what to make of my face-to-face with Annie McCray's son. Certainly there was nothing I could put my finger on—nothing definitive to add to what I already knew, or wanted to believe. Anyway, what with one thing or another, I never got around to printing the story of Annie and Harold and old man Kelly Lamb and I never publicly aired the possibility that Hiram Lamb was attempting to destroy his stepmother's confession. However, preoccupation and procrastination only partially account for that lapse.

Oh, sure, I could tell myself that exposing Butch's mother as an adulteress and murderer or branding the patriarch of the Lamb family as a cuckold and killer did not serve any useful purpose. But if I scratched just a little deeper, I'd have to admit there was no way I could chronicle the sins of Annie and her separate husbands without also raising implications dangerous for Butch himself. In particular, I couldn't relate Annie's story without raising the possibility that her son also had a motive for murder.

It was public knowledge that Butch had the means to kill Hiram, and the circumstances of the alleged accident made it obvious that he had the opportunity. What would be the community's reaction to the possibility that Hiram lured Butch to the old homestead for the purpose of destroying Annie's confession? How would folks react if they imagined that Butch was wise to Hiram's intent? I didn't know what people would think, or do, in light of that information.

I sure as hell was not going to print anything that suggested Butch McCray murdered Hiram Lamb. As a journalist, I was obliged to print facts, sure—but speculation regarding Butch's motivation? Or Hiram's, for that matter? Was a job for mind readers, not journalists, I told myself. A newspaper doesn't print rumor. That said, there was one fact

I'd noticed on the day of Hiram's death, one small detail, that I could not let go.

Spring was headed to summer before I finally approached Sheriff Buchanan with my concerns. I began by asking Colt point-blank if he thought there was any possibility that Butch McCray knew or believed that Hiram Lamb was hell-bent on destroying Annie's confession.

"What about it, Colt? You think it's possible?"

"Did you tell Butch that Hiram wanted to get rid of his mama' confession?"

"No, of course not."

"Well, I sure as hell didn't. And I know Thurman didn't."

"Maybe we didn't need to tell him. Maybe Butch isn't as stupid as we like to think."

"You got any evidence to back that up, Clara Sue?"

"The shotgun shells," I answered.

"What damn shells?"

"In the bedroom. You remember when we found Butch there was a box of buckshot sitting right there beside his stool?"

"Those ones, sure. Two shells minus a full count. What about it?"

"It was raining. It was bone-cold wet out of doors and that box of shells was dry as toast. Now, Butch told us that Hiram had him bring that box of Number Ones along with the shotgun out to hunt. Butch would've had to drop that box in the mud and rain if the rest of his story is true. If Hiram's homicide was accidental that box should have been soaking wet.

"But what if Butch lied to us? What if that box of buckshot never left the house?"

"You lookin' for a headline, Clara Sue?"

"Dammit, Colt, you know Hiram was carrying his carbine. Why would he need Butch to bring a shotgun in the first place?"

"Cause it's a hell of a lot easier to kill a running deer with a shotgun than a rifle. I got me as many bucks with my Marlin as I have with my Winchester."

"Fair enough," I allowed. "But if Butch intended to kill Hiram, he wouldn't need a whole box of shells, would he? Butch was carrying Hiram's Remington, the over 'n' under. If his purpose was to make Hiram's death look accidental he couldn't use more than the two rounds already loaded. He sure as hell wouldn't need a box."

"That's a lot of 'ifs' and 'woulds,' Clara Sue."

"I'm just saying that if Butch murdered Hiram he would not likely be carrying an entire box of shells out of doors, which would give one explanation why we found that ammunition clean and dry in the room."

Sheriff Buchanan scanned the street casually left and right.

"Am I on the record, Clara Sue?" my cousin asked privately. "An' you better be damn sure of your answer cause I don't want any misunderstanding between us."

"Why should there be a misunderstanding?"

"Answer my damn question: Am I on record?"

I realized right then that I did not want the sheriff on record for this story, any more than I wanted to go on record myself.

"No. Not on the record," I said, and then added, "I'm probably making things too complicated."

"I believe you are," Colt agreed.

"Butch probably brought the box of shells back in with him after the accident. Plenty of time to dry out by the fire before I showed up."

"What I'm thinkin'," Colt said, nodding. "Most likely."

I could have pressed with more questions—and should have. It shouldn't have mattered that Hiram Lamb was a mean and despicable man. It shouldn't have mattered that I detested the son of a bitch. In fact, my bias toward Hiram ought to have obliged me to push even harder to find out exactly what happened on the last day of Lamb's life. But I didn't. I did not publicly challenge the dominant opinion that Hiram's death was accidental. I did not probe the very real possibility that Butch McCray not only killed Hiram but had the wiles to conceal his crime.

Was Butch ever the simpleton we imagined? I'm not sure. I don't know what to believe, and in the end, I decided I did not want to know. I wrestled it over on my own, and with Randall, but at the end of the day, I took off my journalist's hat and walked away.

Safer to cover flying saucers or the appearance of the Virgin. That and football and the splendid accomplishments of the Future Farmers of America. Of course, sometimes real news sneaks in. Sheriff Colt Buchanan has announced he'll run for a fourth term in office and my readers are thrilled to hear that President Trump wants a shot at his second. I'd like to know whether the tax cuts enacted on The Donald's watch have created jobs or simply ballooned the nation's debt. What about the impact of legislation on health care? Immigration policy? The never-ending contest with jihadists worldwide? I have my opinions, of course, but am no longer in a frenzy to pen a column. There will always be zealots on all sides of any question that matters; that is to be expected, but I have come to understand that even in a post-factual world there is a difference between true believers and those who truly believe.

The UFOs are long vanished, by the way, along with visits from the grave and other unsettling manifestations. It wasn't long after Hiram Lamb was buried that those reports began to dwindle sharply in both variety and number, and by Christmas things were back to normal. Local ministers invoked divine intervention to explain the rout of alien influence. The demonic subdued by the divine. Up to you whether to buy that explanation or reject it.

Believe what you like.

After all—I'm just the reporter.

ACKNOWLEDGMENTS

I always enjoy thanking folks who in one way or the other help me as I craft a narrative. I am especially glad to thank Barbara Anderson and all the folks at The Permanent Press.